STRANGE
ATTRACTORS

STRANGE
ATTRACTORS

REBECCA GOLDSTEIN

VIKING

FIC

VIKING
Published by the Penguin Group
Penguin Books USA Inc., 375 Hudson Street,
New York, New York 10014, U.S.A.
Penguin Books Ltd, 27 Wrights Lane,
London W8 5TZ, England
Penguin Books Australia Ltd, Ringwood,
Victoria, Australia
Penguin Books Canada Ltd, 10 Alcorn Avenue,
Toronto, Ontario, Canada M4V 3B2
Penguin Books (N.Z.) Ltd, 182–190 Wairau Road,
Auckland 10, New Zealand

Penguin Books Ltd, Registered Offices:
Harmondsworth, Middlesex, England

First published in 1993 by Viking Penguin,
a division of Penguin Books USA Inc.

1 3 5 7 9 10 8 6 4 2

PUBLISHER'S NOTE
These are works of fiction. Names, characters,
places, and incidents either are the product of
the author's imagination or are used fictitiously,
and any resemblance to actual persons, living or dead,
events, or locales is entirely coincidental.

"The Legacy of Raizel Kaiddish" first appeared in *New
Traditions* and "Rabbinical Eyes" in *Commentary*.

Grateful acknowledgment is made for permission to
reprint an excerpt from "I Went to a Marvellous
Party" by Noel Coward. © 1938 Chappell
Music Ltd. (renewed). All rights administered
by Chappell & Co. All rights reserved.
Used by permission.

LIBRARY OF CONGRESS CATALOGING-IN-PUBLICATION DATA
Goldstein, Rebecca, 1950–
Strange attractors / by Rebecca Goldstein.
p. cm.
ISBN 0-670-83869-1
I. Title.
PS3557.0398S77 1993
813'.54 —dc20 92-50390

Printed in the United States of America
Set in Sabon
Designed by Ann Gold

For Shelly—always

CONTENTS

THE EDITOR'S STORY

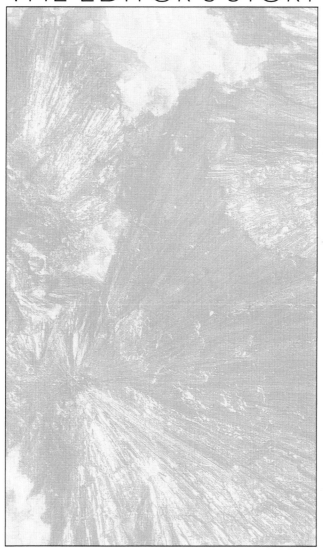

I

BLUESTOCKING

Is that seat too close to the fire?

I keep a fire going, no matter what the thermometer reads, all through this dreary stretch of a season. I can't remember a bleaker January in New York.

Yes, of course I've always lived in Manhattan. I could never have thought of living elsewhere, could you?

Oh, you don't say. Whereabouts in New Jersey?

Well, then, that's not too bad, is it?

I moved up to this place years and years ago, when Owen Hargreaves & Son moved uptown. We used to be, don't you know, oh, for years and years and years, down on Hudson Street, one floor up, in one of those indestructible old cast-iron buildings. We were a strictly no-frills affair back then: bare concrete floors, exposed shafts and air ducts and hot-water pipes. We've come quite a good long way up in the world since then, don't you know.

But I loved the old place. Never could feel quite the same about the new.

The old place, you know, it *smelled* of books. Literally smelled of books.

It was my father, of course, who founded the house. But, then, you must know all that. But what you couldn't possibly know is how peculiar his doing so seemed to all the people he knew—his set, if you know what I mean. They had lost

—well, almost all of them had—a few generations back, the habit of business.

You know, don't you, that what the term "gentleman" used to mean, years ago, was simply a man of property and of no occupation. Well, the old New York that my father knew as a young man held pretty much to the same definition, with the exception made of a few lawyers and bankers. But none of them worked very hard at it. Everyone had the time to lunch quite decently. Nobody really saw what my father's point could be in turning his perfectly acceptable diversion —his own father's family were known to be awfully fond of books—but of taking this perfectly nice hobby and turning it into a regular occupation, so that poor Hargreaves—I think everyone called my father "poor Hargreaves"—was spending his every daylight hour in that hideous place over on Hudson Street, forced to see all sorts of people.

Of course, it wasn't that my father became a publisher with the vulgar intent of actually making money. In that sense, he always remained a gentleman. I don't believe he was ever guilty of the bad taste of turning a good profit.

And, then, you know, little by little, just about all of his private fortune was sunk into the house, just to keep it going. Over the years, one slice after another of precious Manhattan real estate was sold off.

So, you see, it hadn't been the mercantile instinct at work at all in my father. It had been sheer love—which didn't, of course, make it seem any the more reputable to the people he knew, all of whom shrank from any sort of irregular enthusiasm.

There's no way to get round it: my father had jumped the track, in going, as his people put it, "into the trade." I saw, even as a boy, that the rest of his family saw him as a sort of maverick—though, of course, a maverick of the mildest sort, with all the manners and instincts of the gentleman perfectly preserved.

He died when I was a young man of twenty-seven. That was 1907.

Yes, that would be a year before *Chimera* was published.

I like to think, don't you know, though perhaps it's just a foolish conceit, that Owen Hargreaves & Son would never have dared to acquire *Chimera* under my father.

He was a very fine reader, my father was, really a reader of enormous gifts. But he was, when all was said and done, a product of the nineteenth century; whereas I prided myself on being thoroughly *au courant*. I had a tremendous interest in all that was taking place in the very vanguard of all the arts, especially, of course, in all that was literary.

You know, the century was still so new then, so untried and unspoiled. We were, especially we young people, so awfully conscious of being twentieth-century. It seemed to us a thing to be proud over—a source of *personal* pride and possibility.

It must sound awfully naïve to your ears. We had nothing remotely like the washed-out cynicism you young people wear with your blue jeans. It makes me feel really quite sorry for you.

We thought of the Future with a permanent uppercase "F." It was *our* chosen "f" word. But side by side with this luminous vision of the Future was this creeping dread, don't you know, that Doomsday might be lurking just ahead.

It made for the most remarkable tension, when all was said and done, a really remarkable and creative tension. Well, just look at what it produced in its day, the great explosive energy in all the arts, all the experiments with form and content we now call Modernism. You can't tell me it wasn't the very best time there has ever been in which to be young and creative. To be young when the century itself had been young.

There was a great charged sense of excitement in the air, a love of experiment for the sake of experiment.

Ah no. I can't say I follow you there. I can't see any sort of a parallel at all between that time and now.

Can't see it at all.

I always had my nose up in the air, sniffing for something new, the really significant Something, the magnificent Something I was certain the new century would give us. I was just waiting for a book like *Chimera* to happen, though, of course, I couldn't have known it would happen personally to me.

We were a very small house in those days. But the job that I was left with, after my father's death, was still several sizes too large for my frame, don't you know. I might have fancied myself a bold young Modern, staring straight into the glare of the hard bright Future, but I was awfully lacking in the kind of ballast needed to keep a publishing house, no matter how small, afloat. I felt sometimes like a small boy, dressed up in his father's clothes, tripping about on the trouser legs.

The only asset I could claim—and it's by certain people's accounting a very negligible one—was my unbounded love of books.

Well, to be perfectly frank—and I'm too old to be anything else—my relish was mostly reserved for the novels. My eyes have always pretty much had the habit of glazing over a page of anything else. My father was exactly the same. His passion, too, was all for the novel. But he, don't you know, he thought the nineteenth century had said the last word on the novel —whereas I, of course, went about with my nose in the air, sniff, sniff, certain that the twentieth century would soon give us a work with an entirely new kind of perfume.

We really put out only fiction back then, don't you know. Oh, didn't you?

Indeed yes. In those days we were small enough to indulge our eccentricities quite wonderfully. Only my poor mother didn't think it wonderful. She was the only really sensible business head in the family. On her mother's side she was connected to the Van Luydens, one of New York's old Dutch families, and the mercantile element still ran pretty thick in her blood. I suppose she regarded my father and myself as awfully unsteady. Not quite unreliable, though. "Unreliable" was one of her most damning descriptions.

It's not, of course, that my mother looked down on the publishing business, per se. Books were a perfectly respectable product, so long as one could get them to yield a profit. But what she couldn't for the life of her reconcile herself to was my father's and my sense of a "calling."

And, then, of course, she tried just about as hard as she could to avoid having anything to do with the authors. My mother had learned to put up with just about everything in the publishing business, except the deucedly awkward existence of the authors. Considering the fact that it was they who supplied us our product, her attitude always struck me as singularly ungrateful.

But the plain truth is, authors made my mother, to the very end of her days, very uneasy. They were the one element of the business that couldn't be reduced to what she understood so well, who made the business so much unlike the sort of import-export business in which her Dutch forebears had so profitably, so *reliably*, engaged.

The authors brought something uncomfortably incalculable into the house. Especially the novelists. The novelists always made my mother queasy. For her the novelist stood in an awfully bad place—somewhere between the black arts of the sorcerer and the equally sordid manual laborer.

And, of course, my father's and my enthusiasm always made her glare. What could be worse for business than flights of enthusiasm? She kept urging us to publish things like cookbooks and illustrated calendars, lucrative items of that kind. But, say what she would about the inexorable logic of the ledger books, we Hargreaves men were hopelessly in love with the novel.

Of course, the house does all that sort of cashy thing now,

in quite a big way. Even when I was still there. We got to be just a little too successful to indulge our eccentricity.

I noticed that the new list—I don't suppose you've seen it?—was awfully weak on the side of the fiction. Especially when you compare it, say, with the cookbooks. And if you were to tally up the pages on either side, the cookbooks have gotten so hefty and the new novels so starved. . . . Oh well. I don't suppose it matters all that much, anymore.

There was a time, don't you know, I must have been somewhere around your own age, when I thought I'd write a novel or two myself. I've always fancied I have a special way with a phrase.

Why, thank you. I don't mind saying that there's many a phrase of my own mint that's been hammered into the books I've put out.

But perhaps the Dutch element ran just a little too thick in my own blood as well. And they also serve who merely sit and read. And excise and query. And you didn't make the trek all the way here from the hinterlands of Princeton, New Jersey, in order to have me dig up all my moldering old conceits for you—now, did you.

But let me tell you that there are mysteries that go into the making of a good editor, too. Lesser mysteries, I grant you. But mysteries for all that.

A midwife's no mother, but many a babe would perish without her timely intervention, don't you know.

There are moments of a special sort of vision, when you see the book that the writer himself hasn't even seen yet. And there are those moments, too—and they're awfully fine, I can tell you—when you pick up the manuscript of some unknown writer, and you feel the telltale prickle traveling up the whole length of your spine.

Here it is, you think. It's the real thing this time.

Did I prickle when I first saw *Chimera*? Ah yes. Indeed I did. It was a most prodigious prickle. And that was very artfully done, young lady. Steering me onto your chosen topic like that. I commend you upon your tact. Don't think for a moment that I've forgotten the reason that you've looked me up.

It was a most prodigious prickle. I can call it up still. It's probably my greatest claim to literary fame. When all is said and done, it's perhaps my only claim to literary fame. I'm a sort of footnote to the history of that book.

Sixty years, you say?

In August? Yes, I suppose that's right. That would be right. August of 1908.

It was really awfully clever of you—quite the little scholar—to have tracked me down, small and buried footnote that I am.

You're what we would have called, in my day, a bluestocking. Oh dear, yes, of course we still used that expression. Even in the house. Most especially in the house. And the young ladies in question really did wear a sort of bluish-gray hosiery. Very fetching some of them looked, too, in their blue stockings.

But it's blue jeans you young ladies prefer now, though I don't think it's meant to signify the same thing at all. Ah well, I don't suppose it makes all that much difference, anymore.

In any case, it's of *Chimera* that you wish me to speak, not of our bygone little bluestockings.

I'll tell you the whole story behind that book, if you like. I'm at that age where reminiscence seems the most engaging form of mental activity. To be perfectly frank, it often seems the only possible form of mental activity. And it's always nicer with an audience, don't you know. Especially such a pretty one. The story's worth a doctoral dissertation or two.

I'm a Yale man myself. We were a good old Yale house, don't you know. Oh, you didn't. Indeed, yes. There was one old gentleman who was with us, oh, for years and years and years, he was an editor who positively hated books. Couldn't abide any sort of printed matter, not even the illustrated calendars. But, you see, young lady, he had, in his day, disported himself very nobly as quarterback for the dear old alma mater.

But to get back to *Chimera*. It so happens that the day it arrived at the house stands out in my mind most particularly. Not only because of the aforementioned prickle, don't you know, but also because of something very much its opposite. Earlier on that same day I had had a far less enchanted look into the ledger book. Our quarterly statement had arrived only that morning, and its message this time was particularly grim.

I had been in the habit, since my father's death, of putting in sixteen hours a day to the great good cause of solvency. But, in spite of these stalwart, manly efforts, it very much appeared that the house was sliding quite sickeningly nearer the awful precipice. It was the *vertige de l'abîme*, don't you know.

I immediately thought of my poor mother. She knew, of course, that the statement would be in that day, and I began, very feebly, to fret out complications by means of which the message of doom might be obscured. But I soon gave up all that sort of thing as entirely useless. My mother's sense of business was always firmly unperplexable. Indeed, it was something rather awful.

For the first time, I actually considered that the days of Owen Hargreaves & Son might very well be mortally numbered—the dreadful number figuring somewhere in the very low double digits.

I've little doubt now that I was the very last person involved to whom the grim truth came. I've never much liked pushing the facts too far when such an action is likely to end in their revealing something awfully unpleasant, don't you know. But this particular fact required very little in the way of pushing.

I was sunk awfully low, sick with the thought of the scene that would follow that evening with my mother.

I really don't know how I managed to pull myself together in order to do any work at all that day. But I was brought up in the creed—ancient history nowadays—that a good man never forsakes the task at hand. So I manfully squared my young shoulders and sat myself down to the pile upon my desk. And somewhere in that pile lay the brighter Future of the house.

Chimera, I mean, of course.

Ah, so you've seen the famous manuscript, then?

And do you happen to know, young lady, that there were two drafts that came before those literary remains that lie there now in Pennsylvania State University?

No, I've really no idea. Destroyed, I shouldn't wonder.

Quite substantive differences. I shall get to all that—in time. It's rather the main point of my own small footnote, don't you know.

But before we go quite so far into the matter, you might wonder—others did—whatever had possessed the author of *Chimera* to submit the manuscript to Owen Hargreaves & Son in the first place.

Oh, I know I'd cut a more heroic figure in my little footnote if all the great houses up and down wide Publisher's Row had slammed their doors shut in the face of the unknown masterpiece. But that's not how it went. The big houses didn't have the chance to slam their doors—though I like to think they might have, just as I like to think that we ourselves would have done the same had *Chimera* come to us a year before, when it was my father who stood at the helm, making all the final decisions.

But it came to us in 1908, and it came to us, to Owen Hargreaves & Son, first. And the breeze that blew it to us . . . well, it's as eccentric as everything else connected with the book. It's quintessential Worthinghouse.

You see, small and floundering though we were, we happened to have enjoyed the rare privilege of publishing a writer by the name of Sebastian Samowitz.

Never heard of him? Don't fret. It doesn't make you any less the little scholar. I shall not tell them at your university.

The truth is, young lady, no one else had ever heard of Sebastian Samowitz either, not even back then, when we were, in the vigorous pursuit of our eccentricity, publishing his books. Samowitz seemed to have been something of an acquired taste, and only the author of *Chimera* had managed to acquire him—acquired him with a relish, as it turned out, deeming him the most brilliant English writer of the day— indeed, the *only* brilliant English writer, all other brilliant writers writing, don't you know, in French.

You look, young lady, as if I had just served you up a triple scoop of your favorite flavor of ice cream. They'll make you a lady professor yet, before you've even gotten your degree!

Yes, I dare say you can find Samowitz's books *somewhere*. I suppose the house must have copies squirreled away. You can check with young Bob Sales. He ought to be able to tell you.

No, I found out about this passion for Sebastian Samowitz much later. I don't believe there was even a letter accompanying the manuscript. I got the return address—Pittsburgh, of course; that you surely know—from off the brown envelope the thing arrived in.

All that came was that manuscript, which I thought, as I started to read it that summer afternoon, quite the queerest set of words put together for the intent of publication that had ever arrived at any house anywhere.

Imagine it, if you possibly can. By now any undergraduate schoolboy who fancies himself a writer has had a go at imitating that first chapter, the one that buries all the old conceits of how first chapters pretty much ought to go. But imagine, if you possibly can, young lady, what it read like back then, before anything remotely like it had ever been done. The smell of the Future that came in that brown envelope—well, it pretty near made me dizzy.

It *did* make me dizzy. But you know it's one of the mysterious powers of that book that it makes you dizzy without making you sick. The whole pack of derivers don't quite manage to pull that off, don't you know.

Oh dear me, no. Sebastian Samowitz was nothing *at all* like it.

I must have read about a fifth of the book at that first reading. It was rather late in the evening when I finally put it down. My poor mother had sent over our servant sometime earlier in the evening—we lived not too far, over on St. Luke's Place. And I had returned him to her with the message that I was sunk in my work, and that she should on no account hold back supper for me.

Can you imagine it? There the poor woman was, waiting at home for some word of the Future of the house—and waiting was something poor Mother always managed very badly—and I had clean forgotten, if you can believe it, all about that infernal quarterly statement!

Well, Mother waited just about as long as—and even a little longer than—she could stand. Just as I was lighting the lamp—it was August, so the light had lasted me a good long while—the door of my little cramped office was flung opened. And there, filling the portal, was Mother, dressed for dinner and very hot beneath her French-lace collar.

She must have stood there for a good twenty seconds, fixing me with one of her perfectly exquisite glares.

"Tell me," she finally brought it out. "Tell me what it is!"

My mother had a voice—well, even our tender relationship didn't prevent my perceiving it as disagreeable. I've noticed that, wherever in old New York families there was a strong admixture of Dutch blood, the voices were flat, somehow metallic, and the diction was very careless. I've always agreed

with the Bard that a good voice, "ever soft, gentle and low,"
don't you know, is indeed an excellent thing in woman.

You, my dear, have a lovely speaking voice. Even on the
telephone. I probably wouldn't be talking to you right now
if you hadn't.

But I've left my poor mother hanging there in the portal,
with her peremptory "Tell me what it is!"

"Oh," I answered my mother, "it's magnificent!"

You understand, of course, that I was still completely besotted by my afternoon's strong drink of *Chimera*.

The enthusiasm of my response rather baffled my poor
mother—how she hated to be baffled—and she glared at me
again, for another twenty seconds at least.

She finally demanded, with the unimaginative literalness
of her people, "What is magnificent, Owen? The quarterly
statement?"

The question, of course, hurled back at me, hitting me
square with the thud of reality, what the last several hours
of reading had entirely obliterated: the dingy little fact of our
galloping fiscal ruin.

"Oh, *that*," I answered her. "*That* is nothing."

Well, you can just try to imagine how she glared at me
then.

"Or at least," I continued in the gap that her astonishment
made, "at least the statement is nothing, says nothing, that
can't be entirely unsaid by this!"

And I carefully transferred into the arms of the astonished
mater the infant masterpiece.

"This is what is magnificent, then?" She brought it out
slowly.

"It is," I answered with as much solemnity as my giddy
mood permitted.

"E. A. Worthinghouse," she read off the flyleaf. "Is he one
of ours? Is he famous?"

"He shall be!" I fairly proclaimed it.

"Ours . . . *and* famous?"

I think at this I nodded my head. There seemed to be something in my expression that my mother found awfully provoking, don't you know, in all the mixed nuances of the word.

"And you think it possible, then, that this will save us?" she asked me at last, giving the grasped pages a sharp little shake.

I think I must have paused a while before I finally answered her.

"Oh, I think it more than possible," I remember saying at last. "And if it doesn't, well, then, there's nothing more to be said about the publishing business, anyway. We might just as well go into the manufacturing of plumbing fixtures, or ornamental trimmings for ladies' hats."

Well, you yourself must know, or you wouldn't be here, the kind of reckless hold the book takes over one, when once it has taken hold. You're not, for at least several hours after, totally accountable for the sorts of things you're likely to say. Perhaps that's the reason why it was eventually banned in so many cities—the author's own Pittsburgh, don't you know, leading the way.

My mother, who was, of course, in no such state of reckless candor, must certainly have glared at me now.

I seem to have already had my poor mother glaring an awful lot. Well, it was her characteristic way of responding whenever she didn't know what to say.

She glanced back down at the manuscript she was still holding, turning a few pages at random, seeming to read from here and from there. As I watched her, it was my turn to feel mildly provoked.

I had already a premonition—it was really nothing very preternatural—that my mother would never be made to feel the singular power of *Chimera* for herself. The confirmation of my critical evaluation would come, as always for her, only in the straight, ruled columns of the ledger book. I doubted very much whether she would ever even read *Chimera*, though in this I was quite wrong.

My mother's small appetite in literature was wonderfully satisfied by the best-selling female authors of the day. Oh, the bluestockings were very popular at that time. So far as Mother was concerned, the art of the novel could ascend no higher than that stage of development to which it had been brought by Mrs. Oliphant, who, alas, was not one of "ours."

"But, Owen," my mother suddenly looked up from the pages she was riffling to demand, "if the book is truly so very good, how can we ever hope to make it sell?"

I told you that my mother's grasp of business was something rather awful.

II

CACOËTHES

I've apparently decided to tell you something more of the story than I had at first intended, my dear. I seem to have taken a real liking to you. You're such a rare listener.

I'm very glad your pursuit of higher degrees, and all that sort of thing, has left you so unspoiled. Really, what does such a pretty girl as you want with such awfully solemn titles? Aren't you afraid that they'll scare away all your young men?

You asked me yesterday about the differences among the three drafts of *Chimera*. Well, I'm going to tell you, and let you decide what to do with it.

Perhaps you'll decide that I'm not merely an obscure footnote. Perhaps you'll decide to promote me right up there into the text of the remarkable story.

Almost all of the changes had to do with the Antonia sections. Yes, that is right, my dear. And very substantive changes they were.

Was Antonia originally more or less scandalous? That's a

very interesting question—very interesting, my dear. And I shall get to that—in time.

But I'll tell you one thing. The color white was entirely absent until the third and final draft.

Yes, that's right. But, please, do let me proceed to tell you all about it in my own quite linear fashion. I may have encouraged my writers to liberate themselves, *après Chimera*, from the tyranny of the cause-and-effect relation. But I find, especially at my age, that my narratives get awfully shaky without the scaffolding of causality.

I remember that, when I awoke the next morning, my mind was all crammed full of what I had been reading the night before, well into the early hours. It *is* a work most suitably read through the night, with all its strange nocturnal elements.

And, now, this is strange. When I recalled some of the passages that had most deeply impressed themselves on me, I automatically spoke them to myself in French. The inkling had formed itself in me—even while I slept, apparently— that I was reading a translation from a work called *La Chimère*.

Does that make any sense to you, my dear?

Yes, I rather thought it would.

What can I say? I read all that day at the office, breaking off only at one point to dictate a letter to the author of *Chimera*. It was a wildly, imprudently enthusiastic letter. Had my mother seen it, she would have thought me mad. Indeed, she might have thought me unreliable.

A writer receiving such a letter could reasonably infer what no house ever wishes to imply—namely, that vast sums of money would be forthcoming.

But it seemed to me, even then, that I was not so much addressing a writer as, something more along the lines of a Master. And I was not so crass as to touch upon terms at all.

I simply stated my belief that *Chimera* was destined to be recognized by every literate man in the civilized world as one of the epoch-making masterpieces of the English language, and that Owen Hargreaves & Son was unspeakably moved to have been singled out as the means by which this historical literary event would occur.

And I said something, too, about how I was most anxious indeed that we should meet, and meet soon, for there was so much, so very much, that I wished to discuss with the author of *Chimera*.

I was, perhaps, by the end of that day, halfway done with the book. I read all through that night, and by the next day, about midafternoon, I had reached the last page.

Well, no. The ending was not the ending that you know. How could it be, when I've already said that the color white didn't come in until the third and last draft?

But, yes, the color-washes over the characters, it was all done already, done so beautifully, the way they flowed and merged, emerged, submerged. The inky, the indigo wash over Antoine, and the fleshlike colors of Antonia. And then Hector, gray, *gris,* granite, so that Antonia's prose went muddy whenever he came near, but went deeper toward violet with Antoine's indigo. Yes, that was all there in the very first draft, and I can tell you: it fairly took my breath away.

But, please, my dear, do please try not to interrupt me. You were such a good little patient listener yesterday.

You've heard, perhaps, of a cacoëthes scribendi? Well, I had been the happy victim, those last three days, of an answering sort of cacoëthes. A cacoëthes lisendi, if you like. I had not thought a thought, dreamt a dream, that was not somehow different from having read *Chimera*.

I saw a lot—well, enough so that I knew I'd never seen anything remotely like it before. But, of course, I didn't see it *all*. And, as I've said, it wasn't even *all* there yet to be seen.

But I knew enough already to know, though not yet altogether distinctly—I wonder if anyone yet knows altogether distinctly—how ingenious and how new were the techniques that set the whole vast thing to working. And I knew that these techniques constituted some further stage in the art of the novel.

I knew that *Chimera* was the first true masterpiece of Modernism, the first literary payoff on that bold promise made on our frighteningly new Future.

It was the first thundering footstep of that approaching prodigy, the Modern Novel, a chimera whose parts were the genius of E. A. Worthinghouse, Marcel Proust, and James Joyce.

Would you really, my dear?

I hadn't ever myself really thought of placing the formidable Gertrude Stein so very near the top. One of my own requirements has always been that, for a book to be great, it has first to be readable. It can be demanding, it can be damned difficult. But it's got to be readable.

And that, of course, *Chimera*, as magically unlike anything else as it was, always managed to be. It makes you dizzy without making you sick.

I think I mentioned to you last time the special mysteries that attend the making of a good editor, the knowledge of the book-to-be that can come, like a vision, upon him. Well, I had such a vision. I had a vision of all that *Chimera* was meant to be. Even when I didn't see the whole of what it then was, still, I had a vision that it was meant to be something more. I couldn't, for the life of me, have told you what the something more was. I'm an editor, not an author. But I knew, somehow, that the book wasn't done until the colors set down blended in such a way that . . . well, I couldn't have then said, though now it seems so inevitable—it seems so, after the fact.

But that's perhaps just exactly the point. I knew the book required an ending that would seem to be inevitable, after the fact.

There was no way on earth that I could query any page—indeed, any word or letter; even the awkwardnesses seemed deliberate and right—of what I had of *Chimera*. And yet I felt, I felt it keenly, that I had not read enough. Something, somewhere—though I could not tell you what the thing was or where it was to go—had been left out.

I thought, even, that I caught a whiff of the fetid odor of morality, clinging here and there.

Yes, I know how strange that sounds now, after all the squawk of scandal that was stirred up by the book and its author. But you see, my dear, it's of the original draft that I speak. It's of the *unwhitened* version.

And I thought: Did the author of *Chimera* not know this, not know that his book was not yet entire? How could he not, I thought, when he knew enough to produce what he had produced? And yet I've told you of those intuitions and mysteries that go into the making of a good editor.

Though the author of *Chimera* had already given so much, I knew that he must still give. He must be made to give us more.

And, the more I thought about it, and you can believe me that I was thinking of little else by now, the clearer it seemed to me that it was the last Antonia section that was, so to speak, to blame—that there was a something, cold and un-consumed, that lay there in the center of Antonia. For you see, my dear, the first draft of *Chimera* contained nothing, absolutely nothing at all, like the famous, the infamous, one hundred and six pages of Antonia's confession.

How you gape, my dear!

It's true. It wasn't just the blaze of whiteness that hadn't yet broken out into the text. The entire one hundred and six pages didn't come about until the third and final draft.

And now, my dear, now that I've delivered you up into such a state of speechless wonder, I think that I shall leave off.

Shall we meet again this time tomorrow?

Ah well, I see. If you can't, then, of course, you can't.

No, no, no—not at all. It's only that I would have thought, all agog as you only a moment ago appeared to me to be, that you'd be more inclined to rearrange your life in the interest of learning how the notorious white pages of Antonia's confession came to be written.

Yes, yes, I quite understand. Next week, Monday, is fine.

I am, as you can perfectly well see for yourself, completely at your disposal.

III

PIQUE

It was, as well you know by now, practically impossible to draw any portrait of the author of *Chimera* from the work itself.

It's like that, of course, in all the greatest writers, at least it's always seemed that way to me.

Think of the Bard, after all. What, when all is said and done, do we really know about the person who was born to a Mr. and Mrs. Shakespeare of Stratford-on-Avon? Why, it seems almost sacrilege even to consider the biographical question.

The lesser writers, why, their image is looming there on every page they produce, like a petty tyrant, don't you know, who has his face plastered up there on every flat surface in every city, town, and hamlet that he rules.

But, still, I have to confess that I did form some view of the author of *Chimera*. You see, it had already occurred to me, given the extraordinary maturity and the unparalleled confidence of the work, that E. A. Worthinghouse was a pseudonym for an already established writer.

But, I thought, trying to follow out this line of reasoning, would he not, then, likely be one of "ours"? And, try as I might, I couldn't bring myself to imagine that any of ours, not even Sebastian Samowitz—I jest, of course—could have brought off such a thing as was *Chimera*.

Perhaps it's true, some writer or other said it, you can imagine in what a tone of pique, that no man is a genius to his editor.

The thing of which I was most certain was that, despite the present Pittsburgh address, the author of *Chimera* must have lived, and for some considerable time, too, in Paris. And I was certain that he had lived there as no mere tourist, don't you know, but had penetrated into the life of Paris as the light of Paris, the broad light of the boulevards, had penetrated his book, and the sound of the woman's heel echoing off the wet pavement at dead of night had penetrated, too. It was someone who knew all that, don't you know, who knew it all, the wide boulevards and the dead of night.

It's funny, but, you know, I had formed a very strong hunch that the author of *Chimera* was a foreign journalist. For you see, it seemed clear to me that E. A. Worthinghouse, whoever he was, must have been writing for some time. And, then, a journalist would have had just that sort of intimate exposure to the great variety of types and classes which it surely seemed that the author of *Chimera* possessed.

Well, of course, I was terribly impatient to get a reply to the letter I had sent off to Pittsburgh. In fact, I even followed my letter up with a telegram, again offering the author my congratulations and expressing my wish to meet with him— either in New York or even in Pittsburgh—just as soon as might be convenient for him.

Well, I think it took about two weeks for a letter from Pittsburgh to come at long last. A letter—not a wire—signed

E. A. Worthinghouse. The letter was short, really quite un-
telling, and yet more than satisfying for all that. It put me,
don't you know, into the very pink of pleasure, just to see
myself addressed by the hand that had written out that
signature.

The letter itself simply told me that E. A. Worthinghouse
would be at my office to meet me at four o'clock in the
afternoon on a date that was there named, some two or three
weeks forward, I think. I inferred that E. A. Worthinghouse
was a man of some affairs, which affairs required that he
couldn't rush off to New York at a moment's notice.

Well, there it was, finally, the awaited day. My mother, of
course, knew that the author of *Chimera* would be visiting
Hudson Street that day, and I had asked her if she had a wish
to be present for the occasion, which, of course, she hadn't.
But she did very much warn me, since no terms whatsoever
had been touched upon, to, on no account, show the author
how well I thought of him, lest he, as she put it, "got ideas."

"How will our writers write for us, if they don't get ideas?"
I, perfectly tipsy on high spirits, teased.

"You know very well what I mean, Owen," she returned
to me sternly.

It wasn't that she was perfectly humorless, my mother. I'd
certainly seen her enjoy a good laugh, especially if it were at
someone else's expense. But she was in possession of a fairly
extensive list of topics about which one didn't joke, and
Money was certainly on it, if anything was.

My drunken eagerness that morning certainly didn't inspire
my poor mother's confidence. She was, I think, almost inclined to intrude her always steady self into the transactions
between the house of Hargreaves and the author of *Chimera*.
But in the end her repugnance for this class of person over-
came her worries of ownership, and she sent me off to Hudson
Street to deal with the shifty creature—the wretch!—in my
own way.

Well, I sat rather in a shiver all the day. My office—I think I might have said it, my dear—was a very small, very cluttered sort of a place—well, the whole Hudson Street enterprise could hardly have been on a more modest scale—and for half an hour at least, I fretted about the grandeur that would be conspicuously lacking in the impression we would present that day. I wished that I might be able to present the author with a view up Fifth Avenue, say, and with glass-doored bookcases filled with best-sellers. But I loved that old place, you know, and I decided there was no shame in welcoming the author of *Chimera* into an establishment smelling of books.

At about a quarter to four, there came a very sharp knock on my door, which was opened to admit a very tall man with a set of truly magnificent mustaches. He had a wonderfully commanding air and I was not in the least disappointed, for twenty seconds at least. It took me about that long to understand that the impressive gentleman was a representative of a New York charity, come to ask me for a donation.

I quickly wrote him a check, very anxious for him to be gone. No sooner had I gotten him out than there came another knock—it was four o'clock precisely. I called "Come in," my heart rather pounding, as I rose all unconsciously from my seat to meet at last the author of *Chimera*.

The door opened, and there, barely reaching a third of the way up the doorway, stood something very small and very drab.

What can I say? My first thought was that E. A. Worthinghouse had been detained, and had sent along his wife or sister to tell me so.

She, meanwhile, closely watched me, as I stood there looking, no doubt, the very image of the fool she had set me up to look like—or so I, at first, in my heat and haste, assumed.

That, perhaps, was my third or fourth thought. The second, of course, had been the realization—it fell on me like the crack of a whip—that that prim little person supremely staring me down—she looked, you know, so exactly like a Methodist minister's daughter—was none other than the E. A. Worthinghouse I had, with such consummate reverence, already christened the Master of the Modern Novel.

She, meanwhile, had not uttered a syllable. She didn't smile in greeting or move in the slightest a muscle of her face. It seemed to me a very chilling, a singularly remote, expression she wore with which to scrutinize me.

You know her face, of course. Those wide, gray eyes that had such an unnervingly steady stare, the very rounded arched ironical brows, the cheeks a trifle too full. The famous portrait by John Sargent—you've seen it, I suppose, it was I who set that up for her, don't you know, when she came to New York again, after *Chimera*'s great reception—well, that portrait frankly flatters her.

In that day, no woman could be considered pretty who didn't have a complexion. Beauty was unthinkable without a complexion. It would be hard for you in this day, my dear, to picture the shell-like transparency, the luminous red-and-white, untouched by paint or powder, of the best complexions of that day, in which the blood came and went like the lights of the aurora. The women that I knew, certainly my mother and my future wife, Lucy, went to great lengths to protect the treasure of a good complexion against the disasters of sun and wind. And with such ineffable results!

Well, to put it with an ungentlemanly accuracy, E. A. Worthinghouse had no complexion of which to speak. There certainly was nothing of the luminous about it. Indeed, it was rather rough and blotchy, especially on that first occasion when I saw her.

Of course, she had been working very hard. She had been writing her *Chimera* night and day, and when I saw her she was still, I think, in a state of semi-exhaustion. There were great dark circles beneath her eyes. She told me, later, that she barely slept the whole time that *Chimera* was working within her.

But the truth was, she hadn't a complexion, and she hadn't a good carriage either. Sargent's celebrated brushes had lent her a stature, a grace of bearing, that she really hadn't at all.

You know how small she was. And she had no figure at all, at least she hadn't what was then considered a figure. She was very slight, like a child really. And the fashion of that day was all for large women, of whom my mother, by the way, was a most splendid specimen, as was Lucy, too, for that matter.

Here they are: my mother and Lucy. This was taken quite soon after our marriage. They look a trifle oversized, no doubt, by the reduced standards of today. But let me tell you, young lady, that in their day they were a glorious thing to behold, those gallon-sized beauties.

Of course, when the fashion for largeness changed, my poor Lucy had to try to change with it, and her life was made an endless misery, what with the diets and Trilene tablets and chin-straps and what have you.

Nineteen sixty-eight might have favored Eugenie far better than 1908. Who knows but that E. A. Worthinghouse might not have looked very fetching indeed in a pair of faded blue jeans.

But in the fashions of that day, the great abundance of clothing that women carried on their backs, and with every conceivable sort of trimming, little women like Eugenie were just lost in all the drapery. They looked like nothing so much as piles of washing.

And, you know, even at the height of her fame, her brilliant celebrity, not to speak of notoriety, she never managed to expand herself into a felt presence. She never had any sort of presence at all. Small as she was, she always seemed to be trying to press herself into something even smaller, as if she would vanish altogether if she could. It used to make me feel so sorry for her, but also so awfully impatient. She had, you know, this ridiculous way of ducking her head when you asked her a question.

When she came to stay with us, after *Chimera* was published, well, whatever there was of society in New York was standing ready to lionize her. But she continued to carry on her life like a little mouse. The only concession she made to fame was her sittings for John Sargent, who was one of the most gracefully cosmopolitan men it's ever been given to me to know. He was the very soul of affability—which certainly contributed to the brilliance of his career—and he even got Eugenie, who usually hated to be looked at, to relax before his easel.

But John Sargent was really the only person, besides my mother and myself, that she came intimately to know in New York. Of course, she kept bringing up the name of Sebastian Samowitz. But aside from him, there was no one she wanted to meet. She had a horror of meeting new people that you simply couldn't imagine. It bordered on the pathological.

You've no idea how many there are who get the idea of writing a book simply because they think it would be a good way to meet new people. They've been told by some irresponsible source that everyone's got at least one book in him. Well, perhaps that's true, though who says it's a book anyone would want to read?

But for Eugenie, of course, it was entirely different. I've never known an author less willing to pass through any of the doors celebrity had opened. Any suggestion I'd make her to meet this person or that—of course, only people of consequence—but she always greeted such suggestions with a look of starkest panic and a volley of feeble excuses.

I don't think it was only that, given the brilliance of her name, she dreaded disappointing people by her person. I'm quite sure that she was almost as shy before she became so famous. In fact, I've always believed that there was no other explanation for her having taken so very long, from the time of my first letter to her, finally to come to New York to meet me, but her morbid shyness. She might never have managed to bring it off except for the very great assurances I had already sent her, that I truly admired—that I venerated—her work.

But, yes, perhaps it's true that the inclination to make herself disappear intensified under the glare of publicity.

I remember—well, this is a great leap forward in my little footnote. But, you know, it paints the portrait of her so much more tellingly than that flattering picture by John Sargent.

It was maybe six or seven months after *Chimera* was published, in the midst of the great sound and fury that was unleashed upon the book. E. A. Worthinghouse was all the rage—oh, all the rage in both senses of the word. She had already been banned in Boston, and, of course, in Pittsburgh, and there were rumors that New York would soon follow suit. It was all the more intense, of course, both the sorts of rages, because she was a woman. And a Methodist minister's daughter thrown in! Ah, nobody could let that lie!

Well, Eugenie came to visit me in New York for three weeks. She stayed at our home, of course, with my mother and myself, on St. Luke's Place.

At that point, with the fame of her name, she could have met just about anyone she really wanted to meet. Everyone was clamoring for an introduction to the author of *Chimera*. But, of course, the only one *she* wanted to meet was that impossible little man Sebastian Samowitz, who was playing hard to get, making it just about as difficult as it could be for me to set up an introduction.

It was awfully trying for my mother, those three weeks that Eugenie stayed with us. My mother had never so put herself out for the sake of an author. Well, there was the good of the house to consider. Already, don't you know, the

Worthinghouse name was beginning to draw others in. She saw, of course, my mother, with her genius for the practical side of life, exactly where, as she would have put it—in fact, *did* put it—"our bread was buttered."

So my mother covered her aversion as best she could, which, with all the good manners she could marshal, was very good indeed.

And yet Eugenie, with her very different sort of genius, saw clearly through it all, saw clear through all the beautiful manners, to the absolute horror she aroused in my poor mother. And I'm pretty sure, too, that she divined the true source of the horror.

For you see, my mother's mistrust of Eugenie went far beyond that general queasiness that authors always aroused in her. I saw her, the entire three weeks that Eugenie visited with us, closely watching Eugenie, with a very lively scrutiny peering from beneath the beautiful manners.

But all that, of course, was kept unspoken and unacknowledged. On the surface my mother put herself completely at the disposal of our celebrated author.

And in that spirit my mother and I convinced Eugenie, one evening, to go out with us to attend a public lecture whose title we thought would be intriguing to the author of *Chimera*. It was something like "The Idea of Doom and the Vision of the Artist."

Well, we went, the three of us, to this lecture. We arrived, as I remember it, somewhat late, and had to sit near to the front.

This lecture, my dear, turned out to be nothing other than a focused attack on the author of *Chimera*! I think the speaker described the book as a twisted, contorted, howling monstrosity, in which only the very basest of sensibilities could find anything to which to relate, much less admire.

The speaker—I think he was a doctor of theology—of

course could hardly have known, we ourselves only decided the very last minute to go, that the author of *Chimera* was herself in the audience.

Well, don't you know, it went on. I was sitting right there beside Eugenie, my mother was at her other side, and I, of course, was most particularly curious to see the effect that the words of the doctor of theology were making on her.

She just sat there, looking exactly the little stick she always looked. Not a blush, not a tremor—just that same wooden stare that was her most habitual expression, especially when she was out in public. Only her thin lips went a little whiter. But to look at her you wouldn't think she had anything at all in particular to do with the work the doctor of theology was calling a misshapen, howling monstrosity, from which all right-thinking Christians ought really to avert their gaze in pity and terror.

And, you know, it occurred to me, sitting there right next to her, as the doctor of theology raged on—it occurred to me that perhaps little Eugenie hadn't after all written *Chimera*. It occurred to me that maybe it had, after all, been the dead brother, the brilliant older brother, Laurie, who was the author of *Chimera*.

Just the thin black tail of an idea, which swam quickly past me, and was gone. For, really, what could be a worse thought to be entertained by the publisher of a celebrated book? That wasn't the sort of scandal we wanted at all.

But for just a fraction of a moment I thought: Perhaps it was the dead brother after all.

Of course, we all know it wasn't. Eugenie Amalie Worthinghouse was, strangely enough, the author of *Chimera*. The great revisions prove that. Those one hundred and six pages of Antonia's confession that she wrote for me.

But you could never have guessed it, looking at her, guessed what it was she had within her. Nothing of the fire within got through the layers and layers of drab she had wrapped round herself.

I looked at her for a reaction after the doctor of theology had finished his attack: not a flicker, not a spark.

All that she did was to whisper, very hurriedly, into my ear, that she wished to leave the lecture hall immediately, before the audience's questioning could begin. So we three —I walked ahead, my mother and Eugenie following behind me—started up the aisle. And everyone's eyes were on us.

They knew who she was, you see. The word had made its way up and down the rows of chairs in the auditorium. Somehow they all knew that the author of *Chimera* was there in attendance.

The people in the aisle silently made way, so that little Eugenie, her eyes pitifully sunk to the floor, could hurry past.

And poor Eugenie, so my mother told me afterward, was simply clinging to her, her head barely reaching my mother's shoulder. She clung and trembled like a dried-up little leaf in the wind.

That was E. A. Worthinghouse, you see. That gives you the picture of Eugenie Amalie Worthinghouse.

My mother told me that, by the time they finally reached the door, Eugenie was so leaning on her for support that my mother was all but carrying her out!

How little enjoyment she was capable of extracting from her celebrity. She was able to feel, with great intensity, the stings—but she couldn't, for the life of her, sip a single drop of the honey.

However, all this, the stings and the honey, they all lay far ahead, as I surveyed the small figure staring me down from the doorway of my office, as I struggled to take in the truly awful idea that it was she who was that heroic Modern who was ushering in for us the awesome Future.

Well, you know, my dear, I've always been a man who has liked, thoroughly liked, don't you know, women.

And, being, at that time, a young man, a young man of twenty-eight, and a single man to boot, well, I was very fond of the company of women.

I thought I understood the ladies pretty well, don't you know, the feminine point of view and all that sort of thing. I had certainly read my share of the female novelists of the day. And I liked them, so far as they went. I liked them very much indeed.

But it was very hard for me to allow, in that first brutal lash of a revelation, for such a thing, in the general scheme of things, don't you know, as the author of *Chimera*. I simply couldn't quite get her, the *idea* of her, to fit in.

She, for her part, had, as yet, said nothing. And I, for my part, could not yet speak for my fury.

Yes, I was furious. I felt I had been played a very low trick.

The woman is a monster!—this was perhaps the next thought to come to me in the confused succession of my thoughts.

I was really a very mild young man. You mustn't think that I was easily given to rash flashes of temper. But what young man likes to feel he has been toyed with, made to dance on a string like a silly marionette, especially when he looks up and discovers it's some woman that's jiggling his cords?

Actually, I think at that moment I saw her less as a playful puppeteer and more as a sort of ghoulish scientist, a ruthless experimenter in the field of human behavior, staring into the cold lens of her microscope at the poor squirming specimen, the little one-celled worm, she had all expertly pinned down on her slide to observe.

And I thought again: I've never encountered such a she-monster! I've never known such a thing as she could be!

All this, you must understand, transpired very rapidly. Outwardly, I think I regained my composure soon enough, prompted as much by my desire to sabotage her little experiment with me—the turn of the worm, don't you know—as by anything else.

"So, you're the author of *Chimera,*" I said to her as I came out from behind my desk and ushered her into my little office.

She gave me a very quick nod of the head, glancing all the way up to me—well, of course, I simply towered over her.

I really can't exactly recall how the conversation between us began. Quite badly, I think. She offered me very little help. She was, don't you know, completely at a loss if the conversation was directed on her, and that was, of course, the first way that I tried to direct it.

To ask her a question about herself was to be made witness to a very curious and painful sort of spasm of self-consciousness. She went pale, she went miserable, her eyes darted first this way and then that. And she made that awful ducking motion, as if she were dodging a missile.

There was nothing in the world of which the author of *Chimera* cared less to speak than of the author of *Chimera.* How very unlike most authors she was.

I did manage to learn that she was the daughter of a Methodist minister. And her mother had died many years before. But the father, you probably know this already, the father had died only two winters previous.

I think she'd never have written *Chimera* while her father still lived. She certainly wouldn't have thought of publishing it, but I doubt even if she would have been capable of writing it. And, of course, he was sick for many years, and Eugenie was his sole nurse for all those years.

Well, we continued for a while, making desultory conversation, both of us quite evidently at a loss. How, I was wondering, would I be able to discuss *Chimera* with this little dry person, how demand of it that something more, I felt, must yet be given?

Well, we groped, she and I, rather miserably along. And then I, simply grabbing at one thing and another, happened to ask her why she had chosen to send her manuscript to Owen Hargreaves & Son.

Eugenie forgot to duck at this one, and I learned for the first time the place of Sebastian Samowitz in our little saga. In fact, I think Eugenie herself managed to ask what sort of a man was the author of *Charades*—that was her favorite of his books. He was, in fact, a difficult, self-important bore, whose demands to us had always far exceeded what he could materially supply us. No doubt the man had talent, though I think Eugenie rather overdid it. But he was as self-promoting in his dealings with us as he was unscrupulous on the point of the cleanliness of his neckties, and I always came away from him feeling that he almost came up to my mother's low view of the authors.

But I certainly didn't let any of this on to Eugenie, who was expressing, with timorous breathlessness, the great hope she had long cherished that she might some day be able to meet Sebastian Samowitz. She nearly—nearly, don't you know—blushed when I assured her that her desire could almost of a certainty be met.

I happened to have on my desk a new manuscript from Sebastian Samowitz—he was a prolific devil, I got at least a manuscript a year from him—and I indicated the object to Eugenie, reading off its title, which I can't remember now— much as I remember once a man who had a beautiful old Austin Healey I was interested in picking up several scraps of paper from his desk and telling me they were all bids for the car.

Well, that strategy worked that day on me—the man got very nearly his price. And I must say that my mother would not have glared had she seen the rapturous eyes that Eugenie rested on the manuscript on my desk.

After that, the conversation simply flowed. I told her a very little bit about the manuscript on my desk—the truth is I don't think I had altogether read it—and from there the conversation went on to other authors she admired, all of whom, except, of course, for Samowitz, were French. She hadn't, it seemed, read a single one of the best-selling female novelists of that time.

I was awfully surprised by the names she mentioned. No lady I knew would ever have read—would ever even have heard of—such books as she apparently had studied with great application. Even the sordid fantasies of the unspeakable Marquis had passed before the Methodist eyes.

It turned out she had an absolute passion for Emile Zola.

Well, there was another shocker. Eugenie placed Zola, don't you know, right after Samowitz.

I, too, had rather a passion for Zola.

After we had spoken of such things as Zola, I felt I could bring up with her the delicate subject of *Chimera*.

"You've written a very strange book," I said to her, at last.

"Oh," she gave a small gasp as if with pain and seemed even to make a small flinch—I was awfully irked to see this theme of *smallness* so worked out in the author of *Chimera*. "Oh, I thought from your letter that you liked it."

Her voice—have I said it?—it was a very low voice, in fact a very sweet voice, though it often hesitated over the choice of a word.

"Oh, I do. I do like it," I quickly hastened to assure her. "Indeed, 'like' is too pallid a term to describe my reaction to your . . . to *Chimera*."

I had found, on the trying, that I was not yet able to say to her "your book." I think I preferred, for the moment, to think of the book as essentially unattached and unauthored.

"I can't remember the last time I was so excited by a new work as I am by *Chimera*," I continued. "I was completely fascinated, overwhelmed—and not just a little bit appalled."

"Appalled?" Again she seemed to flinch.

"Well, yes. It is, don't you know, appalling—perhaps in the way that all very new things are appalling."

"*Is* it very new?" she asked me, quite stupidly. "I wasn't terribly conscious of its being very new."

Really, she seemed to me then as just not terribly conscious at all.

"Not new? Really, tell me another author who does anything remotely approaching what's done in *Chimera!*"

"You must think me oddly dense," she said, reading my mind. "I think I'd be quite at a loss to say what exactly *is* done in *Chimera*. I'm too much in it."

This, of course, brought me face to face with the unpleasant fact I had been trying hard to pretend all the time wasn't there.

"But how did you come yourself to *be* in it? It's altogether extraordinary that you *should* be there, don't you know, Miss Worthinghouse."

Again she considered for a very long time, staring down at her childlike lap.

At last she said, "I suppose I must have come to be there because of Laurie."

I do dislike it awfully—don't you?—when people simply mention a name quite out of the blue, and expect you somehow, as if by magic, to know of whom it is that they're speaking.

"And who is Laurie?" I asked.

"Laurie was my brother. He's dead. He died young."

"Oh, I'm most dreadfully sorry," I said.

"He died in Paris," I think she continued. "He was twenty-eight."

"My age," I said, quite irrelevantly.

But, you know, my dear, I've talked myself up into the most raging thirst. I'm parched dry with all my talking. Are you parched dry with all your listening, your very excellent listening?

And now why don't I ring, and we can have some of Mrs. Duffy's indecently good tea and little cold sandwiches? And I rather think the fire needs tending, don't you know.

IV

LAURIE

Well, you do know, you must, of course, the whole sad story of the dead brother, Laurie.

It was the next day, when I went to see her at that awful boarding house for respectable transient women she had booked herself into over on Tenth Street, that she told me all about it.

I remember how we sat in the hot, faded parlor, and talked. There was a rug with a picture of a Newfoundland dog rescuing a child from drowning laid before the chimney, and a row of chromolithographs on the wall.

It was Zola once again that got us started. Zola always was the theme that broke the ice. Eugenie could fulminate with all the outrage of a Methodist on the topic of the would-be keepers of the public's morality. The man, don't you know, had been kept out of the French Academy, by these ever-busy keepers, though he had stood for it no fewer than nineteen times. And then, you know, the Englishman who had translated Zola's works had actually been imprisoned on charges of obscenity.

But, of course, Zola wasn't altogether the martyr Eugenie would have had him. In fact, he seemed to have done a bit in the way of fanning up the ready ire of the keepers of morality, knowing how very good for sales such scandal always is.

But Eugenie was adamant on the point of Zola's martyrdom. She was one of those who were convinced that his death—he died, don't you know, from the poisonous gases that entered his bedroom through a faulty flue in the chimney—but Eugenie was one of those who were convinced that the death hadn't been an accident at all. The murderous critics had fixed that flue.

It wasn't, of course, Zola's style that so much interested the author of *Chimera*—of course, you can see how very little she owed him in that direction. But she was very much taken with the use Zola makes of Christian symbolism, his translating such concepts as "original sin" into so-called naturalist terms.

But of course, my dear. Of course Zola had a concept of original sin. Only he didn't call it by that name. He called it an "organic lesion."

He had believed something like that human weakness, madness and vice and all that sort of thing, was the result of what he called an "organic lesion" in one member of a family, and that this fatal frailty was, without fail, transmitted to all the doomed descendants. It was only a fluke if any of them happened to escape.

This idea, you know, of seeing the seed of doom implanting itself in the psyche of a person, and watching it work itself out in the generations, work itself out in pages of singeing, black poetry, well, all of this had penetrated itself awfully deep in the mind of the author of *Chimera*.

Meanwhile, this talk of seeds of doom and such led directly enough to talk of the dead brother, Laurie.

He was the elder, by, I believe, six or seven years, a boy of enormous talent and promise. They had all completely doted on him: the father, the mother, and, of course, Eugenie. None of them was ever quite certain, least of all poor Laurie himself, what it was that he would end up doing, but there'd never been any doubt that, whatever it would be—science or music or art or theology or letters—for his genius was almost atrociously adaptable—whatever it was he would finally end up doing, it would be, don't you know, on a very grand scale, on the very grandest scale. He would change the flow of the tide just by the stepping into it.

Changing the tides. It's the moon that does that, isn't it. Not the right image at all for Laurie Worthinghouse. Laurie was the very sun of that family. They all revolved about him. They all saw themselves in relationship to him. Eugenie was the moon, the dark circling moon. That's how she continued to think of herself, long after he was gone.

That's why she was so completely nonplussed when one asked her anything about herself. She saw herself as the dimmest sort of figure. No real shape or color or substance to her at all. No real self. A sort of shadow of a self.

And that's also why she always was at such a loss to take in the thing that she had become. After the publication of *Chimera*, I mean. She never could take it in, you know. Never could see what it was she had done with the doing of *Chimera*. The acclaim just made her feel like a fraud, like an awful humbug and a cheat.

Perhaps, if she had lived a little longer in the company of her fame, it might have changed her. Something of what the world took her to be might have penetrated in to her. Though I somehow doubt it. She never did seem to be making any sort of progress in that direction.

So, when she said to me, that first time, that she was the author of *Chimera* because of her brother, Laurie, she quite literally meant it, even though the poor boy had been dead for seven years when she finally came to write her book.

And it's not as if he himself had written anything at all like it in his life, though he had been working on a book— well, in a manner of speaking—during that period that led up to his death in Paris.

It was to be a book of theology. He had left thousands of pages of notes—only notes—and she had spent perhaps the first two or three years after his death trying to sort them out and make sense of them. She was hoping, of course, to reconstruct the great idea and give him, at last, his immortality.

It had broken her heart to have to give it up, finally, as impossible.

That's how, I suppose, she came to write a book at all— out of her failure to piece together Laurie's book. She'd never have taken it on otherwise.

It's strange, but I can really tell the story of Laurie Worthinghouse so much more fully than I can Eugenie's own story, because, of course, his was the story that *she* could tell.

Laurie Worthinghouse had been, as Eugenie told it, an absolutely fascinating person, with all that presence I had looked for in vain in the author of *Chimera*. His conversation was an education in itself. That's how Eugenie had gotten herself an education.

She had made herself his little slave, I think, from a very early age, for I remember her telling me that she would often do the drudgework of his school assignments for him, and in that way earn for herself the reward of being allowed to stay near him for the evening, so long as she didn't make her presence too much felt.

Now that I come to think of it, the little girl must have been awfully precocious to do the drudgework of a brother seven years the elder.

Do you remember the place in *Chimera* where you get, all of a sudden, that funny little sideways glance of the child Forchette, walking beside Antoine, trying to keep up with him? The pain in her side you're given to feel for a moment as she struggles to match his strides? It's strange—and strangely affecting, too—the way that fleeting image of her comes. Just for a moment you see the walk over the Pont Neuf from down at the child's eyeview, the child only trying to keep up with Antoine and the stitch in the side that's making it so difficult for the little thing to draw in a breath.

Well, don't you know, I've always imagined that the five or six sentences of that fleeting description make for the only truly autobiographical moment in the whole vastness of *Chimera*!

I imagine that the little sister, Eugenie, used to struggle in just such a way, with just such a stitch in her side, to keep up with her brother, on those occasions when he allowed her to walk beside him, and allowed her to catch snippets of the wonderful thoughts he was thinking.

Belief in his genius had been the passion of her young life. She had been fiercely—oh, fiercely!—ambitious for him. If there was anything that made her feel that she was different from all others, that she was a person somehow lifted above the level of the ordinary, it was that she was Laurie Worthinghouse's little sister. It was to be, for her, an occupation in life. She had never dreamt, as a young girl, as other young girls do—I mean of husband and home and all that sort of thing. But she knew, as it is given to very few women to know, what it is to have that great hungry beast, Ambition, stalking one's breast.

Even when I met her, years after he was dead, the traces of her passion were there on her yet, despite the awful disillusion that had come to her from the years struggling alone with Laurie's notes.

She didn't, not on that morning at least, there in the parlor on Tenth Street, let me know the secret she had come finally to extract from the thousands of pages of notes—though, of course, when I came fully to understand how it was that she had been able to write *Chimera*, I understood it all.

That morning she made it sound as if the failure to assemble her brother's thoughts into a book had been all her own— that he himself would surely have done it, poor boy, had he been allowed to live out his life.

Well, you know, he had been given to great dramatic crises

of faith, which made him take wild leaps in all sorts of strange directions.

I don't suppose young men suffer those crises of faith anymore the way they used to do. I don't suppose there's enough faith around over which to suffer a crisis.

He had gone, in his late adolescence, I think, through an intensely religious phase, during which his father's Methodism had seemed a pretty damnable attenuation of the real thing. He began to study—of course in secret, though Eugenie knew all about it—with a Jesuit priest. He was intending to convert to Catholicism.

And little Eugenie, she must have been about ten or eleven at the time, had known that she, too, must convert. She formed an image of herself in a nun's black habit.

But then something happened. I don't know if she herself ever really knew exactly what it was that made Laurie abruptly give up his Jesuit, and refuse ever to talk of Catholicism again.

But the Roman religion always did continue to hold an almost unwholesome fascination for her, don't you know. You can see it right there, can't you, in *Chimera*, in the dark flitting figure of the young Jesuit priest. One can never quite figure out what he's up to, can one. Oh, a very great number of learned papers have been written on the ambiguous figure of the Jesuit priest.

In any case, after the Jesuitical plan was dropped, Laurie enrolled himself in Harvard, and began the study of medicine. But he gave that up, too, after about a year or so.

It's amazing the exorbitant demands the young man made on his parents' fund of indulgence, which must have been pretty near limitless. But, then, their patience was the answer they all made him to what they saw as his own inexhaustible quality. So he had much to answer for, too, this young man. He had no choice but to be the genius they all of them believed him to be—the only problem remaining his fixing upon the shape into which his genius would finally settle itself.

But this was the one problem Laurie's genius couldn't resolve. It moved about in Laurie's life—that quantity of genius—like a goblet of mercury rolling about on one's palm.

Laurie withdrew from the Harvard Medical School, only to enroll in the Harvard Divinity School, now with the idea of training for the ministry.

Of course, another one of those crises of faith interceded before too long. They seemed to have been coming at quite regular intervals by now.

Again, he asked to study medicine, but this time he begged to be permitted to go to Paris, to the hospital where the famous Charcot had given the lectures on hysteria and hypnotism that had implanted themselves in the mind of the very young Freud.

But the investigation of hysteria didn't send Laurie Worthinghouse off to create a new science of the mind. Instead it sent him hurtling like a shuttlecock back to theology. There seemed to be nothing like the study of medicine for making Laurie yearn after theology; just as there was nothing like the study of theology to determine Laurie to be a doctor.

So, before long, he had left the hospital, and had plunged into a deep and solitary study of the New Testament.

Eugenie only knew that in the course of that solitary study Laurie uncovered—or believed himself to have uncovered— a secret that was buried in the text of the New Testament, a secret that was to make Christianity forevermore impossible. Eugenie never knew from Laurie the chapter and the verse, and even his notes were written in an increasingly elaborate and Byzantine code, for Laurie was tormented by the suspicion that everyone he knew—but most of all his younger sister!—was determined to take his idea from him.

The more she begged him in her letters to tell her what he

knew, the more he suspected her of treachery. And scrawled all over the margins, in a frantic hand that was only just decipherably his, were the words "I shall burn this," which Eugenie believed to have been written at the eleventh hour, before the terrible thing happened.

She hadn't any idea why he hadn't acted on the intention scrawled in his margins. Perhaps he simply couldn't bring himself to do it. Perhaps he'd only found the courage, at the end, to destroy his own life, but not his idea. Who can say, since Eugenie couldn't, or, in any case, wouldn't.

But the thousands of pages of notes came to the father on Laurie's death, together with all his other personal effects. And the father had handed them over to Eugenie.

He wasn't sleeping, you know, all the time that his great idea was working within him. Sleep had become almost physically impossible for him. He kept a diary—it's worked into the theological notes—of the few minutes of sleep he'd manage to snatch from the ordeal of wakefulness.

He threw himself into a surfeit of sensations, trying, perhaps, to tire himself out. This, too, began to work its way into the thousands of pages of notes. No wonder poor Eugenie had finally given up trying to resurrect something like a book of theology from out of them!

But, you see, that is how Eugenie, the poor drab creature out of poor drab Pittsburgh, that is how all the frightful knowledge of *Chimera* had come to be hers. She was trying to grasp for herself all that he had felt in those maddened weeks before he died. And so she imagined for herself her poor brother's terrible descent into a world of pleasures and pains so far—so incalculably far—from her and her Pittsburgh.

That's how, in the end, she came to be the author of *Chimera*.

Yes, my dear. She did in fact tell me almost all of this

during those hours I spent with her in that awful parlor on Tenth Street.

At first, she had spoken so stiffly, so stiltedly. Strange, to think of the author of *Chimera* as uttering anything stilted!

I think, don't you know, that she was very unused to talking. Well, think of it. With whom did she have to talk, now that all her family, now that Laurie was dead? I don't think she had a friend in the world before I came to be her friend.

Why, yes, of course. Of course, I was her friend. Not just her editor. Do you think she could possibly have done what she did if she hadn't thought of me as her friend?

But she lived buried alive in such a tomb of solitude. Who was there suitable for her in Pittsburgh? Who could there be with whom the author of *Chimera* could speak?

I think she was startled, at the beginning of each conversation, by the sound of her own voice.

I glimpsed this that morning, there on Tenth Street. I glimpsed a bit of how hideously lonely the author of *Chimera* was, how even her writing *Chimera* had been, in some way, a long terrible shriek of the loneliness and the longing she felt for her dead brother.

In some ways that doctor of theology had been quite right. *Chimera* is, for all its wild beauty, a howling, pitiful thing, too. Its genius doesn't exult in itself. It despairs.

I seemed, while Eugenie spoke to me that morning, to be staring down such a deep frightening well of solitude—and seeing those solemn gray eyes of hers peering back at me in the darkness.

It made a tremendous difference, that long sad conversation we had together that morning. We came out of it with something somehow having been enacted between us. There was a space we could both now enter, and when we entered we spoke as we spoke to no others. It made possible all that was to follow.

I could speak to her there of her *Chimera*, of the something more that she had still to give me.

At first she was quite horribly upset to hear me say that she must plunge herself once more into her work—that she must follow further the course of her dead brother's undoing.

"But they have stopped," she said very simply. "The voices, I mean. I no longer hear them. I think that means the book is finished. In any case, how can I write more?"

"Oh, when you see the more that's needed—and you will, I know you will—they'll come back to you. All your wonderful voices."

"You're quite certain? Certain that the book isn't done?"

"Yes, I'm certain. There's more in you that's waiting to come out."

"I only hope that I can do it," she murmured.

"I know you can do it!" I told her, just as I had told other authors before her, and many more since. Never, of course, with quite the results it was to have now.

"Give me more," I said, when I had grasped her little hand and squeezed it in farewell. "Genie, *give me more!*"

And so I sent the little author back to Pittsburgh.

V

DAGUERREOTYPE

How is the walking out there, my dear? Not too slippery, I hope. I see you're wearing very sensible boots.

I can't remember a more dismal February, can you?

Come take your place by the fire, and we'll get right back down to it, shall we?

Well, as I told you last time, I had sent the author of *Chimera* back to Pittsburgh with the plea to give me more.

It must have been about three or four weeks later that I received a little note from her, saying that she would be coming to New York again, and that she had thought of a turn in the story that might give me what I was wanting, but that she wished first to discuss it with me.

Well, of course I readily agreed, and before another week was up the author of *Chimera* was back.

She was still staying at the awful little place on Tenth Street, but she had very much changed in her appearance—smartened herself up a bit, don't you know, hobble skirt and all.

I was at first quite startled by the change. But then I decided that she really looked quite nice, that the change was very much for the better.

My mother was always very hard on Eugenie's little attempts at fashion. Well, of course, my mother was a true mistress of style, and she always said—I told you that she had a sense of humor—that little Eugenie looked as if she had gone quite wild with a Sears, Roebuck catalogue.

I remember that it was a most brilliant day in October. The foliage—well, what foliage there was, in the lower part of Manhattan—was at the peak of its colors, and I proposed to Eugenie, for I couldn't really stand another session in that awful parlor, that we take a cab up to Central Park and stroll there. She almost clapped her hands with glee at the suggestion.

There was, when one knew her better, a certain amount of play that peeped out from beneath the prim of Eugenie. Well, there would have to be, wouldn't there, a sort of playfulness, too, in the author of *Chimera*?

There really was very little left of the stick about her that afternoon. She was still diffident, unused to hearing the sound of her own voice, but she seemed ever so much more easy and alive.

And she was really quite excited about her new idea. It was the voice of Antonia, of course, that had started to speak to her. Her frankness in telling me of it was really quite wonderful, and I was, of course, wonderfully excited by all she had to tell me.

I remember, with each of my little comments, she made so much more of them than they really were. She would take the barest hint of a suggestion, cup it in her palm and mumble some magic incantation over it, then open up her hand to show a white dove that would come flying forth, or a streak of colored scarves.

She was a conjurer, Eugenie was. A prestidigitator in a hobble skirt.

Once she became receptive to you, once she trusted you, saw that you liked her, she lost much of the chill of her shyness. And then she could do the most marvelous things with any hint you gave her.

And she had become very receptive to me. She had seen, when I sent her back to Pittsburgh that first time, that what I had said to her had been true. She saw that I had seen something about her *Chimera*, something vital and essential, that she hadn't herself seen, and I can't tell you what a difference this made to her, how awfully receptive it made her to anything I was to put to her.

I knew—and I told her I knew—that she must keep on with this new voice.

"Be open to it, Eugenie," I told her. "Only be open to it, and it shall happen."

"Oh . . . if *you* are open to it!"

"Oh, I am! I most certainly am! Go to it, Genie girl!"

That was the first time that I ever heard her laugh. She didn't often laugh. She had an altogether surprising, a thoroughly *delicious* laugh. So full-throated and spirited. So utterly unlike the woman. Perhaps even a little bit wild. It delighted me, that laugh.

It was a very glorious time we had, tramping together that afternoon through the twisting paths of the old Ramble. Even Eugenie's coloring seemed to have brightened itself up a little in the midst of the brilliant foliage. Perhaps it was just our excitement over the voice of Antonia, but she seemed almost to have, that afternoon, a complexion.

I remember some laughter over her difficulty in keeping up with me, when I would forget myself and walk a little too fast for her, with those awfully short limbs—you know, in those days we would never have referred to a lady's legs— and, of course, that very stylish hobble skirt.

"I shall have to pick you up and carry you if you can't go a little faster," I teased her.

I should never have believed it possible, but Eugenie and I had a very jolly time that afternoon. Well, of course, there was the great excitement of the new idea for *Chimera*, making us both a little giddy.

We took a picture together that day. It was I who suggested it. There was a daguerreotype shop on Fifth Avenue and I thought it would be rather fun, don't you know. To mark the great day when Antonia was all but conceived between us.

Well, as it happened, the photograph turned out to be an awfully bad idea.

The blasted thing had caught Eugenie looking her most sticklike. And she had really looked so nice that day. But she looked terrible in the daguerreotype. Simply terrible.

And I—well, I've always been very photogenic. The camera is always very kind to the sort of looks I had, which I shared with my mother, that blond, healthy ease I had as a young man.

But the two of us standing side by side together in that hideous photograph. She looked like nothing more than a little smudge on my sleeve.

I had looked at the thing first, and when I saw it, well, I did the best I could think of at the moment, which was to laugh.

She held out her little hand for it. You know, don't you,

that daguerreotypes came out in doubles. Well, I handed her her half. And I remember how, when she looked at it, a little tremor passed through her cheek. It was pitiful to see how crushed she was, how terribly, terribly seriously she took the little grimacing image of herself standing there beside the smiling image of me.

She didn't say a word, and she looked so miserable that I couldn't think of a thing to say to her.

But I remember thinking to myself at that moment that the author of *Chimera* would gladly give up all her talent to be pretty.

And then she tore up her half of the picture. Or, rather, she ripped out the part with herself in it, leaving only me. And she begged me to do the same.

But I wouldn't.

"I want it," I told her, even though I saw the tears in her eyes.

Yes, I suppose I've got it still. I'll search it out and have it for you next time.

VI
THE SEA, THE SEA

You know, I never did manage to arrange a meeting between Sebastian Samowitz and the author of *Chimera*.

The man was playing infernally hard to get. He'd never thought I had paid him a sufficient amount of mind, not to speak of dollars, and now he had my attention he was determined to keep it.

It was unforgivably small of him. After Eugenie's death, I found I simply couldn't forgive the man. After all, she had asked so little of me, so very little that I could gratify, and I had all but promised her, that first time, an introduction to the man.

No, I never could forgive him, and I never did publish another one of his novels after Eugenie's death. Nobody else did either, so far as I know.

But I did manage, at least, to give her a day's trip to the sea. It was the one thing she had most wanted—after an introduction to Samowitz—the only other thing she ever asked me for.

She'd never seen it, you see, living all her life, as she had, in Pittsburgh. It was quite an idea with her, the sea.

It was the one thing, she said, that she couldn't conjure up for herself. In her imagination. The sea.

I can't say I ever understood it, the almost mystical power the idea had for her. I had grown up with the sea. It was a pretty prosaic thing to me. As a boy I used to spend almost all my summers at the house my mother had inherited, it was called Land's End, way out on the tip of eastern Long Island, near Montauk. It was a big old ugly wooden house with half an acre of rock and endless miles of Atlantic Ocean right outside its windows.

My mother still owned it at the time. She had a strange fondness for it, big old ugly thing that it was. Well, she had spent her childhood summers there as well. Places one spent as a child, they keep a sort of hold on one, don't you know. That part of Long Island hadn't become at all fashionable yet, so the place hadn't been sold off piecemeal to pay for Owen Hargreaves & Son, as all of our more valuable pieces of real estate had been.

So it was to Land's End that I proposed to take Eugenie that day.

We drove out in my motor—a Panhard-Levassor, a wonderful car. I was, don't you know, a great motoring enthusiast in those days, ever since my very first spin in an automobile—it belonged to an old friend of mine from Yale—in the summer of 1903.

In those days, cars were still pretty much the toys of the rich. But my mother had made me a surprise gift of the Panhard two years before.

You can have no idea what driving was like in those days, the wonderful, wild, free-for-all thing that it was, with no signs or speed limits, no such encroachments by the law— indeed, with hardly any roads to speak of.

As soon as we left Manhattan, I pushed down hard on the accelerator, and we were going nearly fifty miles an hour, over humps and bumps, through ditches and across gutters, windswept and dust-enveloped.

Eugenie was wearing, I remember, a thin little dress—it was an unseasonably warm day in April—and she had a little sailor hat perched on her chignon. But at least I had remembered to bring her my mother's motoring coat—my mother, too, adored driving; I think the gift of the car was as much for her as it was for me.

Of course, Eugenie was completely lost when she put the thing on. One could have made at least three or four Eugenies out of my mother.

Well, you know, conversing was pretty near impossible, what with the wind lashing us in the face. The car didn't yet come equipped with a windscreen. And in any case, once we hit the open space, I became completely caught up in the exhilaration of covering ground so quickly, and almost forgot that Eugenie was there at all.

But at some point I took a glance over at her—she was sitting huddled inside of my mother's motoring coat, still as a stick—and it suddenly occurred to me that she might be terrified, what with the unwonted speed of it all. I'd altogether forgotten she'd never been in a car before.

So I stopped the car and asked her if she was quite all right. Well, I saw, in fact, as soon as I looked at her, that she wasn't. She was white as a ghost, and unnaturally still.

But, you see, it wasn't the driving at all that had made her frightened. It was the sea. The idea of the sea.

"Are we very close to it?" she asked me in a little whisper, looking over at me with those great solemn gray eyes of hers.

"Quite close. I'll have you there in a jiffy, Genie." I laughed back at her. You see, I still simply thought it was the drive that was unsettling her.

"Do you think we might turn back, Owen?"

"Turn back? Whatever are you speaking about? We're all but there! In a very few moments you're to see that great vast sea you've been longing for!"

She simply sat, quite rigid and staring straight in front of her.

"You do *want* to see the ocean, don't you, Genie?"

"I'm not so sure that I really do." Her voice was strained, not at all the sweet thing it usually was.

Well, I was having none of this. I'd set out to show her the sea, and, by George, the sea I would show her.

"Come, come, what's all the fuss?" I just laughed over at her in my most jovial and uncomprehending manner, which I had found awfully effective with her, don't you know. Faced with it, she usually just gave up her point with a little sigh.

And so she did. I heard her give her little sigh, as she huddled herself more deeply into my mother's coat, and without so much as another little murmur from her, we drove on.

Well, it was strange, to say the least, when we got there.

I jumped out over my side and dashed round to help Eugenie. She was as light as a feather, even in the huge coat, which I helped her out of. She seemed almost in a dream, to be moving in a dream.

"Smell the air, Genie! That's the sea air! Marvelous, isn't it? I can tell you, it would put a little meat on your bones, if you were to stay here for a while."

I don't know why it was, but for some reason I always became exaggeratedly hearty when she began to fade out in that way. Well, you know, it made me awfully impatient, the way she did that.

She gave a delicate little sniff, and I heard her murmur, "Ah, I hadn't gotten the smell of it at all."

She didn't give so much as a glance at the old house sitting up in the midst of its dunes and sand-scrubble.

The dunes were blocking our view of the sea. Without a word, she began to walk toward them, in that same dreamlike way, with me by her side making asinine remarks about the boyhood summers I had spent scrambling over these dunes, searching for treasure and whatnot left by pirates.

And then, there was the Atlantic Ocean, spread out before us.

I heard her give a little gasp, and I reached out an arm to steady her, and I felt how she was shaking like a leaf.

"Are you quite all right, Genie?" I asked her, still holding her up.

She nodded, but it seemed to me her eyes were glassy.

"That's France over there," I said, pointing. In fact, the windows of our house looked straight out to the northwest coast of Normandy.

She slightly shifted her head, to stare at where I was pointing, as if the sea might look a little different there.

"Could you leave me now, Owen," she said in that same strained voice I had heard in the car.

"Are you quite sure you'll be all right?" I asked her.

"Quite sure," she answered, even managing to look away from the sea for a moment, and smile quite naturally up into my face.

So I turned and left her there, and went over to the house. I had brought along a picnic basket, and as it was really too windy out there on the beach, I thought I'd get it fixed up on the dining-room table.

Well, the windows of the dining room looked out on the sea, and while I was laying out the contents of the basket I looked out and saw the tiny little figure of Eugenie, walking slowly toward the sea. She seemed so very much like a child to me, looking down at her from the windows of the house.

She was making her very erratic way to the sea. She'd walk a few feet, stop and stand for ten minutes or more, then walk a few feet nearer. It was as if each time she had to stop and build up her courage to continue.

Watching her, I could feel, even from the distance of the house, how completely terrified she was, how much it cost her to stand there all by herself at the very edge of the sea and look out at it.

And when she came back to the house, finally, she was as exhausted and shivering as if she had just swum the English Channel. It was all I could do just to get her to swallow some tea.

But she told me that seeing the sea had been the great experience of her life.

VII
CONFESSION

It was exactly six weeks after our jolly little jaunt through the Central Park Ramble that I got a little note from Eugenie, telling me that the third draft was done.

I wired her back that I was coming myself to Pittsburgh to get it from her.

She lived in a very plain, very shabby house, on a block full of just the same sort of plain and shabby houses. I don't think I'd ever seen a more depressing avenue, and it was astounding, surveying the straight, shadeless bleakness of it up and down—not a tree planted or a garden tended—it was simply astounding to think that this most uninspiring patch had been the setting in which *Chimera* had been born.

My God, I thought, just think what she would be capable of if she were exposed to some little real beauty in her life. And I felt determined, very determined, at least for the moment, to see if I couldn't get some of that beauty to her, in one way or another. I felt it, suddenly, as a sort of sacred duty laid upon me to do what I could to lift the drabness off from the author of *Chimera*.

I had, in the great heat of my impatience, actually made the trip to Pittsburgh in my Panhard. And no sooner had I parked it in front of Eugenie's house than I was besieged by a pack of dirty-faced little urchins. They had seemed, in that universal manner of children, simply to appear out of nowhere. They stood there, gaping, as if I had just descended upon them on a flying carpet.

However, so great was their stupefaction that they kept what seemed to me a safe distance from me and my vehicle. So, with an admonishing few words to them, not to draw any nearer or I should have them all behind bars, I went up the sagging steps of Eugenie's little porch.

She answered the door herself. She was looking very well, despite what must have been a sleepless period for her. My merciless mother would have said that poor Eugenie had been busying herself again in the pages of the Sears, Roebuck catalogue; but I thought she looked really very nice.

She brought me into her little parlor. It was awfully dingy, the furniture was indescribably hideous, but it was all very, very clean. Eugenie, you know, had no servant at all. She did all the housework for herself. She had been left terribly little by her clergyman father, and had to account for every cent that she spent. It was only a poor coal miners' parish that he had ministered there in Pittsburgh. And, of course, there had been all of Laurie's crises of faith to be paid for.

She asked me if I were thirsty or hungry.

"Only thirsty and hungry to see what you have written for me!" I answered her—and it was true.

She hurried out of the room and up the narrow, dark stairs out in the little hallway. In half a minute she was back, cradling her pages in her arms.

"Here it is!" she said, suddenly handing it straight out to me. She blushed like a bride.

I was sitting on the awful little horsehair sofa, the manuscript on my lap, and she was standing right before me. I looked down at the manuscript, and then smiled up at her.

"It's a good deal heavier," I said.

"It's one-sixth of the entire manuscript heavier," she answered me, smiling.

"All of it Antonia?"

"All of it Antonia."

I continued to smile up at her.

"You're not going to tell me another thing about it, are you?"

"Not another thing!"

"Well, then," I said, leaping up. "There's not another thing for me to do but to rush straight back to New York and read it for myself!"

Which, of course, I did.

It was the very last draft, you know, that she handed over to me that afternoon with her strange, bridal blush. Absolutely nothing about it was changed for publication. There wasn't a line, there wasn't a word, one could question.

I read the pages of Antonia's confession over and over again that night, the sweet wild music of the thing sinking into me, again and again, with a fresh surprise.

Even though she had told me before of the voice of Antonia, it came to me as if I had never known of it at all.

Antonia's confession told the story, for the very first time in the history of English letters, of a woman's desires, of what a world made out of a woman's desires would be. And how strange, how awfully strange it was—people have said it, but none of them could feel the strangeness so much as I—that, when the story of a woman's desire came, at long last, to be written in the English language, it wasn't by a cigar-smoking bohemian free spirit of a woman who wore men's trousers, or by a strong-minded, manly-featured woman living with another woman's husband. No, by God, it was written by little Eugenie Amalie Worthinghouse, the clergyman's daughter from Pittsburgh, who shook like a leaf when people noticed her.

Well, what can I say? So much has been said of those one hundred and six pages. Everyone's had a go at them by this time. The doctors of theology, the professors of literature. And now you shall have your turn.

I will say this for myself. I never would have betrayed my opinion of *Chimera*. No matter what the external world had finally thought fit to pronounce on that book, even if *Chimera* had fallen stillborn from the press, had sold no more than twenty copies, I'd have remained faithful to my view that it was the first masterpiece of Modernism. I'd have blamed the world, and not the book, for any of its failure. This may not sound like very much to you, but, coming from an editor, I can assure you that it's something very much indeed.

Yes, my dear. I did say that my mother read *Chimera*. Apparently she did so right after Eugenie's three-week stay with us at St. Luke's Place that I believe I'd mentioned to you before.

The book was already a very huge success. All the scandal was only helping sales.

In those days, of course, one had no such thing as a publicity department. But, really, what publicity department could have done more for the commercial success of *Chimera* than the clergymen and other assorted morality-keepers were already doing?

We were, of course, very much hoping, my mother and myself, for a second novel from the author of *Chimera*. So my mother, as I've told you, put up with her for those three weeks, all the while keeping close watch, through that tissue of hospitality. Watching not just Eugenie, don't you know, but myself as well.

And what she saw—at any rate, what she thought she saw—determined her, just as soon as Eugenie went back to Pittsburgh, to read the book for herself. I'd no idea she had decided to read the book, though, of course, I wouldn't have been able to do anything about it even if I had known.

But one afternoon, perhaps two or three weeks after Eugenie had left us, my door was flung open and there, once again filling my portal, was the magnificent, flushed figure of my mother. She was holding Eugenie's book in her hand, and she stood there glaring at me, in the way she had when words were failing her.

"Well, I've read it, Owen!" she finally announced in the most grating tones of which she was capable.

I simply answered her with a raise of my eyebrows.

"Indeed, you may very well raise your eyebrows, Owen! I have certainly raised mine just about as far up as they can go!"

When I still said nothing, her glare intensified, and she actually hurled the book across the small space so that it landed on my desk.

At this provocation, I arose from my chair, but I still could not trust myself to speak.

"You might, Owen, have considered, if not my sensibilities, at least the sensibilities of your poor dead father. He would never have stooped to publish a thing like this simply to make us some money!"

It just so happened that the hurled book had landed on a paper that I had been studying when she had come bursting in. It was the quarterly statement, which I now handed over to her without another word.

She snatched it from me impatiently and began herself to study it, holding it slightly away from her, for she was becoming increasingly farsighted with middle age, though she refused until she was eighty to wear glasses.

So it took her a little time to make the figures out. But at last she looked up from the statement, with some of the glare turned down in her farsighted gaze.

"Well, this is all very well. I can't argue with figures such as these. And I suppose that there's the added consideration that, with her book to carry us, we can go on publishing the truly worthwhile things. I only hope that that will appease the spirit of your poor father, Owen."

I still had said nothing, and my silence was visibly irking to her. She glared again, then held the statement away from her to squint at it once more.

She finally placed it down quite carefully on my desk, and said to me, her own spirit somewhat appeased, "Get another book out of her, if you can. By all means. But I hope that you will understand me when I tell you, Owen, that a woman who could write a book like that . . . ! My God, she's no woman at all, but some sort of monster!"

She fixed me with one more exquisite glare, and then turned herself about and marched herself out.

I remember that, when my mother said those words to me, that Eugenie wasn't a woman but a monster, I remember that what they evoked in me was only a cold distaste for the woman who had just spoken them.

But those words that she had hurled at me, along with the book, across the small space of my office, those words had found their way into me, though I hardly knew it at the time. They stayed in me, spreading their chill.

My mother's words would never have done what they did if they hadn't been met with other words, of my own, that were very much similar.

But there's been some satisfaction all these years in living in my own small buried footnote, knowing that it was the

space that the author of *Chimera* and I had opened up between us that allowed the marvelous thing to happen.

Give me more, Genie! And she gave me those pages of
scorching poetry. Could any one else, I wonder, have wrung
such pages from her little Methodist heart?

It was strange, but we never really spoke of it, of Antonia's
confession. Even though she stayed with us an entire three
weeks, and I was very much with her, rather to the neglect
of Hudson Street. I even went with her to her sittings for
John Sargent. She was awfully pleased with what he was
making of her. She was very preoccupied with the progress
of her portrait. It was I who had commissioned it. My mother
glared awfully hard over that.

We talked a great deal those three weeks, but never a word
about those pages. Well, what word *could* I utter—except
the one?

And that I didn't do. I don't say that I couldn't have done
it, for I could have. There were times when the word might
have been said, when it was in my mind to say it, but I never
did.

Perhaps it was just the swell of vanity that had seized
me—a man's just pride at having been the prod that brought
forth those one hundred and six pages. I don't really know.
I was never a man very certain of what I was feeling, even
at the moment that I was feeling it. And at this great distance
of time, viewed across all those years of my long and not
unhappy marriage . . . Well, who can say? I can't, so surely
no one can.

And then perhaps there was also that in the situation that
didn't so much swell a man's pride as make it seem awfully
to droop. There was something almost a little annihilating
for a man in Antonia's confession. There was something that
was somehow cold in that desire that could speak itself with
so much genius.

Do you know those words of the Bard: " 'Tis mad idolatry, to make the service greater than the god"?

Well, if they are viewed in a certain way, that's precisely what those one hundred and six pages do. Who was I, really, to have provoked such art? She had constructed something round me that I was as far away from being as the real E. A. Worthinghouse, the little stick of a minister's daughter, was from being a poet's vision of womanhood.

And so she left us at the end of the three-week stay, in the last week of April, with never a word having been spoken between us on the subject of those one hundred and six pages. And by the end of the following June, I was engaged to be married.

I'd known Lucy Endicott all my life. She was a member of our little set, don't you know. In fact, she was a very distant cousin of mine, on my mother's side.

I wired Eugenie my news, and very soon after got back an answering telegram, congratulating me. "I drink the mead of your felicity." A short while later, a cut-glass-and-silver writing set arrived as a wedding present. My mother said her maid told her that they sold just that sort of thing in the Sears, Roebuck catalogue.

Our wedding was planned for the following April. Lucy absolutely insisted on the long engagement that was at that time considered only proper. Any attempt I made to have the date moved up was always answered in exactly the same way: But what will people say?

You see, one didn't want to do anything that might possibly be interpreted as precipitate haste. It wouldn't do to put out a hint that there was any sort of undignified desire on the part of the betrothed pair.

Eugenie had written me that she planned to attend my wedding. But sometime in February I got a letter saying that she had been very ill that winter—I hadn't known a thing about it—and that she was, on the orders of her doctor, sailing for Europe the very next month, on March the twenty-first. It's odd how the date has stuck in my mind.

She was sailing on the *Mauretania* from New York Harbor. Of course I went down to see her off.

She looked very bad, you know. I could see she had been ill. She was thinner than ever, and dressed in just that style of spinsterish drab in which she had first entered my office.

But she spoke to me quite cheerfully. She was going at long last to the Paris she had lived in only in her mind. Zola, of course, was already dead, asphyxiated in 1902. But there were men there who had known him, and would surely be pleased to meet the author of *Chimera*. One of Zola's young disciples was working on *La Chimère,* and she spoke to me of meeting with this young man, and seemed to look forward to it.

So I really can't answer your question, my dear. I don't know. I don't know if she had set out on the trip intending to die, to die in that terrible way she chose, or if she had simply allowed herself to succumb to one of those moments, don't you know, one of those moments one just can't see one's way out of.

It's too awful to think about. After all of these years, still. I've never been able to look out, straight out, at the sea without being stricken by the most overpowering feeling of loss.

Of course, the final irony was that the sickening sensationalism of her death absolutely assured that *Chimera* would sell for a very long term. By the end of the year, we had contracts on its translation into every major European language. It was the last thing she gave to Owen Hargreaves & Son.

I gave her a last gift, too. I had happened to find in a florist's shop, the very morning she was sailing, a cluster of extraordinary roses, very heavy white blooms, with a pure intensity of perfume. I had never seen any quite like them before, and they immediately made me think of the white prose of Antonia's confession, the white flame that had burned up everything clean in her *Chimera*.

I bought the roses, of course, and presented them, in their long white box, to Eugenie.

I remember how she had gasped a little at their beauty when she lifted off the lid. Well, they really were the most intensely white, the most startlingly beautiful specimens.

She lifted them out and held them to herself for several moments, her head down and inhaling.

She was so frail from her sickness, so dried up and haggard, she looked as if she might collapse beneath the weight of the two dozen roses.

I ran to find a porter and got a vase of water for her to put them in. And when I had returned, she handed me back twenty-three of the roses.

"They're too much for me," she said, half laughing. "They'd overpower me here in this little space. This one— just the one—will do me perfectly," she had said, randomly selecting a rose from the bunch.

And she took the vase of water I had gotten her and put it on a little table and settled the one rose in it.

Then she turned back to me, looking up with those solemn gray eyes of hers, and said, "I hope your fiancée won't mind that her two dozen is lacking one."

And those were just about her last words to me.

Of course, that question has haunted me, whether when she said them she already knew that they would be the last she spoke to me. But, in the end, I must simply tell you, my dear, that I don't know. And if I don't know, well, I don't suppose there's anyone that ever will know.

After all, I was the person who could read the author of *Chimera* better than anyone else. I was her editor. I was the one who drew those one hundred and six pages from out of her. The pages that were unlike all others that had ever been written before her, or since. Despite the whole pack of derivers.

But, of course, any woman who could write like that . . . ! Well, I don't suppose it really matters, anymore.

Do you, my dear? Do you really think it does?

Well, then, I think you'll be really quite happy to learn that I've decided to make you a final present after all. Here are the first two drafts of *Chimera*—yes, I've had them all along. And now they're yours. No, yours forever. It's just the sort of thing, isn't it, for a little scholar like you.

And I've something more, too, that I suspect will prove even more invaluable to you. They're Laurie Worthinghouse's notes, the whole mad lot of them. They were sent to me after her death, don't you know.

Look, here are the words in Laurie Worthinghouse's hand: "I shall burn this."

Why do you suppose he didn't, I wonder. And I wonder if she knew.

But you'll find the fatal chimera in there, my dear. I promise you that *that* you will find.

But what you won't find in Laurie's notes is anything like those one hundred and six pages of Antonia's confession. That was Genie's alone. The blazing white poetry that she wrote for me.

Not at all, my dear. I'm overjoyed to be able to do this for you.

I've decided, don't you know, to help make your brilliant career.

FROM DREAMS
OF THE
DANGEROUS DUKE

In her father's great house—half a woman, half child—
In her high cradle bed, she sleeps on to wan morn
When she wakes with a cry—half a whimper, half wild—
From dreams of the sad Duke of Abracadorn!

While a tall woman paces—a tigress, a tempest—
In her eyes a queer light that goes out with the dawn
When she sinks where she stands—the cold stones to her
breast—
As she curses the mad Duke of Abracadorn!

While a good man's young wife—round her white throat a
cross—
Abjures not the sanctified troth that she swore
But remembers her vow—blesses all that she's lost—
As she clings to the bad Duke of Abracadorn!

And I who write trembling—in distress and haste—
My pale, silent sisters in sorrow to warn
Drop down my cold pen—no more words but to wait—
For my darling—my own Duke of Abracadorn!

Little Cragglenook, 1835

*F*riday 25 September: It is late evening. I arrived here, round midnight, with an exhaustion and a despondency that penetrated themselves, with the wet chill, into the very marrows of my abused bones.

The long journey—even as Joseph's brothers sojourned southwards to the land of their bondage—was begun several hours before sunrise. The moors looked eerie and unfriendly in the cold moonlight, and Mother's gravestone was icy on my cheek when I kissed her goodbye. Father, who had of course not bestirred himself at so ungodly an hour, had taken his leave of me the evening before, with the words, hoarsely whispered (for whosoever departeth, yet cometh the Sabbath sermon, for which the clerical larynx must be preserved): 'Well, Emma, I hope I shall not see you again this time so very soon,' by which unembellished fare-thee-well he did wish me some portion of success upon my present venture. His words, as always, flew straight and true, for I found myself with an invigorated determination to see the situation through this time.

The trip ought to have taken a grueling ten hours, but was prolonged to a pitiless nineteen, owing to the rains that accompanied us the entire way down, slickening the roads and on several occasions causing the horses to become stuck in the mud—so that we must all of us alight, to sink our boots deep into the mire, while the coachman lashed and cursed his poor creatures forward. It was an experience in its every aspect tedious and drear, which are attributes I little wish to replicate here, for which reason I shall leave off its narration, only to state that I had to change carriages three times, and that for the entire way between Leeds and Manchester I shared the steaming, malodorous interior of the carriage with a family who had in tow two specimens of the genus *puling brat,* both of them with the nasty evidence of the influenza displayed about their persons, and whose noisome vapours I do no doubt carry even now within me, and very much fear that I shall yet suffer the baleful consequences therefrom. Inauspicious contingencies indeed for an already reluctant governess.

I was too low in body and spirit to take in much of the

surroundings that greeted my delayed arrival. The household had already retired, and I was 'seen to' with brisk efficiency by the housekeeper, a Mrs. Winter. The only details that mattered at the moment were agreeable: my room was plain but comfortable; the servant resentful of the hour and there-fore close-mouthed; the sheets of my bed dry and cinder-warmed.

I slept dreamlessly till dawn, when I awakened thoroughly dispirited with the thought of the hard Necessity awaiting— for me, the most trying in all the world: to meet new people and assay to make myself accommodating to them. I think that I could stare into the poised rifle-butts of a firing-squad with a steadier pulse than that which flutters sickly in me on those occasions when I am forced to converse with strangers. As I lay there, a sinking sensation rising together with the day, I felt all that I had fastened within me—all the rare verities I had sifted out from drossy delusion—violently pried loose from me once more; so that again I knew nothing of myself, nor of the world, nor of my place within it. 'Tis this that meeting new people always does to me.

But the hours since the darkling dawn have somewhat restored me to myself, so that I am again in that state of active determination with which I took leave of my affec-tionate parent. And truly, had I been forced to spend another month alone with him in that house of hallowed silence, methinks I should have been moved in some desperate di-rection. They are not, all in all, domestic scenes to which one ruefully bids adieu: seated wordlessly across from one an-other over dinner—myself the involuntary audience to Fa-ther's methods of mastication; or, again, myself, settled upon the hard settee with my basket of sewing and the ceaseless ticking of the grandfather clock that stands out in the hall. Methinks that when I die and go to Hell (Father's theology has left me little doubt of my destination) there will be for sure a grandfather clock ticking loudly in the outside hall.

But what I most fear now is that the situation here will go too far in the direction of obliviating solitude, so that every single one of my moments shall be delivered up to the resources of my employers, to make of it what they will. I can bear, by now, almost anything—but never that; for, without some little time to think the things I would, I grow as restless as the poet Camilla without her drug.

And yet perhaps—what a sweet promise breathes in 'perhaps'—it shall not be here as it has been before. For truly the omens of this place are good. The promise that I had, all cautiously, read, of circumstances that would prove congenial to my peculiarity, still seems to me to hold up under the more severe pressures of propinquity. They appear to be people of remarkable good breeding and of a decided intellectual direction—rare boons indeed for the governess.

The sisters, who shall together constitute my duties (there is a little boy of four or five, but he—I offer up my praises to our Lord—is under the tutelage of his own nursery governess) are three: there is Ella, who is fourteen; Vanessa, who is twelve; and Anna, who is almost eleven and remarkably pretty. They all of them seem to be intelligent and most becomingly solemn little girls. Vanessa, in particular, has already impressed me with the degree of infantile brilliance with which she answered the questions I put them. All three children are to be sent next year to Brussels to finish their education at a very prestigious boarding-school; and I am here to prepare them for this high advantage. Thus, as I well knew before embarking upon this situation, my employment here is of limited duration. The Madame did mention the possibility of my staying on to instruct the little boy; but I rather think not. In the meanwhile, I shall be instructing the girls in writing, arithmetic, history, grammar, geography, needlework, music, and drawing.

The household is on a very grand scale—quite commensurate, in fact, with the magnificence that had existed only in the fond pretensions of my last employers. We are on the far outskirts of Manchester, quite out of the city's noxious fumes. The house itself is eighteenth-century, very large and well appointed, of white stucco, with a handsome linen motif running all around the upper storey, as well as numerous picturesque balconies and a creeper. It is set in its own park of some twelve acres, and is surrounded by open fields. (The park, they tell me, is unusually beautiful in spring and summer, though the scene it affords now is uncommonly drear.) The drawing-room where I was received is immensely large, with an adjoining conservatory. It has a large grand piano and very elegant furniture by, I believe, Chippendale and Sheraton. On the walls are several very fine oil paintings— mostly Flemish and Dutch—as well as pull-cords for the servants, who are, I believe, eight or nine in number (excluding the two governesses).

The mistress gave me a moment's distress in the drawing-room, owing to that first impression, upon whose reliability I have come to rest so much trust. However, a few moments more of conversation quite lulled my apprehensions, as I saw that these last were largely due to her costume, which was extravagant, to say the least. She is indubitably a lady of very decided fashion, and I anon inferred those most odious qualities of Female Flightiness and Vanity, which are so often the spiritual accessories of a pronounced preoccupation with personal adornment. But, of course, I am little used to people of high fashion, and so perhaps the effect her fine clothes made on me was disproportionately immense. In any case, the conversation that succeeded went some way toward convincing me that, appearances to the contrary, my mistress is an unusually clever—indeed, intellectual—manner of woman, if also decidedly formal and cold. I perceived—it took little acuity—that she was intent on making the precise limitations on our relation quite explicit to me from the beginning. There was nought in the manner in which I was addressed to encourage the fatuous conceit that I was to consider myself an entitled member of the *cercle intime*. It is no matter, for I little crave entry. Indeed, I was not a little pleased—I hope my countenance did not too openly betray the pleasure—to be apprised that I am to take my meals *en solitaire*. Being deemed neither a servant nor a member of the family—neither fish nor fowl nor good red herring—I shall be served my meals by a servant in the privacy of my room, as Edwinna, the nursery governess, has been wont to do.

But such facts as these do not, as yet, frighten my little bird of confidence from off its tenuous perch. M'lady's iciness and hauteur are qualities I can well withstand, if conjoined with the blessings of good sense and good breeding. ('Twas precisely the lack of this alliance which rendered my former situation so mutually intolerable.) And though her costume was so exceedingly smart—it was a carriage costume, with very wide skirt and matching pardessus—I believe there was nothing positively vulgar about it. It is not entirely impossible that such dismay as mine betrays the crude fact of provinciality.

The girls, I am happy to say, were dressed quite simply and modestly, in high-waisted muslin, innocent of flounce and crinoline. (M'lady's was so very wide I wonder that the doorways—built for more moderate fashions—have not required widening.) Ella, Vanessa, and Anna seem quiet, undemonstrative little girls, but they appeared to like me well enough on this first inspection; as I did them—immensely.

But I should blow out my candle now, as I am deadly tired. I shall not dream tonight methinks.

But I recollect that I have omitted to say anything of the Master.

He seems a kinder sort than his wife, less formal and more human. At least he was less intent upon immediately impressing upon me an acknowledgement of the great fact of our social incommensurability.

He assayed some amicable comments about the weather, apologising for the inconvenient sogginess—as if it were a matter for his personal chagrin—and promising that their tiresome winter climate invariably climaxes in the most rapturous springs in all of England. He said this truly; they were his words. There seems an element decidedly Romantic about him. I should judge him, on the scant evidence of this day's offering, as a phlogistical manner of person (*comme moi*), trembling always on the verge of flame. His wife, methinks, is constituted of the cold and watery stuff, admixt with the airs of vaporous intellect. I am afraid I little rewarded his kindly efforts to put me at my ease. (I could see that this was his purpose.) Though my *arias* are not half bad, my *recitative* is habitually off-key; and talk of the weather always ties my tongue into an awkward knot. But his smile did not diminish a whit, and he did not seem to interpret my silence as of the sullen variety, as did my quondam employers. (How sharply still I feel the lash of that last exchange, when the great numeracy of my character defects were copiously catalogued for my chastisement and edification, as if such people as were they could have the dimmest glimmer of what I am, and am about.)

His name is Walter, which designation does little serve to conjure him. He is a man almost handsome—the privation, methinks, is a matter of the chin, of which there is too little—with hair that is dark and thick and worn perhaps a little longer than is quite *comme il faut*. There is an immaculate look which is all about him.

He wears a Byronic tie.

Friday 16 October, early evening: Three entire weeks have gone—have flown!—without my setting a single jot upon these pages, which have hitherto been the receptacle of my every rash mood's outpour. But I am wonderfully taken up here in the life of the house.

The wet and drear outside continue unabated. The girls and I have not been able to go out walking for over a week now, and we all grow restless from such rest. I am afraid that the youngest, Anna, has caught a bad cold.

My wonderful interest in Vanessa grows each day. There is no doubt that she is a very remarkable child. I have never seen a person, of whatever age or sex, with such a remarkable aptitude for deduction. She has a shameless passion for the syllogism; her little face positively screws up in the oblivion of the exercise. One can talk with her on any topic of the day. She is thoroughly informed in politics, spending a good hour with the Manchester *Gazette* every morning, and forming her own opinions on what she finds there. In a house full of radical Whigs she is a most ardent little Tory—and she is pleased to find a comrade-in-arms in her new governess. The four of us engage daily in vigorous political debate, with Ella and Anna taking the part of the Nottingham weavers, and Vanessa and I asserting the rights of the factory-owners.

I wish so confident a guide to the high ground of feminine virtue as the esteemable Sarah Lewis—who exhorts us to leave the grimy life of intellect and action to the men—might have a peek at my invincible little Vanessa, as she applies the chiselled pincers of her cerebrum to some ponderous passage, with all the solemn sagacity of a winsome Aristotle, and plunders it to bits.

And all this dexterity of intellect is yet compounded with the mildest disposition I have ever yet encountered, a fragrant sweetness as of honey and yet without that stinging temper that I have been wont to overlook in myself, having judged it to be a sign of my intemperate intelligence. How tender young Vanessa doth confute my disputation.

The other two sisters seem, by gentle unspoken agreement,

always to defer to the middle child's superior opinion, which agreement redounds to their own very good sense.

The love between these three composes a most affecting family portrait. There seems nothing in the way of the rancour of jealousy and rivalry, and there is only good fun in the manner with which they sometimes tease one another as regards their innocent little foibles: Ella's tendency towards dreaminess, Vanessa's occasional pedantry, and Anna's pert little temper. How well each sister knows the other, infallibly judging when to speak and when to keep her silence, when to make light and when to regard with all due sobriety. I closely study their ways of interaction. They seem to need no other company but each other's, although, because they are very kind, they move themselves—discreetly, so I shall not see the need—to make a little space for me.

I begin to see that what I had been wont to regard as the incomparable splendours of my isolation were lacking in certain warm and agreeable hues. I had not seen these shades before, and therefore, as Mr. Locke has instructed, had not even their conception by which to judge they were not there. Though I would most often prefer the dark comfort of my own seclusion to the garish companionship of the vast majority of my fellow-creatures (owing to which the years I spent at school were an unrelieved agony), I yet begin to see that companionship need not always be perceived in the way of vexatious disruption.

Tuesday 20 October, daybreak: 'Tis a cold dawn now, so cold a dawn as follows a sleepless night.

He came to me last night. 'Tis the first time since I am here, and I could not say whether 'twas more with rapture or revulsion that I looked upon the so familiar figure.

I have thought so little of his world since I've been here— that world that was once all the world to me. And yet, 'tis strange, it seems it did all continue on without me, so that there are happenstances that have been and gone, and left me only their smouldering traces by which to try to know them.

There is none to control him now, since the child Consuela is dead, and the Duchess retreated behind the dark folds of her religion. He seems, in truth, half-mad. And yet such madness as is his gives him a power over others that is no little like a demon's.

Lady Hastings has at last surrendered, the impenetrable hauteur of yore gone, leaving me to wonder what exactly transpired between them to have left her the unladied Lady I find her now, biting her knuckles to silence her cries. Her descent has been perilously quick. The end for so proud a creature as she once was will be terrible to see. And yet to behold him, as I beheld him last night, as he stood gazing at the foot of her bed, the expression in his face half-imperious and half-imploring, is to understand full well that sorry Lady's fate.

But I must hasten now to shake off the visions he has pressed upon me all the night, for my little girls shall soon be stirring, and the very smell of him is on me.

Friday 30 October, evening: The children, who seem little to indulge in confidentialities, preferring more impersonal subject matter, have been telling me this evening of the accomplishments of their brilliant Mamma and Papa. Their modest pride in doing so was very touching to behold. What it must be to have a parent one can both love and admire is a Grace that it is mine only to imagine; but methinks that every shade we place in our pictures of Paradise must be tinctured with the longings left from these old passions of childhood.

Vanessa did not join in the conversation, but sat listening, with a little smile on her serious face, clearly enjoying what her sisters said, but feeling no urge to add any word of her own.

Their father (whose time at Trinity College almost over-lapped the Duke's disastrous term there) has had several stud-ies of poetry published. Methought he had the look of a Poet and Philosopher. And their mother, it seems, is most for-midably educated as well, being now in the very midst of producing a little book on the history of costume. So her interest in drapery is not just in its application, but in its theory. The children reported that she is a most gifted artist and is herself doing all the drawings for her little monograph. It seems to me a rather shallow vessel into which to pour the heady liquor of scholarship.

Saturday 31 October, early evening: A very strange day I have spent today, as does befit the bewitched legends of the date. How frightened I remember being, as a small child, at the grim warnings given, and elaborate precautions taken, upon this night, by my father and my Aunt Nettie, whose strange and foreign rites must have derived with them from the ancient hearth in Ireland.

This afternoon, the rains abating for an hour, I used the opportunity to provide myself with some much-desired and required exercise; for the confinement the hostile elements have forced upon us tries sorely on my spirit. The winds were very strong, great gusts of south-westerlies blowing the clouds swiftly across the sky, making for strange shifting shadows on the landscape. But, so long as there is no wet, I mightily relish walking amidst such wildness of a wind-struck day.

And so there was much to relish in this hour; for the wind was blowing with a savage fierceness, and my grey cape bil-lowed about me. I was half blown back by the vehemence of the winds, which howled round the house and along the narrow gravel walks. I was more pushed upon than chose my path.

There was a strange abandon in the scene. I felt something

within me rising up with the lashing of the winds, and I grew every moment more excited.

I laughed aloud as I walked, and caught myself, now and again, singing into the wind, snatches of old hymns and nursery-songs. I must have cried as well; for when I returned my cheeks were wet, though the storm was dry.

I do not know quite where I wandered within the great park, nor what maddened dreams I dreamt. The more it howled about me, the wilder grew my inward mood. It was one of those episodes (I have known them before) when a dimmed and diminished piece of self, that has broken off and been left abandoned, is permitted to come forth and assume the whole shape of our identity. But even as it raves into the winds, our more persistent self stands aside and waits.

Monday 2 November, dusk: Today, during that weekly meeting in which we discuss the progress made by each of her daughters in their studies, and my plans for them for the coming week (Anna is to be excluded for now, her ailment having taken a turn for the worse), I made so bold as to broach the subject of her research with my haughty mistress, expressing—quite timidly, I should think, for I certainly had to overcome a very real diffidence in getting the words expressed—that I might some day be allowed to peruse her work for myself.

She allowed an exceedingly startled look to cross the formal setting of her face, which face is supported, methinks, with a very firmly controlled system of muscular pulleys and chains, so that the overlying countenance expresses only the emotions M'lady chooses to have shown there.

Matron though she is, the very ice of chastity is in her, and it makes me wonder mightily for my Master.

'Perhaps some day,' she murmured with a fine display of the frozen element, whilst staring slightly to the side of my face.

I see with this how little she knows me—nor cares to know me!

My voice gagged up by the bitter root, Necessity, I made no word to her, but cast my eyes downwards to my feet, so that she might not see for herself what was of a certainty blazing within them.

I am of the fiery substance—and when water falls on me, what can I do but *hiss*?

Wednesday 11 November, evening: Today, all three children being laid up with fever—we had separated them to different bedrooms in an attempt to contain the contagion, but, alas, too late, it seems—I was given the entire day to do with myself as I pleased. (In my former situation my employer should have eagerly grasped at this contingency as providing a happy occasion for my devising an entire new wardrobe for the moon-faced Mathilde's consortium of dollies.)

I sat in my little room, at my table 'neath the casement, and pulled out the pages of my writing. But here I encountered a very strange thing. How well my little Journal, soul-mate of my bosom, knows where it has been that my real life has been led, crushed close beside my Duke; and knows it, too, that, when I have been forced to break the surface of the mystical waters so that I might attend to the meddlesome world, it was always with the application of an effort and a counter-impulse of rebellion.

But now I found it was with a decided strain that I tried to make my way back down into the Duke's domain, to feel again the maddening heat of his presence, and trace the wild wanderings of his nocturnal prowls—which seemed to me now, in my more distant humour, to limn but senseless circles!

I saw him clear enough: he stood before me in his silken cape and hat, slowly pulling on a pair of white kid gloves. The long black waves of his hair were wild round his face, and spilling over the collar onto his slouching back. His eyes were large and liquid and luminous—too luminous. His nose is of an exquisite Hebrew model, but with a breadth of nostril unusual in similar formations; and even these did flare in self-assertion. His full lips were pallid, the beautiful curve of them the merest quiver away from petulance. I saw the dangerous tempest commencing to gather upon his brow.

And yet, though I knew still the very shape of his flaring nostril, he seemed not withal so *real* to me—not even the half of the all-consuming thing he once had been.

I recalled with what an effort I once had tried to break the bad habit of my Duke, praying aloud upon my knees till they were reddened raw, even whilst he stood before me, arms akimbo, laughing at my pieties. I sought to drive him from my presence with angry words of Scripture: Vengeance is mine; I will repay, saith the Lord. There is no peace, saith the Lord, unto the wicked. How oft is the candle of the wicked put out! and how oft cometh their destruction upon them!

And when even Scripture had failed to banish the mocking villain, his beautiful head thrown back in unleashed evil mirth, I would sing aloud the hymns of my childhood, even as I had sung them every evening before bedtime with Father and Aunt Nettie.

> For *in the deep where darkness dwells,*
> *The land of horror and despair,*
> *Justice has built a dismal hell*
> *And laid her stores of vengeance there!*

For a year or more I battled my Duke, charging behind my shield of Scripture and helmeted by my hymns. But he, like all his wild brethren, was born to fight and vanquish; whilst I was born but to resist, and then surrender. And when at last I did surrender, it was to live only by my Duke, and with my Duke, and for my Duke. And it has been so, without the smallest motion of conscience or contraction, until now, when I find I am so suddenly released.

I read over some of what I had narrated before of his blackguard adventures, and found myself untouched, and strangely cold towards it.

I can only reflect that 'tis very odd what the brief term of my residence here has accomplished in the way of my inward organisation.

And so I put away from me my writing things, and wandered down from my little room at the top of the house, finding my way to the library. Of all the rooms in this most beautiful house, methinks this is the loveliest of them all. Its proportions are large and gracious, its furniture well worn and comfortable; there are several sketches by Ruskin above the mantel, the heaving bookshelves go from floor to ceiling, and the aroma permeating is that most wonderful admixture arising from the presence of old books and my Master's cigar; for he is so often there. There is always a good fire kept upon the grate, as all the family is continually wandering in and out, in search of some volume or another, the entire day through.

Today, however, when I entered, I found the room all to myself, and with gladdened ardour took me over its possession.

I immediately went to a particular shelf, got me down the book I knew to be there, and sat myself down on the wood of the window settee, preferring this place of comparative rigour to the luxury of the fireside chairs. A volume of headiest poetry is debauchery enough for a governess and parson's daughter.

So deeply engrossed in my pages was I that I failed to detect any sign of someone's having entered the room. It was the intensified aroma of the cigar that made me look up with a start from the book upon my lap.

'Byron, is it?' said my Master, whose voice—have I re-

corded it?—has a manliness that comes from deep down in
his chest. He squinted, very slightly, as he looked to the leaves
where they lay upon me.

'Yes, sir,' said I, knowing hardly how I found the voice to
do so.

'Is he a very great favourite of yours, Emma?'

'Yes, sir,' I answered, and then blushed furiously at hearing
the dull repetitiveness of the responses I made him. We were
not speaking here of the prosy weather, but of divinest strains
of poetry! And yet I could not break the bonds in which I
am always tied up, that wrap me in the cool indifference the
world adjudges seemly for a woman of my station.

But my blush was of the fiery element.

I do not know how my Master chose to interpret this fire
in my cheek; but, 'I am also a great admirer of the Lord Poet,'
is what he said.

'And your wife, sir?' I for some reason made so bold as to
ask—I could not tell you then, nor now, to what precise end.

'No,' he said, after the slightest hesitation. 'My wife is much
more the Classicist. Dryden, Milton, Pope—those are her
chaps.'

'And Shelley, Keats, and Byron mine!' I blurted out with
little thinking, inspired by my subject to throw off with one
strong impulse the cutting cords of caution.

'Mine, too!' he enjoined with a matching ardour. 'Wait! I
shall show you something!'

And he moved the library-stair to a corner of the room
most distant from the fire, and clambered quickly to the top,
where he reached out to a bookshelf lying just beneath the
ceiling.

'Ornithography!' he called down to me, who kept my
window-seat and gazed up at him with frank astonishment.
'Not one of my studious little girls shows the slightest inclination towards ornithography!'

I took it that he was about to request of me that I forthwith administer to this dearth in his daughters' erudition, and wondered just a little at the *non sequitur*.

Holding two large volumes in his right hand, he now reached in his left and pulled out one much smaller, replaced as they were before the massive two, and returned to *terra firma* with the small volume, which he then proceeded to hand over to me.

It was by Byron: a rare and precious first edition of the *Don Juan*, which, needless to say, I have never so much as held within my hand—a fact of which I tremorously apprized my kindly Master.

'Well, now you are most decidedly holding it.' He made me his smile. 'You might even, if you so choose, take it and peruse it at your leisure.'

'Might I, sir?'

He fixed me with his very mild scowl.

'A person to whom I entrust the education of my daughters must have, I should think, the mental wherewithal to choose her own reading material for herself.'

Methinks my Master is a Radical, in addition to being a Poet and Philosopher. How fortunate are his own three daughters, and how I wish myself a blessed sister to them, a worshipful daughter to him!

But I have no cause—never have I had less in all my life —to make pulish complaint of my own Fate.

They feared no eyes nor ears on that lone beach,
  They felt no terrors from the night, they were
All in all to each other: though their speech
  Was broken words, they thought a language there—
And all the burning tongues the passions teach
  Found in one sigh the best interpreter

Of nature's oracle—first love—that all
Which Eve has left her daughters since her fall.

Friday 13 November, dawn: If I *burn* and I *burn* and I *burn*: is it not because it is in my *Nature* to burn? And is not all attempt to douse this indelicate heat but the endeavour to snuff me out?

And if I *yearn* and I *yearn* and I *yearn*: is it not, too, because I am yearning towards my rightful place whither my *Fire* directs me?

Is not the internal composition that which alone signifies, when it is of the innermost things that we speak? *Like* will go to *like*!

Wednesday 25 November, evening: Ella and Anna have sufficiently recovered their health so as to be able to take their lessons once again. Vanessa still continues ill with the influenza, and remains separated from her sisters.

The two convalescing girls are not yet permitted to sit up for very long, so I am still left with the luxury of great pieces of time for whose occupation I must make good to no one but myself. I detect the other servants—including the nursery governess, Miss Edwinna, whose little charge has maintained unbroken the boisterous spirits of his good health—to be quite resentful of my leisure; but they are none of them of the slightest account to *me*.

I find that with the so brilliant illumination of Vanessa laid temporarily out of sight, the lights of her two sisters emerge with greater clarity. They, too, are very special creatures, unusually intelligent and receptive and fine. I confess I had not seen them so bright before, much as we cannot see the softer stars when they are cast in the vivid sunshine. But both Ella and Anna have their own distinct natures and delightful gifts. Anna, who is remarkably pretty—yellow ringlets and great limpid long-lashed eyes of purest cerulean—has inherited her mother's artistic facility, and can dash off wondrously like portraits of anything that catches her pretty eye, though she is most partial to human faces, and of these her favourite subjects are her own two sisters. She has one, wherein she has caught the precise aspect of little Vanessa when she is lost in the dense abstractions of her ponderings, which I simply could not resist petitioning for a gift; a request Anna good-naturedly acceded to at once, for she seems to hold but little to her productions, perhaps because of the lack of exertion with which she tosses them off.

Ella, the eldest, has more the dreamy soul of the Poet. She has committed great quantities of verse to heart—her tastes are sweetly catholic—and will recite, when encouraged to do so by her sisters, in a very pretty style. She also writes verses, which are not at all bad for one of fourteen years—mostly warbling of nature and her changing seasons, with lots of twittering birds and fluttering butterflies and gustily humming bees. The glowing embers of her young and unstirred soul have not yet been blown upon to produce the rare Fire of true Poetry. We shall have to wait and see.

And yet, of an evening, when the four of us sit before the hearth in our favourite room, which is the library, and I tell the girls my stories—for they love, sweet darlings, to hear them—it is Ella's face that I find myself watching and searching, for the effect my words do rouse in her. The other two listen attentively enough—Vanessa with her grave little face sometimes exhibiting a certain troubled puzzlement by the gross *illogic* of my characters' actions; and Anna often quickly sketching with her pens as I speak, trying to capture in her imagination what I see in mine. She has drawn me a portrait of the Duke of Abracadorn that is nothing at all like him, totally lacking the infernal element that is of his very essence.

But, then, I am glad she cannot see him, and have been careful to leave gaps in what I tell them. And yet at times little Vanessa will turn upon me her grave and questioning eyes; and she asked me once, in some confusion, whether the Duke was somehow not a gentleman—a question which launched anon a spirited altercation as to whether such a doubt might even be raised *à propos* a member of the landed aristocracy. But, even as we four debated, I wondered whether I had not taken my little girls too dangerously far down below with me.

But Ella listens with her entire soul's absorption all gathered up into the shining compass of her eyes. And, I confess, the enraptured attention that I see there provokes me to go deeper into the history of my doomed characters than cooler prudence would advise.

For Ella's eyes *will* water—not with the sadness of my tales, which will often draw forth the tears from Vanessa and Anna as well. But no, the signifying droplets form upon her lashes at those moments when some sudden turn to the story, or the phrases I am given to speak it, suddenly ushers in soft-breathing Beauty; and we feel, she and I, for the brief moment of her stay, the stirred air from her great white moving wings, making for the hair to rise upon my skin, and bringing the water into Ella's brightened orbs.

I have described for them the Duke's vast estates, and the time-blackened Bloodin Castle in Abracadorn; told of how the land and its great powers had been given over to the family a full four centuries before, in reward for the exercise of their vicious vitality, which had served their bepledged King well in his wars with the Franks. And of how these ruthless qualities of character, which had proved so convenient in tumultuous time of war, had continued to flow unchecked in the noble blood of their prideful heirs; so that they were, almost all of them, colourful, violent, and dissolute.

I told them, too, of how the Duke and his wife had had a little girl, and how she had died. And I told them of how the bereaved Duchess had for evermore forsworn the love of her dangerous Duke—thus sealing both their dooms; and how now she seeks only the colder embrace of her new religion.

I tried to make them feel how it was that for the Duchess the death of the infant Consuela was a judgement delivered upon them from a wrathful God for the sins they had between them done—only leaving out what those sins might be; how in her grief-maddened piety she cursed the demonic love that had issued in the being of that innocent daughter. I only said she felt that she had loved the Duke too well—as he had her; with a passion that had made as nought all things that were not in it; as surely *God* had not been; so that there had been nothing left in all the world, but only herself and the Duke; and that this was an annihilation the Lord would not abide.

And I have told them, too, of Camilla, the poet-enchantress; of how it was that the Duke had chanced to meet her when she was still living as a daughter in her father's great house, amidst all the wealth of the vast West Indies' fortune.

I told them of how Camilla, whilst faultlessly performing the duties of daughter in the motherless household, purloined any hour she might in which to study the exacting methods of her Art: in dead of night, after her parent and all the servants had retired, she contended with the rigours of meter and rhyme. She had never the shadow of an intention of making her efforts public; all the struggle was towards unshown perfection.

No one, not even the beloved parent, knew the secret of those hidden hours; only he remarked to himself, now and then, the whitened cheek and shadowed eye, belying the gleaming surface of her gaiety.

And I told them of how Camilla, beguiled by ardent words of praise the Duke had spoken for an obscure dead poet, whom Camilla worshipped above all others, betrayed the secret of her own inventions. And I told them of her meteoric rise to a brilliant, though as yet anonymous, Fame; of how her slender book of poetry had been printed, through the aid and connections of the Duke, under the pseudonym Chance Will; so that Camilla awoke one morning and found herself famous, though her name itself unknown; with all of England wondering who it was who had written these strange and wild verses, telling an unbroken tale of that place called Crystal Country, the beauty of it so inhumanly wondrous—like a piece of perfect melody or an eternal truth of mathematics.

'Were you not the greatest of living Poets,' the Duke had told her, 'you would have been either a mathematician or a musician.'

And is not one of Camilla's abiding images composed of a fine metallic mesh of mathematics, music, and meter? And was not one of her earliest efforts, written when she was but twelve, an ambitious 'Ode to Pythagoras,' constructed in every way upon the number ten, as the Pythagoreans had reverenced the *tetractys*?

And there was, too, another curious little poem she had written, at sixteen, narrating the tragic tale of the hapless Pythagorean who had discovered the proof for irrational numbers, only to be sentenced to a banishment at sea:

> *Thy desecrant knowledge submerged to keep*
> *In the voiceless vast irrational deep!*

The critics, of course, had got everything about her Poetry wrong, foaming incoherent upon her insults to convention, her invention of new words, and her eccentric rhyming schemes.

But their spurtles of peevish pedantry dribbled out to nought, for the wild music had been caught.

I told the girls how it is now that round the tables of the highest houses of society the talk is of Camilla's verse, with half the company dismissing it for its godless passion, and the other half praising it for the same; whilst all alike wonder

what manner of creature could have brought forth such prod-
igies of Art, and whether it be a man or a woman.

But I see I have wandered far distant from my purpose,
which was to set out a description of my little girls. I believe
I had been speaking of Ella.

In looks she is more like Vanessa than like Anna, though
there is certainly a strong resemblance between all three—
they are all of delicate feature and have the same pretty, heart-
shaped face, with the pointed little chin. Ella's hair, like Vanessa's, is a darker shade of blonde, and both girls have very
clear grey eyes. In figure, they are all slight and elegant. Ella
and Vanessa are considered pretty girls; Anna, of course, is
the little beauty.

In terms of character Ella is less forceful than either of her
two sisters, though she cannot be accused of being self-
effacing either. But, quite unlike the other two, she will smil-
ingly give up her point if it arouses a too insistent denial from
myself or her sisters. Being the eldest, there is a something
strongly maternal in her attitude towards the two younger;
she indulges both quite shamelessly. The other two do not
willingly give up the reins of any argument they choose to
ride, but will lash it until it either wins the day or falls down
dead.

I shall record just one example of this vigorous, though
always amiable, tendency towards tendentiousness, one
which I had found particularly droll in its unfolding. It occurred perhaps a little more than two weeks ago—that is,
just before all three children had taken sick.

Vanessa, with her passion for pure ratiocination, had been
studying (as still she does) the *Essay* of John Locke, and had
found herself very much excited, upon reaching Chapter VIII
of Book II, to learn the distinction the philosopher does make
there between primary and secondary qualities of matter.

Anna was sitting at the table with her box of water-colours,
adding pigments to a pencil drawing that she had done of

their little brother. She was just that moment in the process of admixing several shades of yellow and some white, for the purpose of deriving the tawny blondeness of his hair.

'Only think—' Vanessa suddenly put down her book to say to Anna, 'that those colours you admix do not really at all exist in the external world!'

'Do not exist in the external world? What nonsense is this, Vanessa? Pray tell, where *do* my colours exist? For I certainly know them to exist *some*where!'

'In your mind alone, Anna sweetest! There are no colours *as we see them* out there. Unperceived matter hath no colour—nor smell, nor sound, nor taste. These are only ideas in our own minds.'

'And is, then, everything only an idea in our own minds, Vanessa?'

'Not at all! These ideas with*in* us are produced by real material bodies with*out* us.'

'And these real material bodies have no colour? How do you *know* that, Vanessa?'

'Because they have only those properties that can be fully expressed in mathematical terms—such as the properties of extension, bulk, figure, number, and motion. Those are all the properties you need provide them in order to be able to account for all that we observe of them, and thus—do you see, sweetest Anna?—one can be justified in according them no others—including those very pretty colours you are putting on our dear Robert's hair. Our ideas of colours—and all the rest—are only produced in our own minds by the operation of insensible particles of matter upon our senses.'

'And do you *really* believe this, Vanessa?'

'Of course I do! The arguments for it are as sound and true as ever I've seen. Oh, they are wonderfuly good arguments!'

'But is it not very awful to believe the world outside to be so unlike the pictures we carry of it within us? It takes the darling world so far away from us—makes of it something so distant and so formal and so . . . so colourless! I do not like it to be so!'

'And I think it is very wonderful that it is so. It excites me no end to think that the world out there is nothing like the ideas we have of it. And I think it is a proof of God's love for us that He has made our minds to comprehend mathematics, and by this divinest gift has allowed us to escape our ideality and leap beyond into His lovely mathematical matter!'

'Fie on mathematics!' erupted little Anna—for whom this is the very least favourite of all school-subjects, and who—as well I know as her governess—has just cause to dispute that God's love for His children is expressed in His bestowing on them each a comprehension of the exactest science.

No, little Anna loves too well the pictures of the world her cerulean eyes bring her to let them be argued into insubstantiality by the brutal Mr. Locke. Too dismal a thought that the wretched mathematics might lie between her and all grasp of what is out there. And so she stood her ground, for once defying the superior intellect of her elder sister, and stamping her little felt-slippered foot in her vehement denial of any argument that could lead to so baleful a proposition.

'I believe much more in all my beautiful colours than I do in yours and Mr. Locke's horrid mathematics!' she concluded, with more dazzling a show of spirit than of logic.

Friday 4 December, dawn: Such strange fancies have been assailing me all this night.

There is another figure now who would roam that place below.

He grows stronger in the dimness, imbibing the strong narcotic that is there.

Below he has been re-christened Mandrake, like the man-shaped plant of potent magic.

There was a book about the mystic mandragora in my father's library. It was this plant that barren Rachel bartered from her sister, giving Leah in return to lie that night with Jacob. The Ancients made a soporific of it, with which to deaden pain. And, too, they mixed it in their love-philtres, for there is in the fleshy root a juice that has it in its power to put to sleep the day and awaken night.

And yet 'tis fatal, too; and he who would gather the Mandrake must do so with careful ritual. He must take a virgin sword and draw the magic circle three times round about it, even as the Greeks did encircle the inspired Poet.

And he must, above all things, have made sure to stop his ears with cotton and seal them shut with pitch. For the manly root, wherein all the potency does lie, shrieks as it is pulled from out the ground; and whosoever hears the hideous shriek grows mad at once, with a madness so violent as to end for sure in death.

But I shall not grow mad, for I have obeyed carefully the rituals of my own making.

And I will surely keep my Mandrake down below, where none can hear the shriek.

Sabbath day 6 December, late afternoon: They are not so formal in observing the Sabbath here. They appear never to go to church, and I have found I very little miss the omission for myself. They, of course, asked me when I first arrived whether I would be wanting the carriage on Sundays to make the trip to church; and I found, something to my surprise, that I made errant use of the freedom that the question revealed to lie open before me. And so I have not been to church *once* since coming here, this, then, being the eleventh Sunday that I have missed.

And yet I find that the especial qualities of the Lord's day do enter in and permeate, making sweetly redolent even this habitation of free-thinkers. The very air is transformed into sabbatical stillness, even as it was at home. One does not need the outward trappings to arouse those finer feelings—which are the only justification for all the cumbersome stuff of creed and cant and commandment anyway.

So stands for today my little sermon on Natural Piety. And with what fiercely flashing eye and clenching jaw would come the hoarsely whispered rebuke of my less naturally pious parent:

'Nay, Daughter! Constrict thy throat, for it is the cunning voice of the D' that riseth nauseantly within it! If thou art of the frivolous frame to make light of thy True God's Presence, think thou upon the day of thy Death, which cometh sooner than thou judgest, and think thou now of the Eternal Damnation that thee then awaits!'—which paternal advice, it is true, has always proved a most effective antidote to my finding any solace in the proffered balms of my religion.

'Tis, no doubt, a heavy sin to see our parents as they are, when what they are does not bear looking at.

Monday 7 December, dawn: I have been praying all the night upon my knees for my sweet Deliverer's saving Grace.

What godless voice have I been heeding? In truth it goes too far, too far. I shall fight it now, I have found the strength, and I shall resist with all the grimness of my father's Faith, and with all the Virtue of my poor dead mother.

If only he did not look at me with so much kindness, and lend me books by my Lord, Byron.

The girls have all taken sick again. I wish to God we were recovered.

Monday 14 December, dusk: We are back again into the discipline of our studies, and I welcome this return to sovereign sanity.

Ella and Anna are now completely recovered, though they are weak and wan yet from the influenza, which has proved of a most virulent strain. Vanessa still must keep to her bed. But she is able to read for a few hours each day, and this comforts her immensely. She is, the little prodigy, continuing to assess John Locke's *Essay,* in which she finds much to commend, yet also emend. She is at this very moment all intent on plundering to pieces the unfortunate philosopher's conception of substance—which she adjudges to be an example of metaphysics at its worst.

I confess I work hard to keep apace of my little charge's forceful rushes upon the fortified walls of guarded learning. And yet, though she makes me breathless, it is with the most triumphant surge of spirits.

It seems never to have traversed the pathways of Vanessa's incomparable little brain that she cannot think because she is a girl. No-one in this household has ever let drop such an idea into her mind; and methinks it is not a thought to occur naturally.

And so it is that she proceeds at her own fleet pace, unimpeded by the drag from doubt. One could never hope to construct, through no matter what enlightened theories of education, such a creature as is she. They are born—once in a very rare while. All the effort must be directed to keeping such a one from being destroyed. But I do not fear for her somehow. Instead she infuses me full with strong purpose and high optimism, she is so essentially wholesome and well-minded.

Ah, but it is good to return, in the beloved company of my charges, to the province of sweet reason, after my brief spell of truancy. I had felt myself, with the relaxation of my duties brought about by the girls' convalescence, to slip back under the drugging waters, and to breathe again of that sweet narcotic element, and feel it becoming the more natural—while the other, the sunlit world above, grew murky and unreal. How the girls do bring me up again. And most of all the little paragon of rationality, whom I have just left in her room, propped up upon her pillows, dismantling the illustrious philosopher!

I had not hitherto known that the very place wherein I choose to dwell—whether above with the others or down below with my Duke—might depend upon my intertwined-ness with a fellow-creature. Having never felt close to anyone before, it is a surpassingly surprising discovery for me to have made.

Wednesday 16 December, midnight: This evening, when I went to the sick-chamber to say my good night to Vanessa, I opened the door to find there the mother, sitting upon the daughter's bed. It did appear that they were playing a kind of rhyming game, and both were giggling like girls—which Vanessa of course is, but seldom acts as if she were. Their heads were close down together, so that they did not even see me standing upon the threshold. I had never heard Vanessa show quite so child-like a face, nor make so child-like a commotion, and the sight of them together like that kindled in me a great fire of shame for all the jealous thoughts I had been thinking; so that I hurried out before either of them had taken any notice of me.

And now mefinds myself in a strange sad mood of reverie, recalling as I have not done for many years the great love I had once lavished upon my own mother, in whose hour of death I was born.

Of the threat to her life there had been no foreboding at all. She had been young and hale and hearty. In the crisis that ensued my birth I was deposited into some out-of-the-way corner, where I was, I have been told, forgotten for some time, so that, when I was finally retrieved, I looked more a puling chicken than a child, and it seemed that I would but little survive her.

I have read somewhere that a newborn gooseling will attach itself to the first moving thing it sees, and love it as its mother. But what is true for the goose did not prove true for me. I did not very much attach myself to either my father or my Aunt Nettie, who had come to live at the parsonage in order to care for the infant. She herself died when I was thirteen. I remember the event well. It was an ugly, apoplectic death, which shocked me greatly with its violence. But I cannot recall its having made, in the long run, very much difference to me; for she had been hammered out from the same piece of granite as had my father.

Yet my child's love did find itself an object, as does the gooseling's; and this in the vision it formed of its dead mother. She must verily have been a loveable creature, for methinks my father never did stop grieving her. And even Aunt Nettie, so hard and so cold, with so formidable a face and so towering a figure as my father's, spoke with a softened gaze when she spoke of my dead mother, and called her springtime's flower.

Father I never heard speak of her. But, then, when did I ever hear him speak, but of a Sunday, when he stands high upon his pulpit, castigating the congregation for its sins, and Parliament for its Catholic Emancipation Act?

The little graveyard lies immediately behind the parish house, so I could, through all the bleakness of my lone sad childhood, look out from my window and see the moonlight shining pretty on her gravestone, and wish her each night a 'sweet dreams!' And, as there were no suitable children for me to play with in our parish, which was of a rough and heathenish sort, I spent many of my days at her side. I kept her low home free of nettles, taking even a small pleasure from the sting I suffered on her account. And I would recite my little poems and sonnets for her, and seem to hear her crystal voice declaring me that rare fine thing, a Poet.

I have lost, in its entirety, the sense of her that I once carried always in me, and I cannot say whether it is because her soul has truly withdrawn itself from mine, or from some other cause. But she was once the great figure for me, in the days before the Duke had come, and 'tis strange how I had all but forgotten.

Friday 18 December, dawn: The world is turned topsy-turvy; all is thrown from its rightful place, and God alone in His All-Awesome Sovereignty knows what shall become of us— who implore Thee, Master, Whose living Name is Love, to hear the prayers of the guardians of Vanessa.

I can write no more.

Noon, same day: I set down what has happened.

Last night I lay for a very long time unable to find sleep, suspended helplessly in that half-world that lies somewhere between wakefulness and slumber.

'Tis a dangerous place to be. I have known it before, pinioned in an attitude half-active and half-passive.

And in this state I saw again the Duke. He awoke in the County of Abracadorn just as the sun was sinking, and his mood was of the blackest.

The Duchess was safely ensconced in the ornate little chapel she has built herself down the stone steps in the deep recesses of Bloodin Castle, hidden away there with her Father Bride, that dark and sinister representative of unwholesome Romish mummery, who has all her devotions now, since she has made for herself a retreat of pious dementia.

The Duke did not even bother to seek her out—he despises her now completely—but went through the ablutions of his fastidious toilet without giving her a moment's idle thought. He donned his immaculate evening wear, the silken gibus-hat and satin-lined cloak, all the time a deepening scowl impressed upon his darkening face.

As I watched him I felt nothing like the wild thrill that used of old to course through me as he prepared himself to venture out into the night of the County Abracadorn; but instead felt come upon me a strange and chill foreboding. I saw that he had upon him the fatal restlessness, and my mind struggled to leap ahead to the consequences that threatened.

He ordered his carriage prepared, peremptorily dismissing the coachman, and taking the reins himself—as does he always when the dangerous fury is come upon him.

I watched him on the box, as he half stood in his impatience, lashing the poor thundering foaming horses. I saw the fixed ferocity of his scowl, and could feel upon me the hot breath streaming through his flared nostrils. In such a mood, he seems more beast than man.

And now the carriage was at the crossroads, marked by the guide-post; and I saw with a cold flood at my heart that he took the road to London!

In mind-shrunk time he was there, penetrating swiftly through the city's gas-lit places, his carriage rattling loudly over the cobbles as he made straight for the dark quarter that he sought. I know not its name, though I have seen it many times ere this night, the Duke being no stranger to it. Of all London's sins and mysteries, here lie coiled its rarest and most deadly.

The streets are very narrow and very murky, for the street-lamps here are few. He abandons the carriage when the road becomes too narrow for it; and stoops to pass beneath a low gate in the wall that reveals an atmosphere yet more dense and more decrepit. The thorough-fares here are little more than alleyways, leading off in darkened squalor to nameless establishments, in which can be sated—I hardly know what! Unwhisperable dissipations.

But the Duke inhales deeply of this death-perfumed air. Indeed, he is not the only man in full-dress evening wear to walk this indescribably sordid scene. Several times he passes such another, though instinctively each presses himself closer to the dampened and beslimed stones of the wall, and shrinks from looking the other in the face.

And at one bleak alleyway he halts, and ducks quickly through an unlatched door.

He is in a room, almost completely empty of furnishings, and with so low a ceiling that the Duke, with his great manly height, is forced to stand quite crooked, his noble neck hunched down.

There is no light at all in here—there seems hardly a window—and the Duke, cursing low in his hoarse whisper, lights a match, even his gloom-accustomed eyes straining to see, whilst he growls out a name.

A small low moan answers this uncordial summons, and leads him to a filth-strewn corner where, on a small wooden bench against the wall, sits the poet-enchantress, Camilla, her arms wrapped round her knees, which are drawn up against her chin, rocking herself to some unheard internal rhythm, and looking absolutely non-human.

It is one of the few mercies still bestowed upon this God-forsaken creature—her eyes burnt-out black and all else about her ashen—that her faculties are in a state so perpetually disrupted that they do but vaguely convey to her the pitiless shape of that arch that Destiny has cruelly sculptured her.

The Duke gives her his crude fondle in greeting, and quickly reaches beneath his satin cloak to produce the brownish stuff with which he feeds her genius of delusion—that bitter draught that makes for such sweet verse! He wishes to hear now the strange wild music of the stories she would tell, which might still find their way into his humour, and quieten its darkening despair.

As the cracks in her earthly vessel have perilously spread, the Poetry she serves up has taken on an ever more strange and irresistible potence; so that now, as she is poised upon the very edge of her disaster, her verse quickens with all the pulse and passion anyone could ever have asked of life. The colours she admixes into her Crystal Country have heightened into the fiery upper reaches of the spectrum, straining inwards towards the pure white light Camilla says is there: the blinding streak of searing white at the very centre of the Crystal Country.

The Duke has listened to each word as it is delivered in a speech ever softer and more slurred; he has listened with a mounting wildness of impatience, thinking: Now! Now! I shall see at last what she sees at that whitened centre!—only to be cheated yet again, as the opiate dream gives out, and his sorceress slumps spent into her voiceless stupor.

But cheated he will be, unto the very end, Camilla eternally lost to the Duke's reach now. She wanders irreclaimable ,within the frozen lattice, the cold vast void in which she wanders alone. Perhaps she is become one with its whitened centre. Whatever she now is, she is no more in words.

She turns upon the dubious patron of her Art a countenance as fully remote and empty of the human element as are the spirits of her own inspired verse. Unable to arouse her with his barked commands, he grasps her listless form to him, applying those burning lips that had never failed as stimulants to her fancy before. But she is beyond their brutish power now—and he lets her go with a snarl of disgust, leaving impressed upon the emaciated whiteness of her inner-arm four bluish marks.

She sinks, with a low gasp, into a filthy heap of tattered dress and tangled hair, matted thick with elflocks. She seems not to breathe, and her eyes stare black and vacant.

He kneels and feels for her faltering pulse. He abruptly stands, looks down at her rigid form once more, then steps over her to reach the door and leaves.

His mood is now become even fouler; for even here, in this most infamous quarter of London, he cannot tell what it is that he wants, and must search out the exotic liquor with which to slake the pitiless thirst.

There are women on the street, blowzy and hideously be-painted, who call out to him in caressingly familiar tones, many of them speaking his name, which draws forth from him each time another deep growl of disgust. He knows not what it is he wants—but he knows it does not lie in them to give it!

A boozy strumpet stands in a pool of dingy light 'neath a gas-lamp, wrapping herself round its post to steady her lurching dizziness, as she throws back her head to break into a song that, though but a few weeks old, has attained an instantaneous success.

The tune is delicate, haunting—I hear it now—the beauty emerging even through the besotted rendering.

The words are Camilla's, taken from her celebrated book of Poetry:

> We do not know what notes they were
> The Ancients struck on dulcimer—
> But know we that this music Greek
> 'Twas madness perilously sweet!
> It gave the eye a ghastly gleam
> And scattered the philosopher's dream—
> I've heard it in the place I've been
> Caught in vaults of crystalline.
> It echoes low in crystalline.

It enrages him beyond endurance to hear Camilla's Verse sung in such streets, upon such lips. He goes to stand before the affronting songstress, gnashing his white teeth, and raising his arm with the intent to silence her.

But she freezes the heat of his violence by the brazen un-frightened look she gives him—she *laughs* him in the face! He strikes her, but with a much-diminished force, and her jeering noise, joined by those of her sisters in harlotry, follows behind as he turns his back to them and quickly strides away.

But he is stopped, several blocks further on, by the timorous, thin sound of another soliciting his attentions. He halts, intrigued by the quality of its diffidence; and, reaching down his hand to cup the creature's chin and raise it up for his inspection, he sees a woman-child.

She stares up at him, assaying with difficulty to assume upon her pudding-like face that gaze of brash indecency that alone befits her defilement.

He holds her with his steady gaze. Seeing him, as she sees him, I understand too well the secret of his fatal art. It is that he shows a woman with his look that he knows her better than she knows herself. He shows her what she is—with what he'll have of her.

And the wanting wanton droops down her head before him, covering her shamed face with her tiny trembling fingers.

He laughs at this rare exhibition, and mumbles some words into the child's ear, which words do make her cry. And as he watches her, with his full lips curled into their scornful mirth, there comes suddenly into his eye a gleam of wicked resolve. I know it!

And he is gone from these squalid streets of London, finding now a new destination, whipping his horses with that centuries-steeped savagery, as he takes a road leading northwards from the city.

I know the road he takes; and I grow faint with my dread knowledge.

I see him travel through country I myself have travelled, though approaching from another direction. I see him enter the gates of the park, lashing the steaming horses almost to their death, in the mounting crest of his excitement.

And I wonder: Do they not hear him? Can they not yet stop him? For I cannot. I lie helpless, struggle though I might to break through the force of the evil vision.

He drives his horses onto the gravel path in front, raising

such a racket I pray to God that the inmates must surely hear him, or that the dogs will be awakened from their watchful sleep, and sound the alarm. But he has always had the Devil's luck to aid him in the Devil's work.

He enters unmolested through the front door, for all the world like an invited guest. Nay! like the very Master of the house himself, he flings open the door and strides across its threshold.

I see him mount the stairs. He walks not quickly, nor yet not slowly. Calm and fully confident betimes he comes.

He is there now, in her room, approaching the bed where she lies unprotected in child's sleep.

I see him stand there and gaze down at her with his burning, basilisk eyes. I see him, God help me!—bending down over her, so that he hovers just inches above, making ready to enter, to penetrate her life and her dreams, to take possession of all the faculties of that unsullied sphere—where ere this blackened hour only queenly reason has held her tranquil sway.

And now that I see him actually bestride her, that I see the unspeakable thing that shall come, my anxiety is sufficient at last to vanquish the fatal paralysis. I snap at once its catgut cords, and leap from my bed, snatching up and lighting my candle—and I flee to my Vanessa's room!

She is moaning in her sleep, her small body jerking as if it would toss from side to side, but cannot move.

"My head, my head," she whimpers.

I put the candle to her face, and see the purpled flush upon her. I touch her brow—*and it is on fire.*

I run to rouse the sleeping parents, beating with both my fists upon their bedroom door. My mistress opens, even her composure gone, her eyes going frenzied with the look they see in mine.

We all three rush back to the child's room. Now the other

two sisters are standing over her, frozen in their terror. They are hurried out, and a servant is despatched, though it be still the middle of the night, to fetch us here the doctor.

We three remain with her in her room, whilst we await his coming, the mother vainly trying to bathe the child's forehead with cool compresses. But Vanessa flings them away in the violence of her delirium.

She half sits up in bed, clinging at her mother's skirt, as she stares across the room with her glittering, wild eyes. They are affixed at a point some two or three yards distant, and they follow slowly back and forth as if with the movement of something that is there, as she whimpers with a terror too horrible to hear.

'What is it, my child?' cries out the frantic mother.

'A man, Mamma! A man!'

'Hush, sweet precious. There is no man here. 'Tis only the fever makes it appear so.'

But still the child's fixed eye follows the movement of the phantom-figure, and she clutches at her mother and cries:

'He is here, Mamma! A bad man in this room! *Oh, help me, Mamma!*'

The doctor arrives. It has taken him but a quarter of an hour. It takes him even less time to give us his diagnosis.

The high fever, the excruciating head-pain; but most of all the rigidity of the neck reveals the deadly nature of the illness.

It is brain fever.

The doctor holds out almost no hope at all to us.

Saturday 19 December: It is just past two in the afternoon. Nothing we can do has yet succeeded in breaking the deadly high fever, and she still continues unconscious in tormented, delirious sleep.

Doctor McTurk is in there with her now, but there is little he can do. He lets us know his helplessness and gives us no cause on *earth* to stir our hope—telling us only to pray. And we have all of us, servants and masters together, gone down on our knees to beg Him for His Mercy.

Did not the Presence Himself appear to Moses, when the saddened leader had despaired of all forgiveness for the sin of the golden calf; did not the Lord Himself appear wrapped in the fringed garment of a sweet singer of Israel, and teach to Moses the liturgy of the Thirteen Attributes of Mercy?

Did He not promise Moses that, whenever Israel sins, they should follow this order of prayer, and they should be—even they—forgiven?

The doctor says that, if the child does manage to escape death, there is even less chance she can escape the permanent severance of all her intellect.

I cannot write more now—only, merciful God, hear our pleas!

Six o'clock: Doctor McTurk says that the crisis shall come in a few hours. If she can but live through this night, then she lives!

She hovers now suspended half-way between this world and the next.

Only live, my precious daughter—*live!*

Sabbath morn 20 December: Vanessa still lives—the crisis is past. I lie down now to close my eyes for the first time since the fever came upon her.

Same day, noon: I am just now awakened by a servant who tells me that Vanessa opened her eyes a few moments ago, knowing her Mamma and Papa, and speaking a few gentle words to them, before falling back into a calmer sleep.

It was a night of agony such as I could never have hitherto imagined, ere I knew what it was to love a child.

There was a time, so long ago it seems now, when I thought death poetic. And the more tragic the death, the sweeter I found the taste of the falling tears. I thought it beautiful to sit quietly in the gloom by the Cocytus, and contemplate its deeps. Almost all my poems were prettily embroidered with images of graves and shrouds, giving cause to a most delicious chill. A chill indeed—for what a cold, heartless thing such shallow necromanticism does appear when one is sitting by the bed of a child perilously ill.

I did not know before how damnably vulnerable is sacred Life. I had not this knowledge, ere I came to love a child.

I wonder how all the people daily bear it—loving others in the knowledge that we cannot keep them from harm. I shall have to study them well, so that I might learn from them. Perhaps, when moments of crisis are past, a dull forgetfulness sets in, making fragile Life again endurable.

But for now the child is safe. She lives, she breathes, she has even smiled and spoken a few tender words. And I offer up my humblest gratitude and love—to the Whomsoever or Whatsoever has seen fit to allow us yet to keep her with us —to God, to Fate, or to Blind Brute Chance.

Same day, four o'clock: Vanessa is dead.

THE PREDICATE
OF EXISTENCE

*E*xistence is not a predicate!

It was the December East Coast Convention of the American Philosophical Association, which was being held this year in Washington, D.C.; and the two young participants Hollander and Sharp were facing each other off at a very early morning session, so that the few philosophers attending must have been of a devoutly stoical cast of mind.

But, though the hour was so inauspiciously near to that boozy dawn at which most had finally called it a night, the very young and very handsome Professor Hollander was giving to it, or to the twenty minutes of it that were his, his very all, which was considerable.

He was responding to a paper that had just been read by Sharp; a most unfortunate paper, to judge by the tone Hollander was taking.

Existence is not a predicate!
Is this not one of the few, one of the pitifully few, conclusions that philosophy has managed to secure for itself during these many millennia when it has been about its peculiarly unrewarding business?

So demanded Hollander of Sharp, in a stirring sort of snarl.

The very air around Professor Hollander seemed to crackle with a high-powered aggressivity, enhancing the impression already made by his surly good looks: the massive dark head with the Byronic cataract of curls, and the scowling eyes and supercilious lips, which so effectively took up the offensive.

Philosophers are notoriously high-handed when it comes to offending common sense. For what, after all, is common sense?

But it's rarer to find a philosopher who thinks nothing of flying brazenly into the face of logic!

Professor Hollander was wearing a mustard-colored sports jacket, and a carelessly knotted yellow tie, a color scheme that further dissipated any soporific humors still suspended in the brain. And there was something in the way that he held himself, the wide-legged stance of it, suggesting that a well-defined musculature lay beneath the mustard, and that these thews and sinews and what-have-you's were flexing in the very act of the philosophical exercise.

It all made for a most arousing sort of savagery, so that the two or three female philosophers who were there imme-diately woke up, and Professor Schreck of ——— squinted through her bifocals to make out Professor Hollander's ac-ademic affiliation. Peyote College? she asked herself, squint-ing harder. Now where do you suppose that is in relation to ———?

Only the Sharp whose paper was the object of Hollander's remarks seemed wholly unriveted by the explosive style of their presentation, but sat staring straight ahead, her hands calmly folded on the table before her, and a strangely remote little smile playing upon her intriguing lips.

She only smiled a little more as Professor Hollander, finally nearing the end of his peroration, fired off a great volley of big guns, whose victorious report was that Professor Sharp's thesis could not be rendered sensible in symbolic logic; and her green eyes glowed just a little greener as he took his seat beside her.

His own look justifiably bespoke his triumphant sense of the situation, though he tried to make it seem just a little more tentative as he stole a glance sidewise.

For he didn't know, and just a little did care, how Sharp would have taken down the strong medicine he had ministered her system. (He himself now switched his metaphor, from the military to the medicinal.)

She seemed, in fact, to take it down awfully well, for she calmly answered his smile with a look that seemed to indicate she had enjoyed his wide-stanced attack almost as much as the wildly applauding frump of the first row, whose white blouse was buttoned up wrong.

It was Sharp who applied the word "frump." No one else in that room would have retained such a word in his or her working vocabulary. Just as it was Sharp's green gaze (so cool under fire) that observed the ill-buttoned blouse and the direction of the steamy bifocals.

Sharp, in contrast, happened to be so singularly good-looking for the philosophical profession that she had, earlier that morning, created rather a stir upon gliding through the lobby of the convention's hotel. She was further distinguished from the crowd by being exquisitely dressed as well, in Gucci loafers and a pale fur that looked suspiciously unfake. Several people had thought, of course, of asking her; but there was something unapproachable, in her posture and her poise, that had held them off; so that she had made her way unchallenged in real fur (yes) across a room full of ethicists.

The fur was now thrown carelessly back across her chair, revealing impeccable white wool trousers and a cashmere sweater that was the color of champagne and lovely against her fair skin. Her cropped blonde hair was swept off her brow in an extremely modish cut, and around both slender wrists she wore cuff bracelets made of horn.

But a closer inspection, such as that which Professor Schreck (oblivious to the state of her blouse) had vigorously

executed, revealed that the very expertly turned-out philosopher was perhaps not quite so young as *prima facie* appeared. In fact, Professor Schreck (herself an expert in modal
logic) concluded that it was quite impossible to say exactly
how old this Sharp person was, the band of uncertainty widening perhaps (so calculated Schreck) even into the decades.
She might have been barely past graduate school, she might
have been nearly Schreck's own age. And, though Professor
Hollander had gallantly referred to her as "Professor Sharp,"
the program indicated *no academic affiliation whatsoever!*

The "Oxbridge" accent didn't sound, to Schreck's ears,
altogether the right stuff either.

In any case, Professor Schreck entertained a very strong
presumption against any philosopher who could dress as well
as this Sharp person (and she had personally derailed the
careers of a number of young female philosophers whom she
had judged, for similar reasons, unsound). But this prejudg-
ment was as nothing compared with the high contempt en-
gendered by a creature who offered theses unrenderable in
symbolic logic, as very nicely demonstrated by that promising
young man, who surely deserved better than Peyote.

Professor Hollander, on the other hand, no matter how
censoriously he had regarded her paper, found Professor
Sharp's looks very much to his liking. Whatever her precise
age, it was still certainly within the bounds of the desirable.
He happened to be very partial to women with just that sort
of pale, coldly gleaming look. And those mysterious green
eyes and the snooty English accent were irresistible additions.
Had he known how adorably fetching the author of "Fictional Realism" was to be, perhaps he would have tempered
his bashing of it somewhat.

But no. Business was business. And the business of the day
was bashing. If one didn't believe that, what possible reason
could one have to be here at all?

For herein, according to Hollander, lies the nature of philosophy: conversation is essentially combat; and philosophy is conversation raised to its highest form.

Still, a pretty woman *is* a pretty woman—a tautology not altogether trivial. And Professor Hollander was fully hoping to get to know this particular pretty woman—*qua* pretty woman—somewhat better this evening over drinks.

She didn't seem, judging by the little smile she now gave him—ironical but not unfriendly—to have taken any personal offense from his rough handling. It was strange, on reflection, that she showed him so little hostility. Perhaps it had aroused her respect—or whatever—the manly way that he had exposed the untenability of her central contention. Perhaps, as the Brits would say, she rather fancied him for it.

Or perhaps, Professor Hollander thought, for the second time that morning (the same ghastly idea had flitted swiftly past him while she had been reading aloud): perhaps she hadn't really intended her paper altogether seriously.

After all, "Fictional Realism" took up a point of view that was so preposterously reifying, embracing (to quote now from Professor Hollander's own response) a grotesquely bloated ontology.

No one had hoisted the banner of nonexistent objects since Meinong's golden mountains. And the consensus was that Meinong had been hacked to logical smithereens by Russell's theory of descriptions, not to speak of the prior application of Ockham's razor.

But here was "Fictional Realism," arguing for the reinstatement of the discredited distinction between "being" and "existing," so that one might count, among the things that are, a certain number (quite large) that don't happen to exist.

There are more things in heaven and earth, Horatio, than are dreamt of in your philosophy!

So Sharp had declaimed in her mock-serious manner (so much prettier in person than on paper).

Such nonexistent objects, so argued "Fictional Realism," have a sort of "being," though they lack the property of existence. But they are as worthy subjects of predication as are any existent, and include, as a class, by far the most interesting items—for example, just for starters, all the characters of literature.

The rest of "Fictional Realism" had depicted, with a specious picturesqueness, the nature of the nonexistent "being" of the fictional.

Which is why it had of a sudden occurred to Professor Hollander, as Professor Sharp was reading aloud her paper (as it hadn't occurred to him all the weeks when he had been preparing his assault), that she had only, after all, meant the thing as a sort of English—as a sort of *Monty Python*-esque—joke.

It was her tone that suggested this; it was so unaccountably light and playful. Her voice, with the beautifully exaggerated modulations of a very upper-class Englishwoman, had always half a tone, or more, of amusement mixed in. And then those remarkable green eyes had shown themselves, when she raised them to the audience, to be coldly glittering with an inappropriate humor.

She seemed, most particularly and perversely, to relish the emphatic unsympathy with her position that Professor Schreck of ——— was taking no pains to hide, shaking her head in exclamatory contradiction and delivering herself of disapproving grunts.

For her part, Rona Schreck had never seen such indecent frivolity on the part of a philosopher. Philosopher indeed! Really, where was the APA getting them? The committee responsible for the selection of this year's papers had been shamelessly incompetent, as Rona would inform them in no uncertain terms, than which she possessed none other.

It had been a very off-putting idea for Professor Hollander to conceive, which is why he decided, finally, it was inconceivable: to wit, that the paper to which he had lugged his high-tech arsenal of analytic weaponry had not been seriously meant.

No one—not even someone who wore real furs to the APA—could possibly have been capable of a stunt of such terrifying proportions of recklessness and effrontery. For the joke would then be not only on him, but upon the entire American Philosophical Association, a *reductio ad absurdum* if ever there was one.

Thus it was that Hollander concluded that Sharp had really been asserting the supernal speciousness of "Fictional Realism"; and that her persisting air of insouciance must mean that she had not yet taken in that she had been ground into the dust by his response, which he had entitled "In Defense of Horatio's Philosophy."

Oliver Hollander was a young man of ambitions, none of which, as Professor Schreck had immediately intuited, were being met by Peyote College. The invitation to respond to "Fictional Realism" at the December East Coast Convention of the APA had caused him, therefore, considerable gratification. So the profession had heard of him at last. And he had been even more delighted, on reading "Fictional Realism," to see what a piece of cake it would be to demolish it.

Why should he have thought that "Fictional Realism" was anything other than what it seemed? He was used to all varieties of fallacy and muddle. He taught, after all, at Peyote College. And his sense of his own intelligence, in relation to everyone else's, was such as never to make him hesitate in the grossness of the confusion he was ready to attribute to his interlocutors.

So he had simply thanked the Powers That Be for sending him a colleague's work that he could consummately carve to pieces in this delightfully public manner.

And tonight, over drinks, he would, with a private gentleness to compensate for the required public aggression of the morning, detach the enchanting reifier from her deviant ontology—that is, if she still clung to any illusions after this morning's session.

And that old girl in the first row (his private vocabulary wasn't really much better than Sharp's), upon whom he appeared to have made such a favorable impression (for she had made herself busy, all through his reading, vigorously nodding her assent and grunting her approval), might be, for all he knew, someone worth cultivating. Indeed, she had to be someone important, to have made her approbation and disapprobation so keenly felt all round. He tried, in the short interlude before the question-and-answer period began, to see if he could read the old girl's name tag.

Then he felt, with a start, that his neighbor on the podium had fixed him with her glance, and, turning, he saw that she was regarding him with a disquietingly penetrating stare, her green eyes very green, and her ironical smile very ironical.

She whispered to him, "Ah, your conquest!" as the old girl of the first row rose to her feet, with the first question.

"Professor Schreck of ———," the conquest had introduced herself in the very brusque manner well known to the members of her profession. Even among the fighting men of philosophy she was known as a bully.

"Ah, Schreck of ———," thought Hollander, almost squirming with understandable delight.

Professor Schreck directed her question to—or, rather, as was her wont, against—Professor Sharp.

"Professor Sharp," she demanded, drawing her eyebrows together in an overstatement of perplexity, "I'm sure we're all very interested to hear what you have to say to Professor Hollander's masterful demonstration of the fundamental absurdity of your claims."

"I confess myself unconvinced," Sharp returned, altogether gamely.

"How odd," said Schreck, in a tone that had proved itself effective, time and again, in reducing others to a prepubescent level of self-esteem. "Well, then, perhaps you would be so good as to tell us how precisely you would render 'There are nonexistent objects' in formal logic?"

"I think that's *fairly* trivial to do," Professor Sharp had calmly answered, so drawing out the word "fairly" that it was made to sound awfully like a taunt. "Though I don't myself *particularly* see why you'd ever want to—but all you need do is introduce some sign or other for the predicate of existence. Make it an 'E,' why don't you?" she added with just the faintest trace of asperity.

"The predicate of existence!" Rona Schreck had exploded, throwing up her arms so that the tug on the ill-buttoned blouse popped a small pearly button. "But existence isn't a predicate! Can't you be made to understand that?"

"Existence *is* a predicate . . . *if* there are nonexistent objects," returned Professor Sharp, her mischievous gaze upon the blouse.

"You're begging the question, Sharp!"

"And I say you are, Schreck—at least, that is to say"— she added with a gracious nod—"from my perspective."

"Touché!" came a voice from the last row, and Rona Schreck whirled round in her chair to glare back at the offender.

It was Professor Quinton of Yale, an old enemy of hers, who had, in her opinion, always a great variety of reasons, ready to hand, for making a fool of himself. The presence of a woman such as Sharp would do for him just as well as any other.

"Oh, *really*, Arthur!" Professor Schreck had snapped back at him, then whirled herself frontward again in her seat.

"And what of Ockham?" She fired her question off like a missile. "Professor Hollander, why don't you ask her why she doesn't just cut out all this crap with Ockham's razor?"

"Oh, Ockham." Miss Sharp gave a smiling little sigh. "I can personally report that he couldn't regret more the use that's been made of his shaving equipment."

"I think you're mad," said Professor Schreck, in perfectly even tones, so that it was perfectly horrible to hear them. "Professor Hollander, do you think that there's really any point in continuing on with this? This isn't philosophy—it's pathology."

Professor Hollander, for all his flexing musculature, was sickened by the vicious turn the discussion had taken. Perhaps Sharp *was* rather out of her depth here. Clearly she had been made for things other—perhaps even better—than analytic philosophy. But surely that didn't excuse the tone that Schreck was taking.

He turned now with a protective urge that was out of his character; and was once again astonished to see how very self-possessed—how very, even, entertained—Sharp continued to look.

"*Is* there anything more you'd like to say?" he asked her, quite gently, so that Rona Schreck snorted through her nose.

Professor Sharp shrugged her slender shoulders and seemed to consider for a few moments, her beautiful brow delicately knitting. "Oh, why not?" she finally said, with another flash of green in her eyes.

"Look," Rebecca said to Oliver (for so, I think, we may by now refer to our Professors Sharp and Hollander), in a voice as lightly playing as before. "Do you remember that demonstration that G. E. Moore gave his Cambridge undergraduates for the proof of the external world? You know, here's a hand"—and she gestured with her elegant right hand—"and here's another"—and she gestured with her left. (Oliver noticed there was no ring.)

"Oh, G. E. Moore! Who thinks about G. E. Moore anymore?"

And Rona Schreck made a noise that was something like a Bronx cheer. G. E. Moore's legendary Cambridge colleague, Ludwig Wittgenstein, had once commented that one reaches a point in philosophical discussion when all one can do is make some inarticulate noise; Rona's usually sounded something like a Bronx cheer.

But Oliver was smiling; the gestures with the hands had been adorable. And it was touching somehow to see how the woman, slight as she was, refused to give way beneath the irrefutable weight of Rona.

"Well," continued Rebecca, and she raised her green eyes altogether to his face, so that he saw for the first time how truly extraordinary they were, both in their color and expression. "Would you be satisfied if I gave you a proof very much in the spirit of G. E. Moore?"

Oliver simply nodded his head, so that Rona again snorted through her nose. Peyote was probably a good deal better than this young idiot deserved. She began, with some commotion, to stuff her arms into the sleeves of her plush-pile coat.

"Here"—and Rebecca brought her horn-cuffed left hand up to her slender neck—"is a nonexistent object, and here"—and she gracefully swept her right arm out—"is another. And you can all see that I, just like Moore, can also do it now in numbers of other ways. There's no need to multiply examples."

"Whatever is she babbling about?" demanded Rona. She craned round in her chair again. "Do *you* know what she's going on about, Arthur?"

Rebecca's green gaze rested now on the bristling bulk of Rona, with a sneer that was not a pretty thing to see.

"You're a kind of latter-day version of Miss Pinkerton," Rebecca said to her, with a very slight shudder, "Dr. Johnson's special friend. And you're still quite as incapable of understanding a thing that I'm saying!" Rebecca's laugh was no more pleasant than her sneer.

Rona Schreck continued to stare at her blankly, so that Rebecca said to her, quite impatiently, "Look, doesn't my name mean anything to you at all? 'Rebecca Sharp'?"

Rona's stare continued as fixedly vacant as before, so that Rebecca leaned over and whispered into Oliver's ear, "*Illiterate,* as well as nonexistent!"

Meanwhile, a look of dawning horror had begun to spread itself over Oliver's face, and he shrank back in craven terror from the touch of Rebecca.

"Are you saying"—and his voice, with his face, had suddenly gone quite bloodless, so that there was nothing left in them of the vanquishing philosopher-warrior of the wide-legged stance. "Are you saying that fictional characters can *acquire* the property of existence? Is that what you're asserting?"

"And the Word was made flesh and dwelt among us," there came from the back of the room the quavering voice of old Quinton, who truly *was* losing it.

"Well, no," responded Rebecca, with charming archness. "That really *would* be absurd. *Some* things can acquire existence—but never *these.*"

"But, then," inferred Oliver, who really *was* too good for Peyote. "But, then."

But he couldn't bring himself to say it.

"Yes, precisely," Rebecca spoke it for him, calmly folding one beautiful hand over the other on the table before her, and waiting for the implication to sink in all round.

"I'm afraid," she said, turning back to Oliver, "it's an awfully slight piece, written by some very minor contemporary."

"Minor contemporary?" Oliver whispered, going yet a shade more insubstantial.

"Very minor, indeed. She had the half-baked idea that I'd make a fairly decent analytic philosopher. Of course," she lightly laughed, "*I'm* game for anything. It's in my character. Though there's not an awful lot I could have done about it, in any case, if you understand what I mean."

And then, with one of those ephemeral gestures of genuine concern that came upon her once in a very great while, she laid her hand upon his shoulder, ignoring its ungallant flinch, and saying softly, "And you'd do well to understand it, Oliver."

And with that Professor Rebecca Sharp gave a quick efficient shuffle to the pages of her piece and then stood, giving a last glance to the now fully deflated figure of Oliver Hollander, who sat slumped forward onto the table, his hands entirely obscuring his face.

"Well," said Rebecca, once again sweeping the room at large with a smile, than which no more satisfactory a summation could be expressed, "on the whole, I'd have to say that this was really a great deal more fun than I had anticipated."

And, indeed, she looked as if it were.

Oliver Hollander continued to stare sightlessly into his hands, already abandoned to the blotting action of his despair; while Rona Schreck, her features beginning to dissolve in the tremors that were taking her over, watched transfixed as Rebecca, her supreme sense of self firmly in possession, glided down from the podium and out through the door, there to mingle with the philosophers, for so long as it shall please her; and from thence to sally forth into the greater Vanity Fair beyond.

MINDEL GITTEL

When I was a young schoolboy, going off each morning with a book satchel on my back, I had to read for class a story, it was in German, by some famous German writer, I couldn't tell you his name or the title of his story. The fact that I remember it at all is to me something of a miracle.

But somehow or other this story stuck in my mind. It was about a married pair, both of them dwarfs, but yet people who were exceptionally refined, elevated, full of the highest culture. These two dwarfs lived only for books—books of poetry, of philosophy—and for art and music. For music most especially, if I remember correctly.

I think that at first in the story you are acquainted only with the man, and though he is, to look at him, a freak, yet you see right away all of his refinement, how all of his tastes are for only the highest things.

The wonderful part, of course, is that, if you saw such a person in the street, you would think "*nebech*" and look quickly the other way. But the writer makes you see inside of this man, and you see he's not a *nebechel* at all. You see that you would be honored to know such a person.

The only thing is that, being so different from all other humans, this dwarf is of course very lonely.

And then, miracle of miracles, it turns out that in this world there happens to exist this dwarf's exact female counterpart, another dwarf who is also in love with all of the beautiful things.

Somehow or other, of course, the two of them meet, I'm sure the writer tells you how, but this I don't remember. But in any case it's as if each of these two lonely people has met that half of himself that was sliced away at birth—you know, there is such a theory about love—and now they are joined together again and they are as if whole. It is, as they say, a *shiddach* that was made in heaven.

I remember that the two play together duets on the violin, but they play it like a cello, sitting on a little chair with the instrument in between their knees, that's how tiny they are, and everything in the house is made small so as to fit them. Maybe this is the reason why the story stayed with me, because of the picture of these two people playing together the violin like a cello. It so happened that in those distant days I, too, took lessons on the violin.

So what happens? This woman gives birth to a child, a boy, and this boy is not a dwarf like his parents but completely normal. Even more than normal, he's a big, strong, strapping fellow, like a regular Esav, who likes only to play all sorts of wild games with the other ruffians in the neighborhood. For the beautiful things, for the poetry and music of his parents, this Esav, he has no interest at all, such things don't touch him.

And the parents, on their part, don't know what to make of this child with these unknowable ways, it's as if they're like to each other maybe Martians. And of course the house with the delicate little chairs and little ornaments is too small for the son. He can't move but it so happens he should break some priceless object—not out of malice, you understand, but only because for him nothing there fits. In this house of strangeness, he's the stranger.

So, somehow or other, it happens he breaks the mother's violin, which happens to be an especially fine instrument, a family heirloom—I don't know maybe *eppes* a Stradivarius, though of course the boy doesn't understand any of this. He mumbles that he's sorry and then dashes off to join his fellow hooligans, just as on the other occasions, when he inadvertently smashed maybe a chair or a flowerpot.

So what happens? What do you think happens? In the end, the boy goes off into the normal world of regular-sized people, where he belongs, he doesn't give a glance back to the house of his parents, and the parents go back to their old life of poetry and philosophy and music as if the boy had never existed.

And I remember that, when I read this as a young schoolboy, living as the only child in the house of my beloved parents, may they both rest in peace, I remember that I thought that here the writer had erred.

All along I followed with him, and I imagined to myself that what he said, it could really be so. But when this writer wrote that a child could leave behind parents and forget that they ever were, and that the parents, on their part, could again take up life as if they had no son, I thought: No. This is not true to human nature. No matter how different the generations may be, one to the other, yet they cannot be sliced away from each other and it happens nobody suffers. And because the writer had described a parting with no heartbreak, because the only heartbreak in the story is when the violin is shattered, this is why I felt that his ending was a false one.

So why, I'm sure by now you are already asking yourself, am I telling you this half-remembered story that was written by an author I cannot tell you who, and which even the little bit I do tell you I'm probably getting wrong? Here is my reason. It's because I want to tell to you yet another story entirely, about a family that I came to know back in America, by the name of Zweigel. This family lived in the same little town in Connecticut that I used to live in. I see already you're surprised that I come from Connecticut.

First I'll tell you how I came to know the Zweigels.

The man, may he rest in peace, his first name was Reuven, a refugee like myself. When I first met him it was already, I think, 1953, and somehow or other, with God's help, I had managed to start a new life in America. We had already, myself and my wife, Sara, may she rest in peace, a little store, in lady's ready-made clothing, and we had bought together even a small house, not far from the store.

In short, I felt that I was putting down a little bit roots, as it was in Connecticut, because for some reason or other that's where the Jewish Relief Agency had told me to go. Why, I don't know. I never met another soul who they sent to Connecticut.

But against Connecticut I never made not one complaint. It was a little town, it looked to me always, you can imagine, a little unreal—in every season pretty like a postcard, the houses all painted white with black shutters, every street lined with such beautiful, big old trees, they made in the summertime like a *chuppa* over the road. Such trees.

So how can such a place be real? I would stand sometimes on the main street, even after I had been there already for years, but suddenly there would come over me such a feeling of unreality, looking out onto what they call there the green, where in the days of the Pilgrims they would put down the cows they should graze, and I would think: Maybe I dream?

Never would I have thought to myself to end up in such a place, but it was very nice. Everybody knew each other, and the people, I wouldn't say they were exactly outgoing, but they were always very decent to my Surala and to me. Over the years we even made for ourselves some good friends, I mean among the Gentiles.

There also happened to live, scattered here and there in the little towns around us, a few more Jews, mostly lukewarm Jews, you know what I mean, but still they called themselves Jews, which is already something. It happened that when I came to Connecticut I made up the tenth Jewish man in this area of Connecticut—I called myself in jest the tenth man of Connecticut—and I took this as a sign from the heavens that we ought to get together a little minyan, a prayer group, at least for the High Holidays.

Actually, to be honest, for myself I probably would have wanted to do this anyway. I only used this talk about the tenth man as an argument to try to nudge the others, most of whom had let such things go for so long that they just didn't want they should be bothered. But after everything that Surala and I had gone through over there, it was somehow important to us there should be a little bit a feeling of a community. We had somehow this hunger.

Of course I was only a newcomer, a refugee, I had always to be careful I shouldn't make myself a pest, it's easy that people can become annoyed. But there were a few, one or two maybe, who felt that they would like maybe also to celebrate a little bit the holidays, at least Rosh Hashana and Yom Kippur, and they pulled along the rest, who said, finally, okay, so long as I took care of all the arrangements.

So what this meant was that I had to find someone he could lead us in the prayers, because for myself, I'm ashamed to say, the little bit I had managed to learn as a boy I had largely lost over there. And in any case a voice I never had.

So I put a little notice in the Yiddish paper—not the *Forward,* you understand, because that was for socialists and freethinkers, but in the other one, the *Morgen Journal.*

As for the fee that we were prepared to pay our visiting *chazzen,* in this matter, too, there was nothing but disagreement among us. We had all to contribute the same amount, and, as is normally the case, it was the wealthiest ones who couldn't be persuaded to add a penny more.

So the fee I didn't even mention in the advertisement in the *Morgen Journal.* Let's see first, I said to myself, if anyone responds. Then first I'll worry about the money.

As it was, I got only one letter, written in a fine Yiddish, the return address a street I happened to know on the Lower East Side of Manhattan, and this letter was from Reuven Zweigel.

And the truly amazing thing was that in his letter Mr. Zweigel didn't put to me any question about money. This already, voice unheard, made me very disposed in Mr. Zweigel's favor.

But the others, of course, they set up a clamor that the man would have to have a regular audition, how did we know he had even a voice, we couldn't just hire the first person who answered the advertisement.

And so with this demand I had, with much embarrassment, to write back to my respondent in New York City, only now I of course mentioned the *gevaltig* sum that we were prepared to offer, because otherwise I couldn't ask a man he should make the trek all the way out to Connecticut.

I expected after this not to hear from Mr. Zweigel. But lo and behold a letter quickly arrived, and this letter made me feel even worse than before.

Mr. Zweigel didn't want I should think he was trying to make difficulties, he understood perfectly the wishes of the community, but it happened, he wrote, that it would be very hard for him he should come to his audition. Mrs. Zweigel was expecting soon their first child and was anyway not so well, and he also intimated that the additional bus fare to our town—he had already found out the exact amount— would be for him a hardship. With many finely put apologies he asked me if it might be possible I should listen to him sing over the telephone. He gave me a telephone number, and this I immediately called.

A female voice, speaking in English, answered the phone. It was not what I would call a refined voice, it was to me an unpleasant voice, and my first thought was naturally that it was to Mrs. Zweigel that I was speaking, even though it sounded like the voice of a very healthy female. And I was a little disappointed, because already I was drawing for myself a picture of the Zweigels.

This female voice answered in a very superior tone when I requested I should speak with Mr. Reuven Zweigel, and from this I immediately knew that I was not, thank God, speaking to Mrs. Zweigel, but to the landlady. After all, I myself had briefly lived, before I was instructed by the Jewish Relief Agency to go to Connecticut, in just such a rooming house, also on the Lower East Side of Manhattan, with also just such a landlady, she stands glaring it should happen that a tenant God forbid gets a telephone call.

I felt I knew already the owner of this bossy voice on the telephone. I began even to smell—I don't know, I have somehow this kind of a mind, my Surala used to tease me that if I made money like I imagined other people's lives I would be at least a Rothschild—but I smelled already the cooking odor of fried fish that used to stay always in the hallway of that rooming house I myself had lived in. To this day I don't eat fried fish.

It took some time for Mr. Zweigel to come to the phone, and from this I already guessed that his room, too, was on the very top floor, in what was really an attic. And, knowing what I knew from these attic rooms—it was, you understand, summer, the month of August, a heat was blowing like out of the furnace of Gehenna, and in such a room in the summer one only prays that the blood doesn't start already to bubble—knowing what I knew from such rooms, I worried all the more about this young couple. Such an attic room in August is no place for an expectant mother to be.

I was beginning to feel a little bit like a criminal for being the messenger of my high and mighty community that consisted of all of ten men, that was standing always so much on its dignity. Believe me, what we lacked in numbers, we made up for it in the sense of our own importance.

So, finally, Mr. Zweigel himself picked up the phone, a

little short of breath, which is not so good for a *chazzen,* and speaking in Yiddish, his voice coming in little pants.

A young man's voice it wasn't, so I had already to change the picture I had sketched of my young father-to-be. He sounded at least my age—I was then almost forty—if not older.

He spoke in such a quiet voice, even when he regained a little bit his breath, that it was necessary that I should strain my ears to hear, which is also not so good when you're considering a man for the position of *chazzen.*

So I had about what to worry. Because that I would not hire Mr. Zweigel was by this time already completely out of the question.

Meanwhile, as I'm worrying, Mr. Zweigel is stammering out his apologies that he should make these difficulties for the community, he should dare to ask for this special favor of not coming first to Connecticut for an "audition."

So I stopped him right there, because frankly I couldn't stand it anymore to hear a man that he should be so humble.

You know, there are some people you can interrupt them very easily, they immediately give way. I myself am not what you would call an interrupter, but there are some people they seem almost to be asking to be interrupted, as if they didn't want so much to be speaking in the first place, and this was true of Reuven Zweigel, who was never anyway a man to speak much, I think this telephone conversation was the most I ever heard him speak at any one time. And when he did speak it was always as if he was hoping any moment the listener maybe he'll interrupt.

So that was how it happened now that I interrupted him. Listen, my friend, I told him, as for a community, that is already too important a term for what we are, we are just a few scattered Jews, barely a minyan, and, if he still wishes it, it would be for us an honor to have him as our *chazzen* for the coming holidays. I also added that somehow, through my own carelessness, I had neglected it should be clear that the community would cover his bus fare.

There was a long pause. And then Mr. Zweigel asked, "You don't want that now you should hear me sing?"

And in his voice I immediately heard that, in my haste and my embarrassment, I had made a very grave mistake, that I had insulted the professional integrity of Mr. Zweigel. I didn't want, God forbid, that he should think I was ready to hire him only because of the sick wife in the attic room and the smell of the fried fish in the hallway and all the rest of it.

But what could I say now, that it should erase my clumsy blunder? I was covered with confusion.

And as I stood, so dumb, Mr. Zweigel began quietly to sing for me the Kol Nidre prayer for Yom Kippur. And I thanked God, the man had a voice.

I was there to meet Mr. Zweigel at the bus stop when he came up the day before Rosh Hashana. He came by himself, leaving Mrs. Zweigel behind in the attic room in New York City. I only hoped the landlady had it in her more kindness than I had heard in her voice on the phone.

So, as soon as he stepped off of the bus, carrying an old-fashioned leather satchel bound around with a rope, I knew already it was him. Mr. Zweigel in Connecticut, you immediately knew it was Mr. Zweigel.

The very first thing that I noticed was that his skin had still the grayness of over there. It was, I think I already mentioned it, the year of 1953, and I had not seen that sort of a gray skin for six or seven years already.

I can't begin that I should put it into words, the feeling in me to see the *chazzen* step off of the bus on the main street of that postcard little town on a sunny day—it was just then autumn and there was in Connecticut such colors that you can't begin to describe it—and here he came off the bus, like an old man bent over, skinny and sick-looking, and the skin gray like ash.

That he was a man expecting his first child you wouldn't think it to look at him in a million years, though unlike me—I was already by that time completely bald—he had still a full head of thick black hair, which it so happened that he kept until the end of his days. His actual age at that time was, I believe, thirty-five.

So, meanwhile, I of course had gone up to him and introduced myself, shaking his hand, and asking about the trip from New York, and to this he responded with a little slight shrug of his shoulders. Or maybe that is just now how I imagine to myself that he answered me, because it was with him a fact that, if it was at all possible he should get away with it, that was how he answered any question. Never have I known such a person—and a *chazzen,* yet—so reluctant he should have to hear the sound of his own voice.

Of course, my having been designated the official *macher* of the community meant that it was for me and Sara to put up our visiting *chazzen.* And on the way over, I'll tell you the truth, I was very concerned for my Surala, because I knew how it would be by her to see Mr. Zweigel.

Sara was already by this time maybe nearly two hundred pounds, maybe, who knows, more. She carried always food with her in her purse so that she could prevent it should happen even the slightest pang of hunger. She was twelve years younger than me, she had been little more than a child over there, and so the hunger was by her a very vivid memory.

I walked in with our guest, and my Sara, when she came out to welcome him, I saw it immediately in her face how it was, and she couldn't for a few moments even trust her voice she should speak.

So for her and for me it was truly an amazing thing that, when we came the next day and brought Mr. Zweigel he should meet the others, to them the sight of the *chazzen* it meant nothing at all. To them he was just one more poor refugee from Europe.

So, anyway, Rosh Hashana came, and Mr. Zweigel led us in our prayers.

The rest of them couldn't even read Hebrew at all. So really what we had was that Mr. Zweigel he performed for us, while everybody sat back nice and comfortable—the synagogue was our living room, a Torah we didn't have, Mr. Zweigel had brought along his own prayer book—and everybody sat and evaluated for himself the *chazzen*'s performance. You know how it is: to be a professional critic the whole world is fully qualified.

As I said before, he had, thank God, a voice: a good sound baritone, you wouldn't ever think it to look at him he could get such a nice round tone out of him. A great voice—I don't want, my friend, I should mislead you—a great voice it wasn't. And don't think that the others didn't give me plenty complaints about this, too.

Also, Mr. Zweigel performed in a very simple, very low-keyed style. A showoff he wasn't, not by any stretch of the imagination. He didn't add on all those fancy flourishes and the sobs and the *tzitter*s that some of them remembered, those of them who knew enough to remember, and this, too, made them critical. You would think, to listen to them, that we should have coming to us, who were all of ten men and their wives in Connecticut, we should have at the very least a Richard Tucker.

I knew from listening to the others that Mr. Zweigel had no future as a *chazzen* in America. And Sara of course she knew this, too, and we both spoke about it, late into the night of that first Rosh Hashana that Mr. Zweigel was by us in Connecticut.

So, anyway, after Rosh Hashana, Mr. Zweigel took the bus back to Mrs. Zweigel in New York, he should travel back again to us for Yom Kippur.

As it happened, right after I saw him off at the bus stop, I went into a little corner luncheonette that I happened to like, in order that I should have a cup of coffee before going to open the store. And as I was speaking to the owner, a very fine old gentleman by the name of Mr. Anderson, it so happened that Mr. Anderson told me that he was getting on in years, which was true, and that he was looking for someone he should purchase the business.

When he said this I knew immediately that somehow or other, with God's help and with mine, Mr. and Mrs. Zweigel were going to have this luncheonette.

So all those days, between Rosh Hashana and Yom Kippur, I worked on this idea of the luncheonette with a Mr. White, who was a very fine gentleman at my bank, the People's Trust of Connecticut.

And so, to make a long story short, that is how it came to be that the Zweigels, Reuven and his wife, Miriam, came to be my neighbors in Connecticut.

Of course, between my discussions with Mr. White at People's Trust of Connecticut and the Zweigels' actually becoming Connecticut Yankees like me, I'm skipping a lot of detail. Sara and I, we had to work a little bit on Mr. Zweigel, he didn't want that he should have to accept our help.

In such a situation Sara was much better than I, who am at such times too embarrassed I should be of much good.

But my Surala, thank God, she could be, when the situation demanded it, very direct. And so she said to him: "Mr. Zweigel, I tell you now the truth: from *chazzenes* you will never be able to support your wife and the child she carries."

So again, to make a long story short, Mr. Zweigel went back on the bus to New York City the day after Yom Kippur, we three having decided between us that he would, if she was well enough, bring Mrs. Zweigel back to Connecticut. Because, I tell you frankly, I was very anxious he should get her away from that attic room in the boarding house of the harsh-voiced landlady.

He brought her back to Connecticut looking more dead than alive.

It isn't necessary that I should describe to you too much Mrs. Zweigel, because I have described for you already her husband, and she was his exact female counterpart.

He looked not like a man, but like a shadow of a man, and she looked like a shadow of a woman. She was like him just as gray, just as silent, breathing in and breathing out sorrow. The air around them, it smelled from sorrow. How people like that could have survived over there, this I'll never know.

To look at her, so thin and sickly-looking and also like an old person bent over, you wouldn't believe it in a million years she was carrying life within her.

"Like the matriarch Sura," my own Surala remarked, because you maybe know that the wife of the first Hebrew, the patriarch Avraham, she gave birth to her only son, Yitzchak, when she was already ninety years old.

Not that I am saying of course that Mrs. Zweigel was in actual years an old woman. She must have then been at that time, like her husband, maybe thirty-five.

When they first came to Connecticut they stayed by us, because it was not possible that Mrs. Zweigel she should keep house for herself and her husband. But actually there was, above the luncheonette, an apartment, it was for them.

The baby, a girl, was born on the first night of Chanukah. Such a time as the poor mother had of it I won't go into. But Mrs. Zweigel, who was already no stranger to the Angel of Death, that night she brushed against him once again.

And now I must tell you that, on this night of miracles, when a shadow of a woman managed to give birth to this child, on this night I learned something truly amazing about Mr. Zweigel.

We were together with him at the hospital, Surala and I,

through all of that endless night. Finally, they brought to us the news that the child was born and the mother's life saved. So then Reuven Zweigel began to cry, without making a noise.

And Sara and I, who needed always very little excuse we should shed tears, we always were ready to cry it should happen someone else cried, we of course cried, too.

And then Reuven he lifted up his head, he turned his head to me, and I saw for the first time in his eyes that they were the eyes of a living man. Only at this moment, all the years I knew him, did I see in his face such eyes.

And then he said to me something I will remember it till the hour of my death.

He said to me:

"It is written that a child who is born on the first night of Chanukah, such a child hastens, even in hidden ways, the final redemption."

So of course I asked him:

"Where is it so written?"

And he answered me:

"It is written so in the Zohar."

Now, when Reuven Zweigel said to me those words, then I felt within me a deep astonishment.

"You know," I asked him finally, "you know, my friend, to quote from the Zohar?"

"Yes, I know," he said quietly.

And now I knew for the first time that Reuven Zweigel was a learned man.

That he knew more than I, that he knew more than any of the other Jews in Connecticut, so this was already a given. So this was already nothing. But a person who can quote from the Zohar, a person who must have studied yet the Zohar as a boy, because, you know, for the Zohar even thirty-five, even forty is young, such a person is not only a scholar but truly something of a prodigy.

I looked into the eyes of Reuven Zweigel that first night of Chanukah when the baby daughter was born, and I saw in those eyes that were for the only time that I ever saw them the eyes of a living man, I saw that they were also the eyes of a learned man. I saw that they were the eyes of a prodigy he had vanished long ago.

After this I could never forget it that when I spoke to Reuven Zweigel I spoke to a scholar.

Once, some years later, I got up even somehow the nerve I should ask him if he were the son of a rabbi, because somehow or other I had such an idea, and he had answered me simply,

"Yes."

And then, after a few moments more, he added,

"And the grandson and the great-grandson of rabbis, too."

And this, too, my friend, made a deep impression on me.

It was my habit to go often to the luncheonette. More often than not, in fact, Surala and I, we ate there lunch, only separately, so that one or the other could remain at the store.

There was a counter in the back of the luncheonette, and there you stood and told, to either the one or the other of them, what it was you wanted they should give you. The menu, which was written in those white plastic letters you stick them onto the black plastic with the ridges, it was hanging on the wall behind, just exactly the same as when Mr. Anderson had the store, everything they kept exactly as it was by Mr. Anderson. There in the back was also the cash register, and then on either side of the room, along the walls, nearer toward the front of the store, there were the tables, covered with oilcloth, and the benches with olive-green vinyl against the wall, and there you carried your food.

So I would sit at such a table, sometimes with Sara but usually alone.

And sometimes there would be a customer who complained, *eppes* something wasn't right, something wasn't fresh, who knows. And I would see the deep humility of Mr. Zweigel, how he felt bad inside, how he tried to make up for what the customer didn't like. And this was for me something terrible to watch. I would think: Here is the son and the grandson and the great-grandson of rabbis, and now he stands behind a counter in a white apron, and he spreads carefully mayonnaise on white bread, and answers with such humility to any rudeness. In this soft-spoken voice of a scholar he apologizes if a customer should complain maybe the lettuce is a little bit wilted.

Not that I ever once in my life regretted that I gave out a helping hand to the fate that had come looking for the Zweigels. Because, believe me, compared with the other fates that were also in the sampling, to be spreading mayonnaise on white bread in Connecticut is already something wonderful.

Other times, too, it happened over the years that a piece of Torah or Talmud would fall from Mr. Zweigel's tongue, or a rare midrash. And whenever it happened it caused me so that I should feel a very deep awe, though never so great as what I felt on that first occasion, when he quoted to me from the Zohar on the night that the daughter was born.

And the baby? Never in your life did you see such an ugly baby! It was actually comical, such a face, such an old-young face you had *taka* to laugh, although, God forbid, not in front of the parents.

Sara and I, we picked out right away the Zweigel baby, it wasn't necessary for us we should look at the name tag on the bassinet. She was there the only baby with a full head of black fuzzy hair, in the middle of all the pink-and-white little Connecticut *kinderlach*.

And she was there the only baby she was lying wide awake, already trying to screw her head in every direction, even the nurses said they had never seen over all the years such an alert newborn. Even the nurses they had to laugh when they picked her up to show us through the window the Zweigel baby.

I have to say, next to that ugly little Zweigel baby, the rest of those babies they looked a little dull, they looked even maybe *taka* a little stupid, although already they all looked better fed than her, even though they were all just a few hours old.

But the Zweigel baby had a look on her, as if the angel Gavriel had forgotten to touch her under the nose, she should forget all the Torah she had learned before her birth.

The next day, when Mrs. Zweigel was already stronger, we discussed between the four of us the name. Why—you ask me, my friend—hadn't the name been discussed before? This was because of superstition, the mother's superstition.

So the Jewish name was Mindel Gittel, which was the name of Mr. Zweigel's mother. But Mrs. Zweigel she wanted also that her daughter should have an English name, she should sound like an American child. I don't know how he felt about this. He said nothing. Mostly at first the discussion was between my Surala and Mrs. Zweigel, there in the hospital room.

I'll tell you the truth, we were none of us such experts at American names. Sara and I, we thought maybe we should call in one or two of the nurses, they should be consulted in the decision, but the Zweigels were somehow embarrassed.

But, finally, Sara slipped out, and she had a discussion there with the nurses, they all got involved, they all trooped into the room, it was like a game by them, a word game, and we four listened to them as they, with such a good nature, they tried to figure out the solution to this problem for us, what to name our Mindel Gittel in English.

So they were coming up with all sorts of names, *eppes* "Melanie," "Millicent," "Melinda"; "Minda," with an "i"; "Mynda," with a "y." We were all four of us, especially the parents, getting already dizzy with the possibilities.

So, finally, one of these good-natured nurses said:

"How about 'Melody'? Can that be the English name for 'Mindel'?"

Melody. I ask you, my friend: could there be in the entire English language a more suitable name for a *chazzen*'s daughter?

"It's *taka* a real name?" we asked the nurse.

"Sure," they all assured us. "It's not exactly common, but, then, you wouldn't want anything common for this little baby anyway, now would you?"

So we were all of us completely happy with this name: the father, the mother, and the nurses, too, especially when we explained to them what it was, a *chazzen*.

And the very same nurse, she had *eppes* some sort of a talent, she came up also with the name "Grace" for "Gittel." So now our little Mindel Gittel was Melody Grace.

The parents and the baby they came back to our house, we should help take care of them. But when Melody was two months old, the mother she finally got back a little bit some strength, and they all three moved into their own little apartment over the luncheonette.

For some time after this, our house was very quiet and empty. You know, for us children were not possible, and now that Melody was gone we heard more loudly than ever before the silence in the house. A faucet dripped, it was like the sound of thunder. Finally, I went out and bought Sara a television set.

But Sara was over there with Mrs. Zweigel all the time, and a day couldn't go by I wouldn't stop in to see little Melody Grace Zweigel, to stare into that comical little old face, into the eyes that spoke of all the ancient wisdom, and I would wonder at all that she must know. I would imagine to myself how it would be if she should suddenly start to speak, the wisdom dropping from her toothless mouth.

Meanwhile, when Melody was maybe three months old,

all the black fuzz on that little head fell out, and now the poor little thing was so bald as I sit before you now. Until she was maybe a year and a half, not a single hair did she have. But even so she got a little better-looking, she filled out, and she lost even that look of ancient wisdom that was at once so awe-inspiring and so comical.

And then it was truly something amazing. The hair began to grow back, and it was hair of pure gold. Not only this, but the child was becoming beautiful. As ugly as she had been as a baby, that's how beautiful she was becoming now.

By the time she was two and a half years old, you couldn't walk down the street with her, strangers would stop to exclaim. Her skin, against the golden hair, it was like peaches and cream, and her eyes were light gray, clear like the air in the mountains, and rimmed all around the outside with a deep blue. Such a coloring you never saw in your life. Even her teeth, her sharp little milk teeth, they were to me something of a miracle, so white.

Mrs. Zweigel, even though she worked all the day beside her husband in the luncheonette, she made at night all of Melody's clothes, beautiful little clothes, little blue velvet dresses with lace collars. There was not another child there in that town with more beautiful clothes. Or maybe it was that, no matter what you would have put on that child, it would have turned out it should look beautiful.

So Melody she would spend all the day with her parents in the luncheonette, sitting on the floor behind the counter, she shouldn't be in the way, chattering all the day long to her dolls, singing all sorts of funny little songs she would make up for them, laughing a laugh gold like the hair.

If a stranger came in they couldn't stop exclaiming over the child. That such a child could belong to those two gray people, they would take your order without looking at you, and then hand you your tuna sandwich or your salami on rye without a word or a glance, that this child was theirs, you could see a person blinking as if maybe they're dreaming.

So what happened? What do you think happened? Before I knew it, Melody's days playing behind the counter in the luncheonette are over and she's starting already kindergarten. And then it seemed to me that her childhood started to speed up, it seemed to go past before me in a golden blur, that golden child always in the middle of a golden blur: of friends, of school-doings, of sports, of everything. What didn't that child do?

She did everything what the other children did. At first, I used to see that she asked her parents for permission, just like she saw her playmates that they should ask their parents. So what kind of an answer did they give her? They shrugged, either one or the other of them. And this shrug it meant: What do we know? Do what the others are doing. So after a while Melody already stopped asking them and she just did what the other parents gave permission their children should do.

She was always busy, it became already an occasion Sara and I we should get to see her. But always she was sweet. Always when she saw us she would throw her arms around us with a hug and a little kiss on the cheek. She had a disposition it was like pure sunshine.

I remember once she was complaining to Sara and myself, but comically, full of good humor, about the hardships of her life, all because her last name began with a "Z," because everything in that school it was by the alphabet.

Even to line up to go to the bathroom, they lined up by the alphabet!

"And not just 'Z'! No, that isn't bad enough. I have to be a 'Zw'! Look it up in the phone book, Uncle Sol. We're the very last ones!"

"So, Melody darling, you won't always be a 'Zw.' You'll get married, you'll change your name."

"Abbington," she smiled. "I looked it up. They're first in the book."

You've heard, my friend, maybe of the Brownies? It's like the Girl Scouts, only for younger children.

So, once, I remember, I'm sitting in the luncheonette and Melody comes in with two or three others, all of them in brown uniforms. They have on *eppes* a little brown funny hat, like yarmulkes, and across their chests there's some sort of a sash decorated with all sorts of insignia.

It was the first time I saw the child in this uniform, and to me it was a horrible sight. I felt my stomach turn. Never have I liked uniforms. To me a child in a uniform is a perversion.

So of course she comes right over to kiss me, and I ask her:

"What is this you are wearing, Melody darling?"

"Oh, Uncle Sol, it's my Brownie uniform. You see"—she indicated the other children, who were already trooping to the refrigerator at the back they should help themselves to milk—"we're all Brownies!"

"It's fun to be a Brownie?" I asked her.

"Sure. Tons!" And she slid off my lap she should go get herself some milk, too. They all grabbed some Danish from under the plastic case, and then dashed out the door, their thin little legs kicking out beneath the brown uniforms.

So then I got up from the table and went to the back I should have a word with Melody's parents.

"Miriam," I said. "You think this is right, Melody should go in such a uniform?"

She quickly glanced up from the celery she was dicing and then down again and shrugged.

"Reuven," I said. "It doesn't do something inside of you, you should see Melody in such a uniform?"

He looked up from the large jar of mayonnaise from which he was taking, and then put down the spoon, carefully wiped his hands, took off his white apron, and disappeared through the door that went up to the apartment.

A few moments later, he came down with a little pamphlet, it was maybe twenty pages long, with a drawing on the cover of an orange-haired little girl with just such a Brownie beanie on her head. The pamphlet was called *On Our Way: Brownie Badge Program*.

He sat down next to me on the bench, watching me closely as I turned the pages, there on the oilcloth-covered table.

I have to say frankly I felt a little foolish as I read about Wise Owl, and Busy Bees, and Suzy Safety. The Brownies, I could see, were very fine people.

So maybe I smiled a little sheepish at Melody's father.

"Yes, my friend, you are right," I said to him. "There are uniforms and there are uniforms."

So Melody was for a short time a Brownie. They didn't stick with it long, they gave it up for other things: piano lessons, softball practice, this club, that club. Sara and I we had trouble keeping up with it all, and the parents I don't think they even tried.

I forgot to mention that, with all of Melody's other gifts, she had, too, a voice. In the school shows she had always a big part, usually a solo. People who knew—and if you didn't know you would never in a million years guess—that this pair from the luncheonette were Melody's parents they would come over to where we all sat in the back of the auditorium, on the brown wooden seats, and they would pour out their congratulations on the Zweigels.

"How proud you must be of her!"

And for an answer one or the other of them would shrug, so that Sara and I we were embarrassed, both for the parents and for the kind stranger whose smile would start to dissolve in the middle of the Zweigels' silence.

Now, when I think back, how quickly it all seems to have flown past, the golden blur. Only now, as she got older, of course it was natural there should be also some boys in the blur that was always around her: nice boys, like the girls, from fine families. They would come, all together, to the luncheonette, it was filled with their happy noise. They would greet Mr. and Mrs. Zweigel with politeness, and then, when they would all leave together, they would all say to them goodbye, and Melody would also throw back a goodbye to us from the door.

Now, once, when Melody was already maybe thirteen, it happened that she came into the luncheonette all by herself, and she sat down beside me on the bench where I had been sipping my glass of tea.

"Uncle Sol!" she said, giving me a little kiss. "Long time no see. I see you haven't changed your hairstyle."

It was between us a little joke, she should tease me about my bald pate.

"But you've changed yours a little," I said. "Something somehow is different."

"Bangs," she pronounced, pointing to the fringe that decorated her forehead. "Do you like them? I wanted some sort of a change without doing anything really drastic, like actually cutting my hair."

She had very long hair at this age, all the way down her back, a river of gold.

"On you, Mindela Gittel, I like everything."

So why did it happen just then that I should call her Mindela Gittel? This, my friend, I can't tell you. I only know it came out. Maybe it could be that, because we were talking about a change in the hairstyle, so somewhere, in the back of my mind, I was remembering the black-fuzzed little baby she used to be.

"Mindela Gittel?" She smiled at me.

So I patted her hand.

"You know maybe who was Mindela Gittel, Melody darling?"

"Do you mean the grandmother I was named after?"

So she knew this much. One or the other of them had said this much to her, because with those two you could never assume it that anything had been said.

"That's right, Melody darling. Your grandmother. Maybe you know a little something about her?"

"No, Uncle Sol." She shook her head with the new fringe of bangs. "Really nothing at all. Only that she was Dad's mom. Do you know anything special about her?"

So what, my friend, could I say? The only thing special that I knew about Mindel Gittel was the same what I knew from all of our parents, what I knew from everybody over there.

So it was on the tip of my tongue to ask Melody if she knew maybe where it was that Mindel Gittel had died, if she knew how it was that Mindel Gittel had died, if she knew maybe why it was that her bubby, Mindel Gittel, had died.

But you could see it already the answers, or, rather, what you could see was there were no answers, the second that you looked into the child's face. You could hear it in the way she said those words, "Dad's mom," just exactly like any of her other friends, the other children of that town, they would have said those words.

So, although it was on the tip of my tongue to say something, I said nothing.

But to myself I said:

If a learned man like Mr. Zweigel, who quoted such words from the Zohar on the night that his only daughter was born, if such a man keeps his silence, then who am I, I should breathe the old stench of death on this child?

So that was how it was.

Meanwhile, Melody she started already high school, she was busy, busy, with all sorts of things busy, with drama club, with debating club, swimming, tennis, skiing. And always a student. A+. She brought home an A, Sara and I we would tease her she was getting lazy.

She looked like the young Grace Kelly. That's what everybody in town said. Just exactly like Grace Kelly, she could be her younger sister.

And then, in her senior year of high school, she was voted the president of the entire student body. That was how much they all loved our Melody.

And I will tell you this: all of that town they were all in love with our little girl. All of that town took pride in her. The only ones who never showed any pride, strange as it is to say, were the parents. I never saw they should even smile when people praised their Melody to them.

And when Melody graduated from that high school, she graduated with all sorts of honors. What kind of award didn't that school heap on her? She was the valedictorian, she was the student-council president. There were one hundred and two children graduating, but that night it seemed like it was Melody's night.

She stood toward the back, because they had had them march in by height, the shortest ones first, and our Melody she was a tall girl. And then how did they call them up for their diplomas but by the alphabet, this A-to-Z alphabet that had always made our Melody groan.

But I tell you—I did not imagine it—that the entire auditorium it exploded with applause for our Melody, that there was a roar in my ears from all the clapping as Melody Grace Zweigel stepped up to the front to get her handshake and the piece of paper.

The Zweigels didn't have to pay a cent their daughter should go to Radcliffe College in Cambridge, Massachusetts. The town gave her a special scholarship, Radcliffe gave her a scholarship, the state of Connecticut they even gave her a scholarship. By the time everybody got through giving her, believe me, there were plenty poorer students at Radcliffe College. She had money even for books. Only for clothes her parents and we gave her.

Now it was like, for Sara and myself, it was like when the Zweigels first moved out of our house, they should live in their own little apartment above the luncheonette, and our house it thundered with the silence. Now, for a while, the whole town seemed *eppes* quiet and emptied out.

In Radcliffe, Melody majored in international politics. And it was just the same as in high school. Straight A's. At Radcliffe they don't give any A+'s.

Sometimes she would come home for the vacations, the Christmas vacation, the summer vacation, sometimes she wouldn't, she would go to friends, she would go maybe to ski, once even to a Greek island in the summer, to a home one of her classmates' family owned. I think Melody told us they owned the entire island.

And for us, Surala and me in our dress shop, the Zweigels in the luncheonette, everything went on just the same.

So, in her senior year, Melody's roommate was a girl, also she was interested in international politics. And this girl, her name was Amanda Darnell, she came from a very prominent family in New Hampshire. It happened that her father was a United States congressman, her grandfather had been also I think *eppes* a congressman or a senator.

Melody went to the Darnells' home for the Christmas holidays, and there was there an older brother, of course he falls right away in love with Melody.

So in this there's nothing new. Everybody was in love with Melody. Only this time Melody loved the young man back.

He is already at Harvard Law School, so they see each other in Boston, and soon they're engaged to be married.

The Darnells, they're wonderful people, right away they adopt Melody as their own, just as people were always ready they should adopt Melody as their own. Who doesn't dream they should be so lucky they should have such a child?

Mrs. Darnell she plans everything for the wedding together with Melody. She shops with her for the gown, they pick out together the china pattern, the silver, everything.

And about money, never a word. The Darnells were, I don't have to tell you, very well-to-do. It was old money, the kind that doesn't make a big tumult about itself, and they were never so crude they should breathe a word of money.

And so far as I know they never raised a single word either their son should be marrying a Jewish girl. They were, I don't know that this has anything to do with it, but they happened to be liberal Democrats.

So the wedding was on the grounds of their estate in New Hampshire. It was June, three weeks after Melody graduated from Radcliffe. The boy still had another year at Harvard Law School.

So we drive up there, the four of us, we leave early in the morning, it's still dark. It's an afternoon wedding. Surala and I we sit in the front, and the two Zweigels, silent like the grave, in the back.

And when it grows light, we see it's a very cloudy day, there's low down in the sky a thick heavy blanket of gray clouds, and even some drops fall, now and then, and Surala and I we worry, because it's supposed to be an outdoors wedding.

We drive up, we go through the gates of the Darnells' home, an iron gate with stone pillars, and the name of the home inscribed on the gate—a funny thing, the name suddenly escapes me.

We drive up a long, long drive, under trees like a canopy, on either side a forest, and then suddenly up ahead a beautiful home, stone, like a little castle. And the Zweigels they sit in the back and they say between them nothing.

We come, we're welcomed like royalty into the house, the vestibule is all with marble, it's a beautiful house but with a chill you feel it the moment you step in. Of course, it had been raining, and a stone house has always a chill.

But everybody is very nice, even more than nice. Mrs. Darnell is cooing like a happy dove. She is a tall and stately woman, everybody is tall and stately, like the trees along the drive. But Mrs. Darnell you can see she is a warm person, that underneath all the state she is a genuine person, and there is something even girlish about her, so that immediately I start to imagine what she must have been like on her own wedding day. Her I like.

They don't know yet whether the ceremony will be in the tent or not, because they had planned it for the rose garden, but the weather it's still uncertain.

Mrs. Darnell takes up the mother of the bride and my Surala to the room where Melody is already dressing, and Mr. Zweigel and myself are taken into a library, to speak for a little while with Mr. Darnell, a very distinguished-looking man, and also with very fine manners. So fine, you don't see the manners at all.

But even I am completely overwhelmed by all of this. I don't know how I should sit in such a room, how I should make conversation with such a man, so you can imagine how it is for Mr. Zweigel.

Although maybe, now I come actually to think about it, maybe it was, for him and for me, exactly the same. Because I tell you: in our little town in Connecticut, there was between us, Mr. Zweigel and myself, something of a difference. I was more the Connecticut Yankee. But, sitting here, and maybe even in the view of the Congressman Darnell, there is probably no difference at all. I'm not so sure he can even say at this point which of the two of us is the father and which the so-called uncle.

After about ten minutes, Mr. Darnell excuses himself, he has much to look after before the guests arrive.

And Melody, about a half an hour before the guests are scheduled to arrive, she comes floating into the library, where her father and I sit, and she is followed by Mrs. Darnell and Mrs. Zweigel and my Surala, and Mrs. Darnell her eyes are glowing with tears, and she stands right behind Melody with her hands they're in *eppes* a position like maybe she's praying.

I will tell you this: not on television, not in the movies, not on the stage, never did you see such a vision as Melody on her wedding day.

The wedding veil belonged to the mother, I mean of course to the boy's mother, to Mrs. Darnell. And the gown they had had it made up to go with the veil, at Rosett Pennington, in New York City. Because I was all those years in lady's ready-to-wear, so I can give you a description of this gown it will be professional.

It was very simple, elegant, not an ornament, not a single pearl there was embroidered on it. But the gown it was from silk barathea, which you may or may not know is smooth-textured, not shiny, and it was in the princesse style, with only the long seams, no bodice, and a boat neck, which you may or may not know is across the shoulders cut wide. Melody wore with it only a single strand of pearls.

A train she didn't wear, but only the mother's veil, which was long, to the floor, made of silk tulle and with a wreath of silk flowers.

The names of the flowers she carried in her hands, that I couldn't tell you, because flowers they were never my business. Only women's ready-to-wear. I can only say that the flowers they were white.

But I can tell you that even the skies were charmed by the sight of Melody in her princesse gown of silk barathea. Even the heavens were charmed into submission. The clouds had parted, every bit of them had been swept away. The sun came out, strong like here it shines, and the lawns dried out enough so that Melody was married in the rose garden.

I have now in my mind a picture of this wedding, in the glowing afternoon, you could be the greatest artist you wouldn't be able to paint so much beauty. Only the Zweigels, and no doubt also Surala and myself, we are like maybe smudges on the edge of this picture.

The strange thing was that neither Sara nor I cried at that wedding. All around us were Episcopalians weeping. And Sara and I, with our never-emptied buckets of tears, who will the both of us cry at anything, at a Hallmark greeting card we'll sob, Sara and I we sit there dry-eyed. The Zweigels, too.

Because there is a language in tears, just as there is in laughter. Things you wouldn't know to say in words you say by when you cry and when you don't, when you laugh and when you don't.

Now, the Zweigels I had never seen either of them laugh, never once. I can't for the life of me even begin I should imagine what laughter from them would sound like. I would have thought the Messiah was surely on his way. A smile from them was already a historical occasion.

Him I had seen cry, but only that once, and without any noise.

When did I last see Melody? It was at her mother's funeral. He had died already, maybe two years before, from cancer, and she died of the same thing.

So Melody came with her husband, he was just elected to the State Assembly, he looked already something more like his father, *eppes* a little thicker, and with her also, her two little daughters, both of them beautiful children, they looked just like she had looked as a child. And she had them dressed in just such little velvet dresses with lace collars as her mother used to stay up nights sewing for her.

By this time my Surala she was long gone. It was the extra weight that killed her. She died young, fifty-one years old, from the extra weight she carried because of the hunger she couldn't forget.

So, after I lost my Surala, and then my two dear friends, I found that the roots I had put down in Connecticut they weren't *taka* so deep after all. The winters were cold, there was no luncheonette for me to sit in anymore.

I sold my store and thought about where to go. Miami? To sit and wait for what? Only one thing.

So if I want warm weather I should sit and wait, I thought, why not go to Israel? Let the Angel of Death he should have to travel a little bit he should find me. And so, to make a long story short, that is how you happen to find me sitting here.

And the strange thing is that, between that moment when I saw for the very last time my mother and my father and until this moment that I sit here in this café on Ben Yehuda Street, nothing at all seems real. Nothing except for my Surala and Mr. and Mrs. Zweigel.

I used to stand and stare onto the green and think: Do I dream? And now I look back and I say: Yes, I dreamt.

One thing that happened here I must tell you. I would never have thought it possible, but I found for myself here a relation, a distant cousin. Who would have thought such a thing?

You know that they have such a service at Yad Vashem, you register with them, and they try to see maybe you have still some family. So I thought: Well, I have nothing to lose.

And what do I discover but that right here in Jerusalem is a cousin, she lives with her husband, both of them such fine people I can't begin to tell you. I think maybe I even remember hearing my parents once or twice they should talk of her parents. And now, every Friday night, I'm eating dinner at my cousin's house. So life goes on.

My cousin has a son, he's *eppes* some kind of a mathematical genius, a one-of-a-kind wunderkind, Oren Glube, maybe you've even heard of him, my friend? According to my cousin he's been written about here, several times, in the papers. A beautiful name: Oren, light. He lives in France, at a special mathematical institute, all he has to do is think. They pay him just to sit and think. If my cousin is right—I don't know, because, you know, when it comes to a person's child, even the father Yitzchak thought his Esav a good boy—but if my cousin is to be believed, then her son Oren is at the very least another Albert Einstein. So I have even a little bit of *yiches,* several times removed, in my old age.

So, since I opened with a story—you maybe remember, with the dwarfs?—so maybe now I'll close with a story. Only this one is true, and it's even stranger than the other.

You know, here in Israel we have many zealots, many hotheads. We have unfortunately those who say that they are sick of words, that they must speak another language, with violence, with the spilling of human blood. Some of these people are Arabs and some of these people are Jews. And among these Jews, there are some, I am sorry to say, they call themselves even religious. In fact, some belong to the extreme Orthodoxy.

So, the other day, I'm reading in the Jerusalem *Post* about just such an incident, with two such Jewish extremists, they are arrested.

And there is a picture, they look like any two such very Orthodox young men, with full beards and black hats, but what do I read? One of these two young hotheads he is the grandson of Leon Trotsky!

Now, that Trotsky's grandson should be a hothead making trouble is *taka* not so amazing. But that he should be this kind of a hothead, making this kind of a trouble, this is a little bit of a miracle.

So, when I read this story in the Jerusalem *Post,* I think

immediately of my friends the Zweigels. And this is what I think:

If Leon Trotsky's grandson can wear a black hat and make himself a gangster in the name of the eternal right of the Jewish people to this land, then who knows? Who knows if it won't happen some day a little golden grandchild or great-grandchild or even great-great-grandchild of my friends the Zweigels should maybe know to quote a little something from the Zohar?

THE GEOMETRY OF
SOAP BUBBLES AND
IMPOSSIBLE LOVE

Phoebe Saunders, at twenty-six, is an acknowledged expert on the mathematics of soap bubbles and soap films—and an unacknowledged expert on the phenomenology of impossible love.

Blowing soap bubbles had been one of the few childlike activities Phoebe had enjoyed as a little girl. Her mother, Chloe, a member of the classics department at Barnard College, used to place Phoebe on a couch near the tiled fireplace in the homey Ella Weed room of Milbank Hall, a few doors away from her office; and there Phoebe could stay for hours at a stretch, puffing gently, catching the bubbles on the tip of her wand to create shimmering clusters of infinite variety. Sometimes a Barnard student or two would drift in and join Phoebe in her solemn, dignified play.

But aside from her soap bubbles little Phoebe hadn't gone in much for play, not at least as Chloe understood the term.

For Chloe, play had always meant make-believe. In the absence of any dolls, the child Chloe had dressed her mother Sasha's dinnerware in linen napkins—the spoons and forks were women; the knives, men—and spun out great family sagas, with crisscrossed plots unfolding over the course of days, or even weeks.

But Phoebe's faculty of make-believe had seemed, to say the least, sluggish. Instead she enjoyed puzzles of all sorts, paradoxes, brain-teasers. And, of course, the bubbles. But even in bubbles there's no human element.

It was Sasha, strangely, who had first taught Phoebe chess, though Sasha, with the undiscipline of her nature perfected over the years, only vaguely remembered how the chess pieces move, and beyond that nothing at all. For a few years Phoebe had thought primarily about chess, and so, therefore, had Chloe, who became competent enough at least to play a game engaging to Phoebe.

Perhaps Phoebe might have developed into a chess prodigy, but both she and Chloe had shied away from the clammy atmosphere of the formal chess clubs. Eventually Phoebe's interest in the game had dwindled, as the mathematics she could do deepened.

It was while she was a graduate student at Princeton that she had returned to her soap bubbles, this time captivated by the exquisite geometry of their convergence.

Bright clusters of infinite variety. But beneath the play of iridescence on shifting forms are rigorous description and rules of simple elegance, embodying perfect symmetry, and determining which configurations are possible and which aren't: the "Plateau rules," named after a Belgian physicist who had formulated them more than a century ago:

Soap bubbles consist of flat or smoothly curved surfaces, seamlessly joined together, with surfaces meeting in only two ways: either exactly three surfaces meet along a smooth curve, or six surfaces (together with four curves) meet at a vertex.

The angles formed are always equal—120 degrees when three surfaces meet along a curve, close to 109 degrees when four curves meet at a point—so that all the elaborate, asymmetrical shapes of froth are built of interactions of maximal symmetry.

But beyond the simply stated Plateau rules lies a range of mathematical problems of satisfying intricacy, combining both analytic and geometric techniques into a branch of mathematics mirroring, to Phoebe's awestruck mind, the luminous beauty of the soap bubbles themselves.

Chloe reads the ancient Greeks on such properties as the length of curves, the areas of surfaces, and the volumes of solids, trying to get a clearer glimpse into the work that Phoebe loves; and Sasha, with delight, tells her friends that Phoebe's field is the mathematics of froth.

Phoebe's knowledge of the phenomenology of impossible love also had its beginnings in her childhood. She had been subject, from an early age, to sudden fits of dense passion: fantastic, consuming, hopeless, hopeless love:

At the age of eight Phoebe had fallen in love with Mr. Pennoyer, a deaf octogenarian who lived in their apartment building on Riverside Drive, a little above the boat basin, on West 79th Street.

Mr. Pennoyer, frail and trembly, had shared an apartment, even larger than the Saunderses', with his sister, who was sprier than he. Both had faces so finely lined the skin looked like cracked pottery.

"My brother's deaf now, you know," Miss Pennoyer, silver-haired and ramrod-straight, would explain to Phoebe each time that Phoebe came to visit them. And palsied Mr. Pennoyer, with posture much poorer than his sister's, would smile and nod his head in a way that Phoebe knew was meant to be encouraging.

Mr. and Miss Pennoyer had been born in Manhattan, and Miss Pennoyer still spoke in the clipped tones of old New York. It was Sasha who had first "discovered" the Pennoyers, just as it was Sasha who discovered most of the people who interested them.

Long ago, when the Pennoyers, brother and sister, were young, they had left Manhattan for North Dakota, there to teach school to the children of the Three Tribes—the Arikara, the Hidatsa, and the Mandan. The nine rooms occupied by the Pennoyers were crammed with a world of fascinating objects: boldly painted pottery, beaded bags, a doll made of cornhusks. Mr. Pennoyer was often to be seen sitting in his fireside chair, a blue-and-gray Indian blanket folded neatly over his knees. The pottery of the Three Tribes, Miss Pennoyer had said, was in particular highly prized, and she had explained the significance of its patterns to Phoebe.

Miss Pennoyer very much approved of Phoebe, with her quiet, serious manner, and her intelligent questions. Though Miss Pennoyer had always loved children, achingly loved them, yet she had never mastered the art of speaking to them. She couldn't address a child without, at the same time, trying to instruct him, moved as she was by a deep sense of earnestness that for some reason came off seeming stern. Children had always kept their distance from her, whereas her brother always managed to charm them. Watching him horsing around in the midst of their whooping laughter, or tenderly comforting some small sobbing creature, Miss Pennoyer had ached all the more.

But Miss Pennoyer's pedagogical nature didn't appear to put Phoebe off in the least; and Miss Pennoyer, who didn't believe in compliments, especially not about children, had compromised her principles, once or twice, in order to tell Sasha what an extremely satisfactory little girl Phoebe happened to be; to which Sasha had laughed her deep laugh and answered in her emphatic way:

"Yes, I should say so. I should say that Phoebe is a very satisfactory little girl."

Miss Pennoyer had once also shown Phoebe an old photograph of herself and her brother, the two surrounded by a pack of dark-eyed children, as solemn-faced as Phoebe herself. Miss Pennoyer had turned the picture over and pointed out the date scribbled on the back: 1905. Mr. Pennoyer, watching, had smiled and nodded. Phoebe had only rarely heard him speak, his voice, also old New York, painfully loud; and Miss Pennoyer herself hardly ever addressed him, though she had told Phoebe that he had learned to read lips.

It was the picture that had initiated Phoebe into the secret rites of impossible love:

Miss Pennoyer had been lovely: delicate-featured, but with

a look of composed strength, her hair pinned up and her shoulders squared.

But Mr. Pennoyer! Phoebe had never seen such a beautiful man in her entire life.

He was dressed in light-colored slacks and a white shirt, which he had rolled up over his elbows. He was squatting down, and a tiny little girl in a gingham dress was sitting on his knee, his arm encircling her waist. He grinned at the person holding the camera; he looked as if he might just have heard, or himself have said, something light and funny. Tawny, tousled hair fell over his brow. He looked jaunty and healthy and unbelievably at ease, like one who has been hand-chosen by the gods.

But Phoebe knew something about this shining youth that he himself could never have guessed. She knew the palsied, frail, and deaf old man he would become, smiling his benign smile and nodding his head with encouragement; and it was from this knowledge that her impossible love had sprung full-grown, swelling her poor child's heart with the heat of hopeless, hopeless love.

The object of her passion both was and wasn't the shuffling old man of apartment 6G, just as it both was and wasn't the kindred spirit of the gods, who had squatted in 1905 in a dirt schoolyard in North Dakota. Phoebe had loved a man somehow suspended between these two.

And yet, with all this, Phoebe had seemed to Chloe, who never yet has glimpsed Phoebe's impossible loves, to be a child strangely lacking in imagination, at least so far as any matter remotely human; literal-minded to a fault—what do you mean? that doesn't make sense!—forcing even free-associating Sasha to give some semblance of precision to her fabulously concocted histories. And though Phoebe had rarely ever complained of being bored, she was never able to lose herself to the forms of self-enchantment that had claimed Chloe when she was a child.

Sasha had been very distracted when Chloe was a little girl. By the time Sasha had settled down into motherhood—which hadn't involved her displacing herself, but only shifting the focus of her attention—Chloe's rituals of self-play were firmly in place; and then Sasha had been too charmed by the dramas of the spoons and the forks to spoil anything by providing Chloe with real dolls.

The apartment on Riverside Drive had been filled a large part of the time with Sasha's friends, who would interrupt their arguing just long enough to take a quick sip of the scalding tea they drank with a slice of lemon from glasses resting in silver holders.

But Chloe, lying on her stomach in a corner of the living room, deep inside the clustering plots of her family sagas, could always drown out the invariably vehement voices merging in a polyglot of Yiddish, Polish, German, Russian, English.

And sometimes Sasha, suddenly bored with the circular patterns the arguments were making, would unfold her long, slim legs from underneath her on the couch, and walk over, leaving a trail of ash from her cigarette, to place herself cross-legged on the floor, beside where Chloe lay playing.

"Tell me," she'd demand, in the husky voice that had thrilled the audiences of the experimental Yiddish theater of Warsaw, "what's new in the hectic lives of the Forkowitzes and Spoonozchewskis?"

"What a plot!" she'd marvel after listening for a while.

"This child here," she'd call over to her friends, her finger above Chloe's head pointing downward, "this is the one who should be writing for the Yiddish stage today!"

Sasha was an intimate friend, or enemy, with everybody involved in New York's tight little circle of the Yiddish intelligentsia. I. B. Singer had once propositioned her, but she was already involved with Chloe's father, Maurice Saunders.

"Although, if I'd known then that Yitzy was going to go

on and win the Nobel Prize, maybe I would have acted differently. He himself went on to my friend Tova—she was also a tall blonde, you know Yitzy liked tall blondes—and she had a good time with him."

Maurice had been a journalist/philosopher/laborer/God Himself only knows, who had drifted in and out of New York's Yiddish world, often leaving for crazy places: for Minnesota, for Winnipeg, for Calgary. He had been to North Dakota, too.

Maurice had loved the cold. He used to throw the windows of the apartment wide open in the dead of the coldest winter. The wind blowing off the Hudson would set the Yiddishists' teeth to chattering. He used to freeze Sasha's friends out of the apartment.

He never could sit out a New York summer. Once, in desperation, he had joined a freighter headed for Iceland, offering himself as a cook's assistant. He had figured that all he'd have to do is stir the pots and peel the potatoes. But then the cook had gotten seasick and Maurice had been ordered to take over. Discovered, he had been relegated to swabbing the decks until they reached Reykjavík, where they had put him ashore. He had eventually made his way back to New York, by way of Labrador.

He had always returned, though it could take a few years, to overheated New York, a city he hated. He would come back for Chloe's learned conversation, studded with small ironies; and for the sight of Sasha, her vehemence suddenly turning tender.

Maurice had felt tremendous pride in Chloe's scholarliness. They always discussed books together, or argued over Marxism. He had taken at least one of a father's duties very seriously and that was the instruction of class economics. He himself had thought, when he was young, that he would be a scholar, and he always retained a great love for abstract ideas. But he had spent the years when he ought to have been in a university escaping from Poland, taking the long route: through the U.S.S.R., then by boat to Japan, and by steamer to Calcutta via Shanghai. From India he took a ferry via the Suez Canal, where he was shelled by German guns. When he didn't find Sasha in Palestine, he came to New York. But he never really could settle down, once he was transplanted from Poland. He had gotten the wandering into his blood.

Sasha always laughed when she told her stories of Maurice, of his northward adventures, his sly insults to the Yiddishists, though usually she'd end by muttering: The bum; the no-goodnik. He had been even more unsuited to monogamy than Sasha.

Maurice had died of a heart attack when he was fifty-five. Chloe had returned home from school on the day Sasha had gotten word of his death, on his way back from Nova Scotia, to have Sasha fling open the door before Chloe could fit in her key. Sasha had stood there for a few moments, gaping wild-eyed, trying to find her voice, finally collapsing against Chloe and weeping.

For weeks Sasha had walked aimlessly around the apart-ment, not even trying to repair with makeup the damage grief had done her face.

"Maurice was an intellectual, too," she would sometimes interrupt Chloe's reading to tell her. "He had read more and remembered more than any of those deadbeat Yiddishists who used to sit arguing with one another all day over who was the better stylist, Chaim Pupik or Chaim Pupik's brother!

"But Maurice didn't have weak tea flowing in yellow veins like they did. He didn't have unpronounceable words and flowery quotations where his manhood ought to be!

"It's always that way," she would say. "It's what you call the paradox of sex. The ones who'll settle down, who'll do anything you want, who wants them? It's the others, the bums, the no-goodniks, the ones who disappear for two years and then turn up in the middle of December in order to see their daughter, they're the ones who make you yowl like a cat in heat."

"Never, O never, lady mine, discharge at me from thy golden bow a shaft invincible, in passion's venom dipped," Chloe had recited in the ancient Greek from Euripides' *Medea*.

"Yes? Meaning?" Sasha had demanded.

"Meaning: I hope I never yowl like a cat in heat."

"Ech," Sasha had retorted. "You don't know what you're missing."

Which is why Sasha had begun motherhood in a state of distraction. But Chloe had seemed, and even been, a relatively contented little girl, lost in a book, or in the tragedies of the napkin-draped dinnerware.

So Chloe had thought that Phoebe would by instinct take to the transports of inspired make-believe. But the dolls arranged on the shelves of Phoebe's room remained untouched.

The finer sensibilities of Chloe's Barnard colleagues would perhaps have been rattled: Chloe had gone and bought Phoebe an assortment of Ken and Barbie dolls, with skintight clothes and miscellaneous accessories, having felt the drama latent in their flash.

And when Phoebe still failed to pick up a doll and imagine a life for it, Chloe began to do it for her, just to show her how.

"Let's pretend," she had said, taking up two of the Barbies, almost as undecidably indistinguishable as the dinner forks of old. "Let's pretend that this one is the mother and this one is the daughter. Now we'll make them speak to one another."

"You make them speak, Mommy. I don't know what they'd say."

"They'd say whatever you decide they should say."

"You decide."

"Okay. Let's give them names first. What would you like their names to be?"

"What would *you* like their names to be?"

"Oh, I get to decide that, too. Okay, let's call the mother Hecuba, and the daughter Cassandra."

"Cassandra. That's pretty. Is it a real name?"

"Absolutely real. Greek like yours. There was a beautiful Trojan princess named Cassandra, 'as fair as the golden-haired Venus,' " Chloe had quoted, fingering the tresses of the golden-haired Barbie.

"I've never met anyone named Cassandra." Phoebe paused a moment. "Of course, I've never met anyone else named Phoebe either."

"The Trojan princess had what many people might consider a bad habit. Maybe that's why there aren't too many Cassandras running around."

"Did she bite her nails?"

Phoebe was a nail-biter.

"Not so far as I know. Her habit was telling the truth, always, whether people wanted to hear it or not."

"But that's not bad!"

"The shining god Apollo," Chloe had continued, picking up a Ken doll, clad in psychedelic bathing trunks, "fell in love with Cassandra. Be my girlfriend, fair mortal," Chloe had made the Apollo/Ken declare himself to the Cassandra/Barbie, "and I'll give you the gift of seeing all things, both present and future."

"Okay, Apollo, I'll be your girlfriend. Now show me all things!"

"What do you see, Cassandra?"

"I see a little girl named Phoebe Saunders playing Barbies with her mother."

"Oh, Mom! Really!"

"Oh! I see my bright city of Ilium in blackened ruins,

destroyed by senseless war. I see my father, King Priam, dead, and my brave brother Hector, too. And my mother, the proud Queen Hecuba, taken as a slave to the hated victor, Odysseus, a monster of lawlessness."

And Chloe had made an Odysseus/Ken take the Hecuba/ Barbie by her hair.

"I don't like the gift you've given me, Apollo! I don't want to see all things! Take back my sight!"

"A god can't take back what he's given. And who are you to be ordering me around, anyway? I'm the son of mighty Zeus, and you're a very unruly mortal."

"I don't think I'm going to be your girlfriend after all, Apollo!"

"Then hear what I shall do to you, O reckless maiden. You'll see the truth, and tell the truth just as you see it, but none will ever believe you!"

Chloe's ploy had worked just a little too well. Phoebe sat raptly watching Chloe, and never once ever after did Phoebe pick up a doll on her own. Instead Phoebe would ask Chloe to play with the dolls *for* her.

A great favorite had been Chloe's very free adaptation of Euripides' *Bacchae*. Chloe would have a Dionysus/Ken stride out to declare:

Lo! I am come to this land of Thebes, Dionysus, the son of Zeus, born of my mother, Semele, by a flash of lightning. I have put off the god and taken human shape.

But it was the ending that had unfailingly fascinated little Phoebe: Chloe, simulating a Bacchic frenzy that was part Greek mystery religion, part Charlie Manson, would rip the head and limbs from the sacrificial Pentheus/Ken and fling them all about Phoebe's room.

Chloe, reading books on chess, had been saddened, just a little, by Phoebe's seeming failure to take fire from the games of make-believe.

Of course, Phoebe's love of mental rigor was something

that Chloe could well understand. She herself had fallen in love with the formidable structure of the Greek sentence.

"Some more dead languages for our family!" Sasha had whooped when Chloe, then a student at Barnard, had told Sasha of her decision to major in the classics.

Maurice, Sasha told Chloe, had read *The Iliad* and *The Odyssey* in their Yiddish translations, and had told her that Genesis had them both beaten cold.

"Maybe in Yiddish." Chloe had shrugged.

Sasha read *The Iliad* and *The Odyssey* for herself, in the English translation, to try and get some feel for the stories that had so carried away her daughter.

Sasha couldn't begin to contemplate learning Greek; or, rather, she had contemplated it, for all of fifteen minutes. Instead she had asked Chloe to teach her Latin.

The lessons hadn't proceeded very far. Sasha would immediately begin to make faces at all the rules, until one day Chloe had literally thrown the book at her.

"Rules! Rules! What does a language need with so many rules!" Sasha had shouted, ducking the Latin missile.

"Yiddish has rules, too, Sasha!"

"Where? You show me! I never saw any!"

Sasha had been ever prepared to resist a mother's creeping caution, and accept a life of come-what-may for Chloe.

Never would Sasha become the contemptible hypocrite she had seen so many others of her circle become:

Men and women, who had themselves been so greedy for the gamy tastes of wild freedoms, now as parents become tyrannical bureaucrats, handing out charts and outlines that rigidly plotted the lives they would have from their children.

How was it that a parent could forget what it was to be young, that a mother didn't merge herself with the daughter she once had been?

Sasha could feel it still: the rush that had been sent up the long stem of her body: this can be mine!

Maurice had managed to break all the old rules in practice, and yet to continue to regard them with an intellectual seriousness. How he had managed to do this Sasha had never been able to figure. He, too, had come from a pious family in Poland, like Sasha's own. Only Sasha had grown up in the Galician backwater, in a shtetl called Borshtchev—"where people had the good fortune to live to a very old age, because even the Angel of Death would get lost trying to find Borshtchev!"—whereas Maurice's family was from Warsaw.

Maurice's father had been the cantor of the Great Synagogue, on Tlomacka Street. When Maurice, in his early twenties, had become "enlightened," his father had refused to have anything more to do with him, just as it had been, years before, with Maurice's elder brother, Joseph, a gifted composer. Maurice's mother and his sister, Henya, used to have to come in secret to visit him and his brother.

And yet, in spite of this, Maurice had retained, through the years, a respect and a fondness for the old ways, which Sasha had abandoned with no nostalgia whatsoever. For Maurice, the beliefs of the pious had remained as part of his frame of reference, in a way that Sasha could never fathom, and whenever he met anyone who had a good Judaic background he would try, with no detectable cynicism, to engage him in a Talmudic discussion.

For her part, Sasha had always delighted in outraging those who were easily outraged, and her spirit of rebellion hadn't weakened with the years. When she was a young girl her "liberation" had taken the form of her involvement in the avant-garde expressionist Yiddish theater, a daring experiment which had devoted itself to creating a high art form out of the language and culture of the Eastern European Jews. On the one side there had been the religious fanatics, who forbade all theater; and on the other were the assimilationists, who didn't believe there was anything worth preserving in the heritage. And in between, there had struggled, for a few brief years, an unbelievably innovative theater, from which Diaghilev had lifted many of his ideas, and for which the likes of Marc Chagall had painted the scenery and done the actors' makeup.

But when Sasha had at last made her way to safety in New York (*itself* a story), she found the commercial Yiddish theater of Second Avenue of no interest to her: *shund,* trash. Only a few amateur groups were doing anything at all interesting.

Over the years Sasha's interests had widened, and before you knew it, she was subscribing to *The New Yorker* and *The New York Review of Books,* and was canvassing for the more left-wing candidates on the Upper West Side. Her old circle of Yiddishists sadly shook their heads and said that Sasha was no longer one of them.

Sasha had been prepared to see Chloe grab for all the experience that Sasha demanded for herself, in her own time, which, incidentally, it still happens to be.

But Sasha's stance of radical acceptance was frustrated by the chastely studious life Chloe would lead. Even in her adolescence she had never seemed to think about cutting loose and going a little bit crazy—when there stood Sasha, ready to tolerate, to aid and abet, all degrees of craziness.

Sasha could remember it on her tongue still: the first sensations of freedom, piercingly sweet, painfully snatched from between the cruel thorns of the old taboos.

Passion's venom? Where? She had never tasted venom!

Was Chloe fearful? Was Chloe, God forbid, *insensible*?

During Chloe's early womanhood, Sasha had felt herself baffled, slightly cheated even.

Finally, Sasha had come to the conclusion that her bewilderment was a want in her own imagination. Memory's definitely not enough. Imagination's very much called for.

Phoebe's father was a visiting European classicist. Chloe didn't love him. (Chloe had loved only once—and *he* had been insensible.)

Sasha, one of whose great themes in life is the love of man and woman, has no idea till this day that Chloe had made Phoebe's father promise to disappear from their lives.

Chloe had gotten from Phoebe's father exactly what she'd wanted: Phoebe. If there was one thing she had learned from her mother's life it was that men come and go, but a child is for keeps.

It was odd how few questions Phoebe had ever asked about her own father. Once, long ago, she had asked whether he had liked chess, too, and Chloe hadn't been able to answer. Chloe worries, even now, that Phoebe will suddenly ask her some question about this man that Chloe won't be able to answer.

Sometimes something Phoebe will say, or the way that she'll say it, will suddenly make Chloe see the child's face superimposed over the woman's. She loves this superposition of time-separated Phoebes beyond description in any dead language.

Chloe knows it's stupid, but there it is: in her dreams for Phoebe she reverts to Sasha's great theme. She's gotten safely beyond it in living her own life, but somehow not in dreaming her daughter's. And so, in such moments as these, there's also merged the wish that some day someone else—a man— will see Phoebe as Chloe does, cherishing every quirky little gesture.

"Oh, Mom! Really!"

Phoebe is trying to explain to Chloe a new type of mathematical surface she's been playing around with, two mathematical steps away, she says, from common experience.

They're sitting high over Columbia University, in Butler Terrace, having treated themselves to a luxuriously long lunch, with one glass each of Chardonnay, with which they offer a solemn toast to Hermes, god of travelers. Phoebe is leaving in two days for France, to spend a week at the Institut des Hautes Etudes Scientifiques in Bures-sur-Yvette, about thirty kilometers outside of Paris.

Phoebe, who's usually nonnegotiably negative on the subject of travel, is in a glow of eager anticipation. Her huge brown eyes, always beautiful, are luminous with hidden lights, and there's some elusive shimmery quality splashed about her, so that Chloe can only wonder.

For a mother and a daughter, sealed together and yet separate, questions are a delicate business, and Chloe is always wary of wielding any that come with a point.

Phoebe simply says that the mathematicians in Bures are gods.

"And the ones at Princeton are mere mortals?"

"Oh, Mom! Really!"

Phoebe, a little tipsy on her one glass of Chardonnay, has been wildly drawing her mathematics for Chloe on her pad of lined yellow paper.

"Go slower, Phoebe. This isn't Greek to me."

Chloe and Phoebe don't speak Yiddish, Sasha and Phoebe don't speak ancient Greek, and Sasha and Chloe don't speak mathematics.

For a moment Phoebe's mind slips back onto the man she loves—hopelessly, hopelessly. But there is Chloe, sitting across the table from her, her eyes bright with interest in anything Phoebe has to tell her.

RABBINICAL EYES

We moved around a lot when I was a kid. My father was a very unsuccessful rabbi. His contracts were never for more than three years, and, even though the positions were in cities considered very undesirable—way out in the hinterland, far from any large Jewish community—the congregations rarely renewed him.

My father had a very heavy European accent, which, together with the remote air of a scholar, made him a ludicrously unsuitable candidate for the American pulpit. The main point of an American rabbi is the Saturday-morning sermon, ideally delivered in that oily style congregations require from their clergy, lubricating the hard little pellet of religion so that it slides in with minimum pain. Learned though my father was—and he is of the high scholarly caliber that is called in his culture a *talmid chachem,* literally a "disciple of the wise"—you couldn't understand a word he said. Or so I learned—very early and very, very bitterly—from overhearing the sneers and stifled groans of his congregants.

I was around six years old when I came upon a group of men, a group my father referred to, with a resigned shrug, as the kibitzers, huddled together, out in the hallway during one of my father's sermons. Every community in which we lived—this one happened to be in Omaha, Nebraska—had its kibitzers, men who came to the synagogue strictly for purposes of socializing. When the socializers were women, they were called, with neither more nor less contempt, yentas.

The Nebraska version of kibitzers were going around the

circle, taking turns imitating my father's accent. It was my primal scene of devastation.

One of the sports spotted me and signaled the others, who immediately all fell into an embarrassed hush, having the decency to look terribly shame-faced before the rabbi's little daughter.

I count that moment as among the three or four most painful in my life. Its memory burned in me, night after sleepless night, for a very long time. Within the family my father was such a figure of honor, a *talmid chachem*, whose every request and requirement was treated with reverent respect. The discovery that outside the family he was only a little man with a comical accent was a contradiction I spent my early life trying to resolve.

The amazing thing is that to me it had always seemed that my father had no accent at all.

The various communities we lived in were always very sorry to see the *rebbetsin*, my mother, leave. My mother, who is American-born, is also very learned. She used to study Talmud as a girl every Shabbes afternoon with her rabbinical father, just as I did. Sometimes she and my father still learn a page together.

Legend says that when a pious woman dies and goes to heaven she will get to be the footstool of her husband, as he sits in Torah study. My mother is almost a good foot taller than my father. My mother is also beautiful, with features that can accurately be described as chiseled. And whenever my father looks up at my mother, it's as if he's watching her emerging from the sea, standing poised on a cushion of foam.

My mother always taught in the Sunday schools of the synagogues that employed my father, and she was a rare teacher, managing to get the kids, who were of course seething with resentment at having to go to school on Sundays, almost to like being there. She taught them something, too, trying most of all to infuse them with a sense of their history.

She's a very charming person, so interested in everyone's story, always managing to make good friends wherever we went.

My mother was my father's greatest asset, everyone said so, though not even she could overcome the effect of the accent that sounded like a comedian's bad joke, and of my father's impenetrably standoffish manner. Maybe if he were a taller man, or spoke a beautiful English, he could have carried off what appeared like such misplaced arrogance, a refugee's ridiculous insistence on the dignity and honor of his position, as if he were one of God's chosen ones.

I knew that what must have seemed to his congregants to be intransigence and arrogance wasn't at all personal. My father is personally a very modest and reasonable man. But he was the rabbi—the Rabbi! He was the sole representative of Torah learning among these tragically ignorant Jews. He wasn't arrogant for himself, but for what he carried with him, the learning and the history, out into those hinterlands.

I know that my mother, and I think this is also true of my brother, Gideon, never got a glimpse of how my father looked to those outside the family, what a caricature he cut out there. But I could never get away from the terrible double-vision of my father. And, because I loved him more than anyone in the world, the double-vision of him was very troubling.

My father had been a student at the famous Telz Yeshiva in Telsiai, Lithuania. Telz Yeshiva had accepted my father into the highest class—the top *shaiur*—at the unusually young age of fifteen. He was learning there with men who were twice his age. He was giving his own *shaiurim* to men who already had children of their own.

I learned this from my mother, who, if she learned it from my father, must have learned it very indirectly.

Lithuania was the country most renowned by European Jewry for the quality of its scholarship, and Telz was renowned throughout Lithuania. The "way of Telz" placed great emphasis on rationality, on the logical analysis of the text of Talmud. Lithuania was the center of the *mitnag-gedim*—literally "those who are against," in this case against the mystical, arational approach to Judaism, known as Hasidism. Hasidism had been a grass-roots movement, growing up among the Polish uneducated, in part a rebellion against the rabbinical scholarly elite, who equated spirituality with Talmudic learning. Hasidim don't study their way closer to God, but, rather, sing and dance their way to Him. The scholars of Lithuania responded to Hasidism with little patience, following the implacable position taken by the great Rabbi Elijah Zalman, "the Vilna Gaon," the legendary Talmudic genius of the eighteenth century, whose influence was felt in the yeshivas of Lithuania even into my father's day.

My father's first name is Zalman, and somehow I thought, probably from wishful thinking, through much of my childhood, that the Vilna Gaon had been one of our Lithuanian relatives.

At Telz they didn't train you to be a pulpit rabbi. I doubt that the concept even existed over there. My father was trained to give *shaiurim,* not sermons. He was trained in the *pilpul*—the argumentation—of the Talmud, not the politics of the temple. He had ended up in America, on one pulpit after another, because of Hitler and all the rest of it.

He was the only survivor of his family, which had all been living in some Lithuanian town whose name I don't know, but where my grandfather was the rabbi and my uncles—my father was the youngest of seven sons, born to a second wife and ten years younger than the next eldest—were in various positions of authority and honor. The Sonauers had been the leading family in the Jewish life of this town for generations. I don't know terribly much about it, but I do know that my father was at Telz when the Nazis marched into his town, and that all his family were herded together and locked in the synagogue, which was then torched.

Telsiai was never occupied by the Nazis but, rather, was taken over by the Russians during the war. They confiscated the yeshiva building, and the students were scattered to various Lithuanian towns. A few teachers and students managed to reach the United States, among them, of course, my father.

My father and I look alike to an extraordinary degree, because we both have the same eyes, and these eyes of ours completely dominate our face. These eyes are huge. They make every expression that crosses our face a sad one. They are deep-socketed, heavy-lidded, and very darkly shadowed, the area around them looking almost bruised. Their color is brown.

On the wall above the sideboard in the dining room of whatever house we were occupying, there was always hung an old silver-framed photograph, maybe six by eight, of my father's family, taken outside in a garden on a summer's day. My father had had this picture with him at Telz. There are forty-two Sonauers indistinctly captured in the photograph, counting the children sitting cross-legged in front. My father's six brothers stand in the back, their bewigged wives arranged in front of them. One of my uncles was already a grandfather at the time the picture was taken. His daughter stands near his wife, with the baby in her arms. And in the center sit my grandmother and grandfather, the matriarch and patriarch, she with a rather elaborately coiled wig, he with a raised black skullcap and a long white beard. Nobody, not even the littlest child, smiles. Everyone looks at the camera with an air of studied seriousness.

Whatever gene it is that carries the trait for my father's and my eyes must be a dominant one. For there they were, in the picture of that old family gathering in Lithuania: pairs and pairs and pairs of them. Almost all of those people who were burned in the synagogue looked exactly like me.

My mother had a word for these eyes. Rabbinical eyes, she called them. And it was as much for these rabbinical eyes as for his reputation as a *talmid chachem* that my mother, who was American-born and learned, tall and beautiful, immediately agreed when the young rabbi from Lithuania was suggested to her. She always told me this story when I came complaining to her about how ugly I was, how pathetically puny and sickly-looking and different-looking from any child I had ever seen—outside the silver-framed photograph.

"Ugly?" She'd smile at me. "How can you say that, Rachele? With such beautiful eyes. You have the rabbinical eyes of all your sainted ancestors of blessed memory."

I think my mother really thought that her words would make me love my eyes, love my haunted little face in the way that she did, for all the ghosts that lay behind it. But it doesn't take a doctorate in childhood psychology to understand why it was that my mother's words didn't help me much; that I walked away from them feeling not only an ugly child but a very bad one as well.

My brother, Gideon, by the way, did not inherit the rabbinical eyes. Gideon was lucky enough to be a child who looked like a child, healthy and American-born.

Of course, I have to admit now—I didn't realize it back then—that as a consequence of the pathos that people read into my face I tended to get away with a lot more than I otherwise would. I grew up in the fifties, in the shadow of the Holocaust. I was usually the only Jewish kid in my class—and with *such* a face I stirred up thoughts and feelings that allowed people to put up with a high degree of aggressive behavior on my part, what the professionals nowadays would call "acting out."

My mother's family was also connected with Telz Yeshiva, only the American branch, which is located in Cleveland, Ohio, to which my father eventually made his way. My mother's father was one of the teachers there, her mother one of the leading forces behind the creation of the girls' secondary school. It was a family that very much believed in educating its daughters.

I was born in Cleveland, Ohio, but we moved to Charleston, West Virginia, my father's first pulpit position, when I was a few months old. From there we went to Treesport, Louisiana, where we stayed until I was three and a half, and where Gideon was born. The next place was Savannah, Georgia, which is where my memories start to get distinct, and which we left when I turned six. I started first grade in Omaha, Nebraska, and second grade in Port Jervis, New York. When I was in the fourth grade we moved to Trenton, New Jersey, and we managed to hang on there until I graduated from elementary school.

I remember the anxiety of those first days in new schools, trying to pick out the competition for "smartest kid in the class." It wasn't hard. By the time that I left to go home for lunch—I think in all those places you got to go home for lunch—I knew whom I'd have to do better than.

In Savannah it was a little girl called Cindy Wallquist, who was the only other kid who started kindergarten knowing how to read. But Cindy was just a minor event, since kindergarten was almost all fun and games. And anyway it was clear that Cindy was mostly just creatively guessing.

Omaha is where it started getting serious, or would have had the competition been any tougher than little Daisy Dover, who happened to be a minister's daughter, and the next-smartest kid, after the rabbi's daughter. In math there was just no contest at all.

I can't even remember who it was in Port Jervis. There was a chunky kid called Ira Fistover, who was reasonably smart.

Trenton is where it began to get a little interesting. Trenton was where Frederick Freudenstein—known, predictably enough, as Freddy Frankenstein—had been reigning unchallenged, not just as class genius, but as school genius.

He was a marvel, to look at him, Freddy was. I couldn't believe it when I saw him: just the classic picture of the egghead, straight out of a comic book, with his thick glasses, domed forehead, and affectless monotone. When I first met him I figured his reputation might be based on nothing more substantial than his resemblance to the Professor Peabody character from the Bullwinkle cartoon show. But it wasn't. I think I had pretty much established that by lunchtime of that first day. Freddy Frankenstein worked away at his own sixth-grade math book while the rest of us were given review work from the third grade.

Tears of rage blurred the long columns of tedious addition printed out on the page, that first morning in Trenton. I was completely humiliated to be grouped with the indistinguishable others. There was no way I was going to allow Freddy Frankenstein the uniqueness of his intellectual supremacy.

Freddy made the fourth, fifth, and sixth grades really interesting for me, and we two made it interesting for everyone else. Even the kids in the upper grades learned of our fierce competition. The teachers made special reading and math groups for us, gave us all sorts of special assignments. We were excused all through fifth and sixth grades from attending science class, and instead embarked on a series of unsupervised experiments in a makeshift laboratory at the back of the room.

Kids envied us. Kids actually admired us for being smart. Perhaps it had to do with the way the teachers reacted to us. They were pretty clever, the way they used Freddy and me.

I liked Freddy, and he liked me. My father called Freddy my *chavrusa,* my study partner, and told me that a good *chavrusa* is a gift from God. Freddy once told me that it had been sort of tough for him before I came. Freddy Frankenstein had been a freak before I came. My arrival changed it all around, he said, turned him into a player in what became a school-wide game.

Of course, I could have told him much the same. I really couldn't believe that this was happening to me, that I was having so much fun, that everybody knew my name, said "hi" to me when I passed. I remember wanting to say something like that to Freddy, to let him know that he had made a big difference to me also. Maybe I could do it with a pun on goon and *gaon*.

But even this smelled too much of sentiment. Words of sentiment always end up sticking in my throat. Anyway, he wouldn't have known what a *gaon* was.

Freddy and I competed like crazy, especially in that math group. In the sixth grade the teacher simply gave us a tenth-grade geometry book, and told us to go it alone. We did, Freddy and I, each of us intent on getting the answer before the other.

Trenton was the first and only place I was sorry to leave. Being the smartest kid in the class was never the same again.

My brother, Gideon, two and a half years younger than me, developed his own way of coping with all the moves my family made. Gideon had this incredible knack for making friends. It was a kind of genius in him that left me baffled. I always had to wait for him after school, when he'd finally emerge from the building, always in the center of a group of kids. He was very athletic, which certainly helped. And he had my mother's good looks, too. But it was more than that, though what it was I never could figure out. I just couldn't see how people hooked in so quickly, so automatically, to the fact that Gideon was genuinely lovable. Even the very first day at each new school I'd see him coming out in the center of an easy, laughing group of brand-new best friends.

My brother was smart, good in school, but nothing like me, which left me free to adore him, just like the rest of the world.

I say "my father," "my mother," "my brother." I wonder if they ever say "my daughter," if Gideon ever says "my sister." I was disowned by them all two years ago, when I married Luke, who is a Gentile. My father, my mother, and my brother sat *shiva* for me, as if I were dead.

The funny thing is that, looking back, I think that I probably fell in love with Luke because he reminded me, in some convoluted way, of my father. I had never fallen in love before, hadn't even come close.

I was at Harvard Law School when I met Luke. I was taking a special enrichment seminar they were offering to first-year law students, on legal writing. It was an innovation at the law school, allowing a student some practical training. We were working on drafting contracts for opposing parties with conflicting interests. Basically the point of the exercise was to write a contract that completely protected your own interests, while leaving you as free as possible to demolish the other guy's.

Never since the days of Freddy Frankenstein had my talents in the classroom been quite so applauded as in that seminar on legal writing. My contracts, so deviously subtle, became legends. Everybody asked to read them, to study them, including this guy, Luke McClean—Clean Luke, of course, who looked to me like the very picture of a minister's son.

Clean Luke was having a lot of trouble getting the hang of writing a good contract, and kept asking to study mine. Just to be polite, I asked to read one of his. I was as lost in wonder, reading Luke's contract, as he had been in reading mine.

The thought occurred to me that here was a guy who didn't have a clue how to protect his own interests while shafting someone else's. I doubt that this alone made me fall in love with him, but it's hard for me to say. I was in love with Luke a long time before I knew I was in love with Luke.

Clean Luke was older than the rest of us brash young things at Harvard Law School. (I was the brashest, and the youngest, only twenty.) Unlike the rest of us, so flush on success, he was at Harvard having already tasted of failure. Law was going to be his second career. His first had been as an assistant professor of philosophy at the University of Nebraska. He hadn't gotten tenure.

I had majored in philosophy as an undergraduate at Harvard, but always with the intention of going to law school. The training in analytic reasoning is a good preparation for the law. Just about everybody in my philosophy classes was there with the same idea.

But Luke told me he had been really serious about philosophy. He was an ethicist. He had written a book on how to derive "ought" from "is."

Good God, I thought, a philosopher at law school. An ethicist at Harvard—God help him.

I remembered a stupid joke about the Yiddish word *farblondjet,* which means "lost." The definition of *farblondjet,* went the dumb joke, is a kosher butcher in North Dakota. (Not even my family had ever lived in North Dakota.) Well, now I had a new definition: an ethicist at Harvard Law School.

Luke had taken his denial of tenure very hard, and had tried to hang on in philosophy, taking a series of terminal positions before finally giving up and applying to law school.

"Hey," I said, holding in my hand his latest try at a tough contract, as he told me how he had come to be sitting here, in this seminar on legal writing, for which he showed so little aptitude. "Don't talk of Harvard as if it's total defeat. Harvard's not so bad as compensation. You'd be surprised how many people are really quite pleased to get into here."

"Well, I got in," said Luke lugubriously. "But I don't know if I'm going to make it through here. I have serious doubts that I was meant to be a lawyer."

Boy, so did I. In fact, when I first read one of his contracts I thought that the guy must be stupid. He isn't. Luke is one of the smartest people I know, in his own special way. It's just that his own special way doesn't include any of the strains of intelligence that are likely to show up in the courses you take in law school. He's a slow, ponderous, deep thinker, who questions the meaning of everything. He really *is*—God help him—a philosopher. He's also a creature of unusually generous impulses, which also didn't help him in law school.

"Well, think of it this way. If you had gotten tenure, you'd still be in Nebraska."

"That's exactly where I want to be. I like Nebraska. Hell, I grew up in Omaha."

"You did? Say, you wouldn't happen to know a girl named Daisy Dover, would you? A minister's daughter?"

I was fishing, trying out my hunch that Clean Luke was a minister's son.

"No." He had smiled back at me. "Can't say that I do. We McCleans aren't really a churchgoing clan."

Oh well, so much for my hunches. I'm a creature of analytic reasoning, not intuition.

"So who's this Daisy Dover?"

"Oh, just a little girl I went to the first grade with. I went to the first grade in Omaha."

"You did?" Damn but he looked like a minister's son when he grinned like that. Somewhere down that fallen-away line of McCleans I'd bet you anything there'd once been a clergyman. "First grade, huh? What about the second grade?"

"Second grade was in Port Jervis, New York. Kindergarten, in case you're getting ready to ask, was in Savannah, Georgia."

"Army brat?" he had asked me, trying out a hunch of his own that was so off-base it made me laugh out loud. I had to stifle my laughter quickly, as I realized our professor had entered and was staring at the seminar with that slightly injured look with which he always began. Professor Flew might also have been, for all I knew, a man whose arrogance wasn't of the personal variety, but merely a matter of the dignity and honor of his position. But toy with that arrogance, in any way, and Professor Flew could turn decidedly nasty.

"Rabbinical brat," I quickly whispered back to Luke.

He looked baffled for a few seconds. Then he whispered, "Your father's a rabbi?"

I nodded.

"That's really interesting. You've got to tell me all about it."

I wondered a bit through the seminar as to why I had to tell him all about it. What was so goddamned interesting to Clean Luke of the nonchurchgoing McCleans about my father's being a rabbi?

We went for coffee after class, and I discovered that Luke was a Jew-freak. A Semitophile, a term I had to coin, since there obviously hadn't been a very large demand for such a concept.

Luke's Semitophilism at first made me bristle with hostility. It seemed to me something very near to its virulent opposite. Any fixation on Jews puts me on edge.

I argued with him over coffee that there was just nothing very interesting about Jews. The most interesting thing about Jews was everyone's totally groundless belief that there was something interesting about Jews.

"I hate to disappoint you, but there's really no basis to the mystique. If I were you, I'd just stop thinking all about it."

"You've got to be kidding," he had argued with me at first. "You're going to tell me that there's nothing interesting about a group that constitutes maybe one-third of one percent of the world's population and has garnered maybe about a sixth of the total Nobel prizes in science and literature?"

Oh, yuck. How I hated this stuff. Who goes around tabulating the percentage of Jewish Nobel laureates, anyway?

"Hey, Luke, I don't trust your 'maybe' statistics. Or, better, I don't trust the inference you seem to be making from them.

Have you ever studied probability theory? There are some results there that can seem pretty amazing. Did you know that the probability of any two people having the same birthday in a group of twenty-three is as high as a half? You might think there was something mystical and miraculous going on if you kept discovering two people with the same birthdays —that is, unless you understood the mathematics."

I was trying to end this thing as gracefully as I knew how.

"So you really think there's nothing different about the Jews? I would think it would make you proud. It would me."

"Oh, you think so, do you?" My tone took a turn for the worse. "Where exactly is this famous difference supposed to be lodged? In our Jewish genes? Our Jewish blood? In my opinion, your admiration is a very close cousin to a view widely popularized by a certain housepainter from Austria."

Luke had blushed beet-red at this, looking more than ever like a minister's son. He sort of tilted back in his chair, as if he were being blown backward by the blast of my insult.

I looked at his scarlet face and immediately repented.

"Boy," he said, a little shakily. "I just hope I never come up against you in a courtroom. You really are going to make a hell of a prosecuting attorney."

"Look, I'm sorry. I shouldn't have said that. It was unfounded and unforgivable. It's just that it's . . . well, it's a touchy subject for me."

"I sort of caught on to that," he had said, smiling.

What a nice guy! What a genuinely nice guy. Anyone else would have popped me one after an all-out attack like that. I was getting a little old for acting out. What was I trying to do, prove my thesis that the Jew-lover is easily transmuted into the Jew-hater, by making Clean Luke hate my guts?

"Listen, Luke, I'm really *really* sorry. . . ."

"It's okay. I promise not to admire your heritage anymore. Do I have your permission to admire your legal brilliance?"

"Yeah, sure, go right ahead. No objection raised here to having my brilliance appreciated."

"I bet there's not. And, listen, is it okay with you if I go on loving Isaac Bashevis Singer? You're not going to accuse me of being a neo-Nazi for that, are you?"

It was okay. I deserved that. I'd just take it sweetly, lying down.

"I'm sure it's just fine for you to like Isaac Bashevis Singer. I'm sure your reasons for doing so are of the purest."

"You like him, too, right?"

This guy had a way of setting up assumptions it was a rare pleasure for me to knock down.

"No, I'm not really one for fiction."

"Oh." He seemed disappointed. Just set them up again, sweetie pie, and let me have a go.

"But I have read a few of his stories. I can't say that they grabbed me."

"Really?"

"They're awfully bizarre."

"Really? To you?"

"Yeah. In fact, I'd say, especially to me. See, I told you, we're not just some mystically bonded tribe dispersed throughout the nations of the world. We're not the same metaphysical idea being thought in the mind of the same Jewish God. We find each other strange, too. Singer's world is unintelligible to me. All that supernatural stuff, the spooks and goblins . . ."

"Dybbuks," Luke had corrected me.

"Well, I hate to disappoint you again, but where I come from there aren't any dybbuks, and there aren't any dopes who believe in them either. My family, which happens to be Orthodox, is as far from believing in dybbuks as in Santa Claus. My family's faith is a matter of logic."

He smiled, maybe as if I were a student in his philosophy

class. I suddenly remembered he had been a professor. But I had never been much awed by my professors.

"Is faith ever a matter of logic?" he asked, just *like* a philosophy professor. "If it's all a matter of logic, where's the room for faith?"

I shrugged my shoulders. How could I begin to explain to this guy, who was obviously very taken by the picturesque backwardness of those quaint Jews of Poland, about the way of Telz?

"I think we have a different interpretation of the word 'faith,' " I told him, in such a way as effectively to terminate, or so I hoped, our theological chitchat.

It didn't. Luke pressed on.

"That's really interesting to me, what you say. The contrast between your Judaism and Singer's. You have to explain all this to me."

Again, I wondered exactly why I had to explain all this to him. But I simply satisfied myself by putting forth a disclaimer, to the effect that it wasn't *my* Judaism at all; that I had pretty much left all that behind me.

"Oh?" Again Luke seemed disappointed. For a nonchurch-going McClean he sure wanted his Jews to be true to *their* faith, an observation I would normally have shared with him; but I was still holding my tongue, in the meek posture of penance.

"I saw Singer once in person," Luke went on. "Right after he got the Nobel Prize. He gave a reading in Omaha."

"Lucky Omaha," I muttered.

"Yes, lucky Omaha, though I register your sarcasm, and think it very little becomes you."

He said this in a way that made me remember again that he had been a professor when I was in junior high. I tended to forget this, because in our present context, by which I mean Harvard Law School, I was his natural superior.

"It was a great experience. Singer was brilliantly funny

when it came to answering questions. I remember his saying something like that Yiddish, which logically should be dead, is the perfect language for the Jewish experience, which has always reveled in illogic. Sorry, that's what the man said. And his accent was so wonderful, so perfect for the story. It was 'Gimpel the Fool,' do you know it?"

"I certainly don't *know* it. Maybe I read it."

"I'm going to tell you, though you don't deserve it, something amazing that happened when Singer came to Omaha. I was very good friends with a girl there whose parents are pretty prominent in Jewish affairs, though they aren't at all what *you'd* call religious."

How the hell did this guy know what *I'd* call religious?

"They were just very charitable, charitable people. Aristocrats, in the noblest sense of the term. Anyway, they were the ones who picked Singer up from the airport, Malise's father did, and then Singer came to their home for a short time before going on to his reading."

"Yes?" I, still penitent, encouraged him in the pause.

"Now, Malise's mother, Sandra, is one of the most dynamic, vibrant people I know. She's chairperson of this organization, fund-raiser for that one. Just an absolutely irresistible go-getter. In fact, I happened to meet Malise through her mother, when I was doing some work for the United Jewish Appeal."

United Jewish Appeal? Man, was this guy *farblondjet*.

"But Sandra happened to have spent the first three years of her life, if you can believe this, in a closet somewhere in Poland, being hidden from the Nazis. Can you imagine it? She was a little girl who spent the first years of her life in darkness, in silence. And out of that crazy-making beginning, all that vitality and brilliance.

"She didn't learn to talk until the war was over. Maybe that's why she has absolutely no memory at all of the years she spent in the closet.

"Well, when Singer walked into their house, he just looked at Sandra—she's very attractive, a beautiful redhead—and said, 'You were in the war.'

"Of course, she was astounded. She has no memory of the war at all. And she asked him how he knew.

" 'I see it in your eyes,' he said. 'I see the war in your eyes.' "

And Luke McClean—and his beloved Jewish Nobel laureate, Isaac Bashevis Singer—had made me start to cry.

Luke dropped out of law school after that first disastrous year—I have to say, with my encouragement—and he went on to his third career. He became an elementary-school teacher, and he's managed to hang on to that one. In fact, he's a fantastic sixth-grade teacher, here in New York City, in what they call the inner-city schools, where they sure as hell can use fantastic teachers.

I don't know how long Luke will be able to keep at it. He puts everything into it, he's totally involved with those kids, and the burnout rate is known to be high. I'm pretty certain that there'll be, somewhere down the line, a fourth career. But right now, Luke's a teacher, heart and soul.

I, of course, kept on at Harvard Law School, made *Law Review,* and got a job with a prestigious firm on Wall Street with one of those legendary starting salaries, the kind that law-school students tenderly whisper in their sleep. However, I only stayed there long enough to pay off the debts from law school, which had been my plan all along.

I hated it there on Wall Street. I hated the kind of law I had to do there. Terminally boring stuff. I hated that Wasp firm, which had done the little Jewish girl with the enormous brains such a great favor in hiring her. Of course, my name now is McClean. I took Luke's name, because my own family had disowned me. I made a point, though, during the interviews at Wasp firms, of mentioning that my father was a rabbi, so that they'd know what they were getting, if they chose to take it. Wasp firms. Jewish firms. Where else but in the law can one get away with such crap?

Okay, so now I'm a McClean.

Working there on Wall Street, I was like the patriarch Jacob, putting in his time for Leah so that he could eventually marry Rachel. I was putting in my time on Wall Street so that I could eventually make the very uncool, very un-Harvard move of becoming a public defender. My version of marrying Rachel is the job I have now, as an appellate attorney for small-time drug dealers and other assorted disenfranchised types.

So Luke's in the inner-city schools, battling away to try to keep his students from ever ending up in my office, which is down near the Courthouse, and where, by the way, the burn-out rate is also rumored to be somewhat high. And I can understand that, even though I'm in no immediate danger myself. But I've been here for almost two years, and I can see how the cases begin to get repetitive, and how after a while you get to not believe any of your clients, for the simple reason that they tend to be liars. Really stupid liars, committing contradictions that they don't even see as contradictions. Then there's the other type of criminal, who's very honest about what he's done, because if he did it, it's got to be okay.

Partly what still keeps me fired up is my belief in the right of appeal. There's also the occasionally interesting case where the previous judge really did slip up, often in a way so subtle it's a challenge to present it.

Recently I had a case where the criminal himself was an interesting type. He happened to have been a Hasid, convicted for credit-card fraud. We're still not exactly sure how he and his pals worked it. Guy 1 legitimately had a bunch of credit cards. Guy 2 asks Guy 1 if he'll help him out with his debts, give him the credit cards for about two weeks, and then report that they've been stolen, making up some reason why he hadn't noticed the theft up until now. It happens that my Hasid was Guy 3, who was the one who actually used the credit cards. I won't go into the whole story of how he was caught, which is a pretty amusing one, involving as it does a hooker in Reno whose services the Hasid disastrously charged. Guy 2 was never caught.

The charge against my client was unauthorized use of credit cards. My cute little angle in the case was to claim that, since Guy 1 knew that this was a case of fraud, he *had* authorized their use.

The case I was trying to build got even trickier, since there's legislative history that actually applies to this little gap through which I was trying to slip my crook. A Senate report had addressed this gap, but a House report had left it unmentioned, which absence, I had argued, showed that the House wanted the gap left *in situ*.

In short, what I was building was a nifty little house of cards.

This Hasid was very different from my other clients. Well, obviously he was. But what I mean is that he was really quite clever, almost subtle, in a twisted kind of way. He had a lot of things to say about his own defense, which, of course, made my job that much harder, but still made it all that much more interesting, too.

Whenever the Hasid mentioned anything about Judaism I played completely dumb. Just showed him my blank face. But my particular face can't be made quite blank enough.

"You married a *goy*, didn't you, Rachel McClean?"

I stared at him, startled by the question, even more by the contempt with which he spoke it.

"What was your name before?" he persisted.

"Do you want to tell me what this has to do with your defense?" I finally snapped back at him. I hate it when I feel that hostile towards a client.

Since he's a Hasid, his *rebbe* got into the act, as well. I had
to speak to this *rebbe* a couple of times on the phone. I did
a good job with him, too. My client had told him I was Jewish,
but they obviously figured I was just one of the tragically
ignorant. When the *rebbe* mentioned Purim to me, he felt he
had to add the clause "That's the Jewish Halloween."

"Is it?" I answered.

By the way, my angle in the case, cute as it was, didn't
save the Hasid. Some judges I know might even have gone
for it. But one of the judges we got (in a federal appeals case,
one gets three) is a champion bridge player and one of the
sharpest analytic minds I've ever encountered on the bench.
He gave my nifty little house of cards a very brief appreciative
smile, then knocked the whole thing over.

My boss thinks this judge, who barely ever betrays anything remotely like a smile, maybe likes me. Last week, when
I appeared before him again, he gave me another tiny smile,
and said, "Oh, it's you again."

I lost that appeal, too.

I win maybe 2 percent of my cases, which isn't too bad,
considering that all my clients are probably guilty as hell.

Ah, creeping cynicism. The harbinger of burnout. But I
can't really afford to burn out at this particular stage of the
game.

People had told me, when I was pregnant, that I was going
to feel so conflicted about immediately going back to work,
that every woman, no matter how ambitious about her career,
goes all mellow right after she's had a baby. A simple matter
of hormones, of that almost mystical mother-baby bonding.

There must have been something wrong with my bonding.
My bonding must have sealed not quite right. It all dissolved
as soon as I suspected that there was something wrong with
the baby.

There is something wrong with the baby, and we don't

know what it is. She's twelve months old and she doesn't sit up yet. She doesn't make eye contact. Her eyes are empty.

We've had her in for test after test, ever since she was seven months old, and we began to think there might be something wrong. Up until then we simply thought she was an unusually good baby. So quiet and unfussy. Just the sort of baby two working parents need.

I hadn't had amniocentesis, since I was only twenty-seven. But, anyway, it's nothing to do with genes. One doctor suggested that she be tested for Tay-Sachs syndrome. Stupid, automatic response on his part, since Tay-Sachs is recessive. But it seems that the baby looks like the classic picture of this syndrome, just that sort of vacant lethargy.

But they don't know what's wrong with her, and they don't know what she'll be like, how dysfunctional she'll end up being. Right now they're only saying that she's seriously developmentally delayed, a diagnosis that simply summarizes the problem.

I had taken it for granted that the child I carried would be, at the very least, smart. The smartest kid in the class, just like the mom. I already had devised my theories of education for it.

I remember walking home from one of the first of the visits I paid to one of the first of the doctors, and passing some of the ubiquitous homeless, with their terribly vacant eyes. They were the sort of losers, deadbeats, criminals whose appeals I end up writing.

There was one woman, slouched up against a building. She was horrible to look at, filthy, ageless. She could've been twenty, she could've been sixty. She was snarling out curses to some unseen antagonist.

I actually stopped dead on the sidewalk, the baby was sleeping in the carrier strapped to my chest, and I stared down at the heap of rags and misery, until it noticed and started shrieking out profanities at me.

That moment also has to be counted among the three or four worst in my life. It had just hit me, for the first time, that I was now connected to people of this sort in a new way, in a way I can't bear to be connected.

It's not in the genes. A perfectly wonderful child had been formed, of this I'm certain, and then something had happened. When? I keep wondering. During those terribly critical first eighteen weeks? A whiff of something toxic, some moments of oxygen deprivation? Or during the birth? When?

But something did happen, it's clear, though we don't yet know what, and maybe never will. And now my life is bound up with the kind of questions I can't bear to ask.

I hate this baby for that, although I'm too ashamed to tell anyone, by which I suppose I mean Luke, who loves the baby, in a painful, protective way.

A creature was formed, whom her father and I named Gabriella. A creature who will never do anything good, never contribute, never enlighten, never improve the world into which it was born. A creature who will only be a drone and a failure—a joyless obligation to others.

And because there is this Gabriella, because I have brought this Gabriella into the world, I am no longer in control of my life. Nothing before could ever overcome me. I could think my way clear of every obstacle. No matter how bad a case, if there was any angle at all, I'd come up with it.

The woman who takes care of the baby, Mrs. Foote, still insists that's she's just the best baby in the world. She constantly talks to her, jangles keys in an effort to stimulate her, insists on taking her out for the four hours of fresh air daily that Dr. Spock deems advisory. Mrs. Foote is a find, a marvel. I marvel over her all the time, how it is that she just refuses to give up on that baby. There's something so soothing about her persistence in the illusion of normalcy. She's balm for my nerves.

Mrs. Foote is, of all things, a Jehovah's Witness. Very

occasionally she'll slip into a proselytizing mode, start quoting from the Bible about the great things that are a-coming. But she doesn't press. Years of experience have taught her to judge when a person is likely to slam the door in her face. And I am, of course, just the kind of person to slam the door in a Witness's face.

Mrs. Foote has completely taken over for me, sees that I can't deal with the baby anymore, can't even hold it. She and Luke together manage without me.

She mothers me as well, likes "to do" for me, as she puts it.

I used to resent people's trying "to do" for me. There's no doubt about the fact that I tend to bring out the mother in people. It's a matter of my appearance. I still look about twelve years old, even when I dress up like a lawyer. I'm still puny. I've always been able to eat anything I want and stay skinny. At college my two roommates, who both had weight problems, would go nuts watching me methodically going through my KitKats and other assorted junk. Every night I'd sit down to my books and my junk food, and listen to my two roommates—who were always nibbling on things like carrots and celery stalks—groan about the unfairness of life.

I was a kid who didn't look like a kid, and now I'm a grown-up who doesn't look like a grown-up, so people have always being trying "to do" for me, one way or another.

And then there's the indelible pathos of my face, that reads like a subtext, as the French philosophers say, subverting all my overt aggressiveness.

The baby has my eyes. Her empty eyes are rabbinical eyes. Huge, heavy-lidded, bruised, and sad.

I remember Luke's leaning over me in the recovery room, as I came out of anesthesia. I had had a C-section, my frame too narrow for a natural birth. But the obstetrician insists that everything had gone normally.

"My darling girl," Luke was saying to me as I opened my eyes. "My darling girl," he kept repeating to me.

And then his voice went soft with wonder. "Do you know? Our daughter has the rabbinical eyes."

If only I knew what's wrong with it, what went wrong. I'd know what to expect. If she's bad enough, we can just put her in an institution, and then forget that she ever was.

I'd think it was the curse of my family that had somehow done it to us.

"May you, too, have a child that causes you such grief."

But my parents never said anything of the kind to me. They're not the type of people who would ever curse, not even a daughter they had disowned. And I'm not the type of person to believe in the efficacy of curses.

Those places out in the hinterland where we had lived when I was a kid never had a proper Hebrew day school, for Gideon and me. There were the synagogue Sunday schools, but these were completely inadequate for the purposes of my family. These were meant for the children of those tragically ignorant Jews.

So both my father and my mother taught the Jewish subjects to Gideon and me. There was no gender differentiation in what they taught us. My father studied Talmud with me just as hard and as long as with Gideon. I know that Orthodox Jews are rumored to be sexist. Hell, it's no rumor. One sage wrote that it was better for the sacred books to be burned before they were taught to Jewish daughters. And the Vilna Gaon warned, in a letter to his daughters, that women should stay away from the synagogue, since they're likely to engage there in nothing more uplifting than malicious gossip, which is a fairly serious sin in Judaism.

My family wasn't at all tainted by this kind of bigotry. My father's opinion of people in general tended not to be very high. He saw most forms of human activity as species of *bital z'man,* wastes of time. But I don't think he thought that there were more yentas than there were kibitzers, or that the yentas were, on the whole, of a more vicious or inferior variety than their brothers in *bital z'man.*

I've read some of the angry literature that's been put out recently by Jewish feminists. And truly there seems to be a lot there to be angry about. All I can say is that the kind of mindless dismissal of girls that seems to typify certain parts of the Orthodox Jewish world simply wasn't my experience at all. If anything, my father worked me a little harder than he did Gideon, because I had so much more *sitzfleisch,* staying power.

I was thrilled when he nodded his head at some line of reasoning I had produced. I heard him once tell my mother that I had a good Gemara head, the highest praise.

I loved studying alone with my father, getting all of his attention. My father would have made a brilliant lawyer. His Telz background made him so much more suited to the law than to the pulpit. While he was instructing me over a page of Talmud there was no room for the painful double-vision of him to enter.

I could get pretty intense when I learned with my father. I swayed back and forth, over the massive open volume, faster and faster.

Sometimes my father would suddenly pull away from the text, sit back in his chair, and turn to me. He would cup my face in his palm, smiling.

"Relax, Rachela, there is no contest here. You don't have to go so fast. Enjoy the trip a little. Sit back, look out the window. There's some nice scenery."

This was the absolutely perfect thing to say to me, because another one of the pleasures that my father and I shared was going for drives together. At least this was a very great pleasure for me. Nothing relaxed me, as a child, more than sitting in the back of one of our beat-up secondhand cars—there was a longer series of these than there were homes; cars died on us, one after the other. I remember one of these beauties had a big hole in the floor of the back seat, through which Gideon and I surreptitiously dropped our candy wrappers, thinking it hysterical that we could litter in such an undetectable fashion.

But going for a ride wasn't my active brother's idea of the perfect recreation; only mine. I don't think my father could have enjoyed these drives all that much either. He was a very poor driver, went too slowly. Other drivers yelled at him. But as long as he kept off the highways, it was okay.

We didn't speak to each other on our drives alone together. I don't think my father was really capable of speaking and driving at the same time. He always remained a stranger to the wheel.

But I liked this silence in the car. I'd give myself up totally to the movement. I'd sit back and look out the window, and be completely absorbed in the passing scenes. Savannah, Omaha, Port Jervis. Hell, I even liked driving around Trenton.

Whenever he had to drive me somewhere I always asked him if he could give me an extra ride, just for nothing. And he always did, even though he didn't like driving, and aimless driving must certainly have counted in his book as a species of *bital z'man*.

I remember when I found out that we would have to be leaving Trenton. I had prayed like crazy that I would be able to go to junior high there, together with Freddy, where we could continue the good fight of trying to beat the pants off each other.

We had remained in Trenton for so long, three years, that I had sort of forgotten the air of anxiety that always entered the house around the time that my father's contract came up for renewal.

Only I sort of hadn't forgotten. I knew the meaning of those closed discussions between my father and my mother. They'd go into the dining room, and close the sliding doors, and I would gnaw at my already chewed-off fingernails.

"Would you be awfully sad to leave Trenton?" I asked Gideon.

"Yeah, sure," he said. "Trenton's nice. I have a lot of good friends here."

"You'd make other friends," I told him. "You always do."

"I guess," he said, but sadly.

Of course, when my parents announced to Gideon and me that we would be leaving Trenton soon, not yet certain for where (it turned out to be Chattanooga, Tennessee), Gideon and I said that was exciting, it was getting boring in Jersey, it was time to move on. This was, I said, for me the perfect time to leave, since I'd have to be changing schools, anyway. And Gideon made up some reason also, to explain why it was the perfect time for him to leave New Jersey, too.

I was filled with rage at those tragically ignorant Jews who couldn't see how lucky they were to have a real *talmid chachem* for their rabbi.

My father asked me that evening, after dinner, if I would like to go for a ride with him.

We got into the big old Buick that was currently functioning, not too well, as the family's means of transportation.

We kept driving, slow but steady, out of Trenton, out onto the highway going north.

I forgot a little of my sadness as I watched the trees, interspersed with the occasional diner or store, go past.

We drove all the way to Princeton, got off the highway there, and drove around the quiet streets of the beautiful town.

We hadn't spoken, had kept up our usual silence in the car. But as we circled the rim of the campus, we admired aloud the beauty and sheer massiveness of the buildings.

And then my father suddenly said to me:

"Maybe you'd like to go to Princeton some day. Maybe this is where you'll go to college."

"Maybe," I answered from the back seat.

There was a slight pause, and then he said, so kindly it broke my heart to hear it, "Maybe you'll be able to come back to New Jersey, some day, Rachela."

He was trying to comfort me. It broke my heart that he was trying to comfort me.

You don't need to, Dad, I wanted to say. So I have to leave Trenton. So I have to leave Freddy. So big deal. I can cope with much worse than this.

I struggled, there in the darkness of the back seat, trying to find some safely neutral way of saying this to my father, just as he had found a way to speak to me. My brilliant father! My brilliant father, who shouldn't even have to be here, driving around in the nighttime, trying to apologize to a daughter.

What I don't understand, what I will never be able to understand, is how a father who once loved a daughter so much could sit *shiva* for her while she was still alive.

My father doesn't even know about the baby. I wonder how he would have reacted to such a granddaughter. It was from him that I learned the way of Telz. I was raised on stories of the great *gaonim*. There wasn't any mention made, in our hagiography, of the figure of the sainted idiot.

Luke has said that we must write to my parents and tell them about the baby. That perhaps it will make a difference.

But if we did write to them, and if it didn't make a difference, how would I be able to bear it?

Luke is an amazingly easy touch.

When we walk down Broadway together—we live on the Upper West Side, from where he travels uptown to his work, and I travel downtown to mine—and there's someone with his hand out within a two-mile radius, he's bound to sniff out Luke, and come sidling up to him.

They all get to him: the druggies, the little old ladies with their charity boxes and their orphanages in Israel. All the assorted shnorrers of the Upper West Side.

Luke doesn't refuse to make eye contact and just keep on walking, the way any other sane person in New York City does. He stops on the sidewalk, and attends *seriously* to what the druggie is incoherently mumbling, or the spiel the Hadassah lady is giving him, while I tug at his sleeve, muttering darkly about people who refuse to learn.

The number of charitable organizations whose lists Luke has managed to get himself onto is simply staggering. Obviously there's a nefarious practice of interorganizational sharing of names that goes on, so that the solicitations that arrive here are growing out of control, like something cancerous. Any other sane human being would simply trash the unopened letters, not sit there at our kitchen table, night after night, opening them, reading them, sorting them out according to some system of his I don't even want to know about. Frankly, I've been tempted to do some sorting of my own. But I don't know which of these charities is particularly dear to Luke's heart.

He makes out his checks in multiples of eighteen, ever since I explained to him why it is that those are the sums so often requested by the Jewish organizations, that the letters that designate eighteen are also the letters that spell out the word "life." Luke liked that, and even gives to his gun-control and mothers-against-drunk-driving and save-the-sea-turtles organizations in multiples of eighteen.

The pile is particularly high now, since Luke, still the Semitophile, has managed to get himself onto so many Jewish lists; and this is September, the time of the Jewish New Year, when the appeals come thick and fast.

The other night Luke came into the living room, where I

sat working on an appeal for a small-time drug dealer, my usual sort of case, this one pretty hopeless, since the guy seems to have gotten a fair trial; and Luke wordlessly handed me one of *his* appeals.

"What's this?" I asked him.

"Just read it, Rach," he answered, and went back into the kitchen.

It came from a girls' orphanage in Jerusalem, and I had to admit that they had added a new little twist I'd never seen before. There was a little envelope where you could check off the amount of your donation, that was nothing new. But there was space provided on the envelope for the donor to write in his own little special plea to God, as the accompanying letter explained.

We ask you, once again, to remember our innocent little orphan girls at this very special time of the Jewish year. We have provided a place where you can write in your own personal message to THE HIGHEST ONE. Your appeal will be carried to THE WESTERN WALL by our little girls, and placed by them there between the sacred stones. You can be certain that your words, placed there by these unfortunate orphans of Israel, who are beloved and blessed in THE DIVINE SIGHT, will carry a special power of efficacy in the HEAVENLY REALM.

I was slightly shocked by the brazen simple-mindedness of what I read. I don't believe I had ever seen a metaphysics so unashamedly exposed. My family never would have spoken in terms such as these.

The space provided was not very large. One would have to be succinct. How, precisely, would one do it?

You see, HIGHEST ONE, I have this child. She's twelve months old and there's clearly something wrong with her, but so far no one can tell us what.

But, then, THE HIGHEST ONE would know all that, wouldn't He? Not much briefing is required when addressing OMNISCIENCE.

Pare it down to a simple petition, then. How about: Make it be true that my baby is normal. Only that: normal.

Make it be true? What an awkward choice of words. A verbal clumsiness betraying a logical absurdity.

Make it be true? What could that possibly mean, in the present case? The truth was the truth. The only thing still missing was the knowledge of it. And that would come, sooner or later, without God's help.

What, then, could I write? For I was tempted, beyond reason, to write something. Luke would be giving these people his money anyway. What could it hurt if I scribbled in some chosen words, to be placed within the stones by those little orphan girls of Israel?

But I didn't know how to do it. I had no idea, I hadn't a clue, how to write a letter to God.

What would my father, I wondered, have made of this space provided on the envelope? Would he have dismissed it as another bit of backward nonsense, some more wishful thinking disguising itself as religion on the part of the pious ignoramuses?

My father, of course, addresses God three times daily, and my father is a paragon of rationality. So, then, there must be some logically consistent way to do it. How?

Does my father petition in his prayers? Plead? Ask for special favors? It's hard to reconcile such a possibility with what I know of my father.

What precisely does my father do when he prays? What does he think about while he recites the liturgy?

I once walked into the dining room when my father was saying his morning prayers in there. Normally I wouldn't have done that, walked into the same room where my father was praying. But I had left my math book in there the night before, and I had to get it for school.

My father was wrapped in his prayer shawl, his left arm and forehead bound in his phylacteries. His eyes were closed and he didn't see me. I stood there, waiting for him to notice me and give me a sign that it was okay for me to enter the room and get my schoolbook.

But his eyes remained closed, he didn't seem to have heard me. And then I saw that there were tears streaming down his face. His cheeks were wet.

This, too, was a possibility hard to reconcile with what I knew of my father. He certainly never cried, never betrayed any sign of emotion, when he prayed before his congregations.

I fled the room, forgetting the book.

I wish I had had the nerve, had not been so fatally shy, about asking my father then, when he loved me so much and would have tried to give me an answer, why he cried when he prayed. I wish I had asked him what it was that he did when he prayed.

I can't believe that he was pleading, asking for favors, petitioning for change. But it's possible that what he did, three times daily, was acknowledge his helplessness.

I still have that envelope from the orphanage in Jerusalem. I never gave it back to Luke. It's not, of course, that I don't want him to give his money to those little orphan girls. I'm just still trying to figure out how to write my letter to God.

The baby slept through the night from the beginning. How lucky we are, Luke and I had congratulated ourselves. What a considerate baby we have.

Sometimes I get up in the night anyway, and go into her room. I've thought many times of killing her. She'd be easy enough to suffocate.

I've read a lot about crib death. I believe I could make it look quite convincing. I believe I would get off.

If I killed Gabriella my life would be mine again. But if I killed Gabriella I wouldn't deserve to have Luke's love anymore. And so I almost certainly won't kill her. But I do wish she would die.

The other night I had a dream that the hospital where Gabriella was born called, to tell me that a terrible mistake had been perpetrated in the nursery, the night of the birth.

I could hear that the person on the line was very nervous, afraid of a ruinous lawsuit.

What had happened was that the name tags had somehow become mixed up and we had been given the wrong baby. Our real baby, a bouncing bright-eyed little girl, had been taken home by the Freudensteins, who were on their way over now with her.

Poor Freddy, I thought, for a moment. And then a stream of joy went blazing through my whole body.

She isn't mine! She isn't mine! Give me my real baby, Freddy Frankenstein!

But then, even in the dream, I remembered that the vacant eyes were my eyes. And so I knew that that damaged person was irreparably mine, and everything went dead again inside me.

My unconscious is very big on denial. I suppose they all are. That's supposed to be one of their major functions, isn't it.

I remember the whole series of denial dreams I had after I learned that my family had truly sat *shiva* for me.

Did I think they wouldn't? Did I think they loved me so well that they would, for just this once, ignore what their religion told them they were supposed to do?

Yes, I suppose I did. I knew it would be difficult, a very tricky case, but I was certain that I could win it. I had a deep-down belief, always, in my ability to win. To arrive at the

new school, pick out the adversary, and go get him. I don't
believe I ever entertained the possibility of being defeated by
circumstance. Of course, I could have come away from my
childhood, from the picture of my father, such an American
failure, with quite a different sense of the odds. But I hadn't.
I was American-born, endowed with an Emersonian sense of
self-reliance.

You see, the angle was that Luke loved my rabbinical eyes.
He loved my haunted face, and all the ghosts that came
trailing behind it. Hadn't that been the happy ending that
my mother had been promising me all along, and that I had
kept going back to her to hear, again and again, complaining
to her about how ugly I was, just so that I could hear it once
more? It was, for me, the archetypal story of romance, its
legend. Legend, not just as in myth, but as in the explanatory
code attached to a map. I mean the story of how Esther
Mykoff, American-born and beautiful, had immediately
agreed to meet the young Lithuanian rabbi with the rabbinical
eyes.

So what if in my case it was a *farblondjet* philosopher from
Nebraska? Couldn't my mother, who was always so interested in everyone's story, be able to see that, so far as the
essentials went, the two stories were the same?

I had counted on my mother's ultimate understanding, and
then on her bringing my father around.

Luke had offered to convert, but I, furious at them, hurt
beyond all words that they didn't love me enough, wouldn't
hear of it.

Anyway, no Orthodox rabbi would have converted him
just on the basis of his wanting to marry a Jewish girl. They
would have put him through an interminable rigmarole. And
if it had been anything but an Orthodox conversion it would
have meant nothing at all to my parents. So nothing at all is
what they got.

But I used to dream, night after night, that I opened up

the front door into our apartment, and heard the soft murmur of a voice. And I walked down our long hall, thinking: I know that voice, I know that voice. My heart would float higher and higher as I walked down the long hall.

And then I stepped into the living room. And there was my father, drinking a glass of tea with Luke. Both of them turned to me and smiled.

Last night I got up in the middle of the night and went to stand a long time over the baby's crib. She hadn't been sleeping when I stepped into the room. She was just lying there with her eyes open.

I finally went back to bed and fell asleep. Sometime, it must have been around dawn, I had a variation on my old dream.

I dreamt I got home from work, and opened the door to hear the murmur of the voice as I walked down the hall. And my heart began to float.

When I stepped into the living room I saw my father together with Luke. They were sitting close beside one another on the couch. My father's back was to me, but when he turned around I saw he was holding the baby.

He stood, stretching out his arms, holding out my daughter to me.

MY MOTHER LOVED TO DANCE

My mother loved to dance. Her favorite parties were dancing parties, and the best of these were the masquerade balls. Once she went as Cupid. She wore pink tights and tiny wings.

We lived in Manhattan then, which is a wonderful town for dancing. Only Paris is better, but, then, only during the Season.

What I remember best is that she used to let me stay in her room while she dressed to go out for the evening. I had already had my dinner, in the kitchen, together with Mrs. Knudson and Mr. Knudson and Emily. No one else was allowed into Mommy's room when she dressed, not even Father.

Her room was the brightest in the house, because it was in the southeast corner and had five windows. It was a pale pink, and the furniture was black, which makes a striking contrast. I usually sat on her bed. The cover was soft and satiny, and it was piled high with small pretty pillows. I was always trying to decide which was my favorite pillow.

Sometimes she would ask me to choose her dress. She would take two gowns out from her closet, the one you could walk into, and hold each gown up in front of her, and say something like "I just can't make up my mind between them. What shall it be, flounced taffeta or beaded silk? They tell pretty much the same story, I suppose, only the taffeta says it straight out. The silk's a bit more metaphorical. Choose for me, darling, won't you. Somehow you always know what will be right."

I'd look at the gowns very carefully—she had so many and

they were all beautiful—and then I would close my eyes, and when I opened them again I would point.

"Yes, you're absolutely right," Mommy would say. "I couldn't decide for myself, but now that you've done it for me I can see you're absolutely right. How *do* you do it?"

I never told her that the way I did it was that when I closed my eyes I would picture her, first in the one dress and then in the other, dancing with . . . well, I suppose it would be Father. And I would see in which of the two she was smiling the happiest. I liked her being mystified by my always knowing.

Mommy was in a wonderfully happy mood when she was dressing to go out. She always expected the evening to be divine. Often she'd describe the people she'd be seeing, and sometimes, if she thought it would amuse me, she would do impressions. It was a wicked thing to do, Mommy said, but so much fun, and I wasn't to tell anyone, especially not Mrs. Knudson. That was because Mrs. Knudson had views about children, which made her very suitable for looking after me, but not for understanding everything that Mommy did.

And I rather expect that Mommy couldn't do her imitations for her friends either, since they were *of* them. So perhaps only I knew how well she did them.

It's a rare talent. Mommy was so good at it that, when I was introduced to Dotty Simpson, I knew it was she even before I heard her name by the way she flapped her eyelids open and closed and made the smile Mommy had made for me, with her teeth showing. And *there* was the red lipstick on her teeth.

I always hoped that the evening would be completely divine. Often it wasn't. Sometimes I'd hear her and Father coming in when it was getting light outside, and they'd be arguing. Father would be speaking in the different voice, the one I hated, with the words all running together, as if they were somehow wet. I could hear Mommy answering him, her voice lower than his, sounding very angry. Once I heard someone crying, but I couldn't tell which of them it was.

But when I was with her in her room, her face was always lit up with the thought of the night all opening before her. And then, finally, she'd get up from her dressing table and turn around and say, "Now, darling, will I do?," which always made me laugh, because of course she always *more* than *did*. I always thought that I got to see her at the moment when she looked the most beautiful, before she went downstairs to the others, just then, when she got up and turned around for me, and none of the night had yet happened to spoil any of it for her.

Of course I usually asked about the evening before. And when they'd been to see a play I wanted the whole plot. The parties were usually amusing, but sometimes they were stuffy. Even when they were stuffy, though, Mommy's descriptions of them were funny.

Sometimes she wouldn't tell me about the night before. She hadn't the patience, it was too boring to have to remember. I never asked her when I had heard her and Father coming home angry.

She danced divinely, but she couldn't sing. It was a joke between us. I could actually carry a tune better than she, and I've by no means a voice. But sometimes, if I begged her, she'd sing—or, rather, talk-sing—like Noël Coward, whom we both adored. We always ended up laughing, because the words were so silly, and her singing was so bad.

I can remember the words of all the songs we sang together. Last week I thought I'd lost a line from "I Went to a Marvellous Party." I don't know what I would have done, since there's nobody here I can ask. But then, when I was in bed, it came back to me.

I've been to a marvelous party,
We played the most wonderful game,

Maureen disappeared
And came back in a beard
And we all had to guess at her name!
We talked about growing old gracefully
And Elsie who's seventy-four
Said "A, it's a question of being sincere,
And B, if you're supple you've nothing to fear."
Then she swung upside down from a glass chandelier!
I couldn't have liked it more.

It was the fourth-from-last line that I'd lost.

What Mommy described I could see very well. Her words made pictures for me. I can't always remember the words, but I can remember the pictures.

There's the picture I still have of her floating down the river. Mommy had been sitting at her dressing table, brushing out her hair, which was just to her neck and very black and shiny, and swung altogether when she moved.

And then, suddenly, she turned to me and said something about floating down a river. I can't remember the exact words, something about its all being a bit like floating down a river. You enjoy what you see while you're seeing it. Then it's gone and there's something else to see.

But then, sometimes, she said, something so strikes your fancy, some different-looking flower growing on the bank, that you want to keep it with you. And so you reach out and pick it. But that's always a mistake. The thing just droops in your hand. And then, of course, you're stuck with it. You've picked the nasty old thing, so you've got to keep it.

She was laughing when she said that, and I laughed, too.

Of course, I didn't understand what she was saying. I was only a very young child then, maybe six or seven, and I always laughed when the grown-ups did, especially Mommy, because she had that kind of laugh. "Peals of laughter," I read last week in a book, which is a bit like it. And I suppose she didn't really intend for me to understand. She was simply talking to me as a way of talking to herself, as adults often do with children.

But I've always remembered what she said because of the picture it made for me. And then, after that, when Mommy would talk to me, I'd often see her just in front of whatever it was she was describing, sailing past. Just her head and shoulders actually, and always placed so that she was only half facing what it was she was talking about.

I didn't like seeing her always sailing past like that, always with a kind of pasted-on smile, and I tried to stop it, but most of the time I simply couldn't.

It wasn't until after the Cuban vacation that I understood what she had meant. It was the winter when I couldn't find my feet, which is how Mrs. Knudson put it, meaning that I was in bed sick most of the time. First I had influenza, and then one cold or sore throat after another.

Mommy and Father left in February. They were only supposed to be gone three weeks, but, as it turned out, it was ten weeks and three days. And when Father came back he was alone. He told me that my mother would be coming soon. But a week after that Mrs. Knudson told me that my mother was in Paris, and that she was going to marry Mr. Railton.

I think Mrs. Knudson was very upset to have to be the one to tell me this, because when I asked her if it was just for the Season—I was so young that I didn't really understand, and thought that everything in Paris lasted only for the Season— she didn't even smile, but just said, with her lips stiff in the way I hated, that, no, it wasn't for the Season, and that she was certain the day would come when my mother would remember that she had a little girl, but she couldn't really tell me when that day would be.

That, of course, was a very terrible thing to say to me. And I can only think that Mrs. Knudson was speaking aloud to herself, and hadn't thought about my understanding.

I knew Mr. Railton, of course. He was a friend of my father's. They had been at school together. It's hard for a child to judge, but I think he was better-looking than my father. At least he was taller and thinner, and had a good deal more hair. They must have been about the same age, since they had been at school together, but he looked younger than my father. I suppose I liked him. But, then, I was only a little child, and I liked everybody. Everybody but Mr. Knudson, that is, who was Mrs. Knudson's husband and drove the Bentley for us. I didn't like Mr. Knudson because of his teeth, which stuck out and were very sharp and yellow. And the hairs of his eyebrows, black and gray, were so long that they hung down into his eyes. The affections of little children are often quite quirky. And he used to tell me that the next time he'd be driving *me* to the Copa. And though, of course, I knew better, even then, than to believe him, I still thought it was irresponsible to risk taking advantage of a child's gullibility.

I was surprised, though, that it was Mr. Railton, because I didn't remember Mommy ever mentioning his being with them when they went out, and so I wondered when he and Mommy had had the opportunity to decide to get married. Perhaps it just all happened rather quickly, in Cuba. And, then, I had thought of Mr. Railton as my father's friend, not Mommy's. That was the part that most confused me.

I missed Mommy, of course. I missed watching her dressing for the evening. But it wasn't too bad. Mrs. Knudson was there taking care of me as usual. And then, after a while, I remembered what Mommy had said about picking things one fancied from the bank, and I understood that she had meant my father and me, that we had drooped in her hand and become nasty. And I remember hoping that, now that she had gone on to Paris and Mr. Railton, my father and I might begin to look beautiful to her again. And I even sometimes thought that perhaps, when Mr. Railton began to droop for her, she might come back to us.

But of course that never happened, because the winter when I turned nine Mommy and Mr. Railton died in a plane crash. They were on their way back to New York, and it happened in the landing. Everybody in the plane was killed, my father told me, the pilot and all the passengers.

My father got very sick after that. Well, "sick" is what Mrs. Knudson called it. When my mother married Mr. Railton, my father was sick sometimes, but now he was sick almost all the time. And then I understood that he, too, had been thinking that Mommy might come back to us after Mr. Railton drooped.

And then Father died. He was driving the Bentley, not Mr. Knudson, and he went into a tree. I suppose he was drunk.

I live at Our Lady of Sorrow, which is in White Plains, in Westchester County. The nuns are very nice to me, and don't seem to mind that I'm not Catholic, although of course, now that I'm an orphan, it's their Christian duty to be kind.

I especially like Sister Constance. She's very young and pretty, though, of course, that's not the reason that I like her. I wonder what Mommy would say about someone as young and pretty as Sister Constance becoming a nun. Somehow I don't think Mommy would laugh at Sister Constance or do an impression of her. I don't see how she would, as there's nothing in her to make fun of.

Sister Constance and I like to take walks together and discuss books. This afternoon we talked about *The Secret Garden*, which I've just finished, and which was one of Sister Constance's favorite books when she was my age. Of course, it's about an orphan.

I'm a prodigious reader. I've ruined my eyes and have to wear glasses now all the time. Sister Constance says they make me look precocious and distinguished. But I know Mommy wouldn't have liked them. She'd have said it's better to be pretty and have the world blurry. But I don't agree. I like to see things clearly.

And I also think that Mommy was wrong about things only staying beautiful if you float past them. I know I would have always thought Mommy beautiful. Always.

THE LEGACY OF
RAIZEL KAIDISH

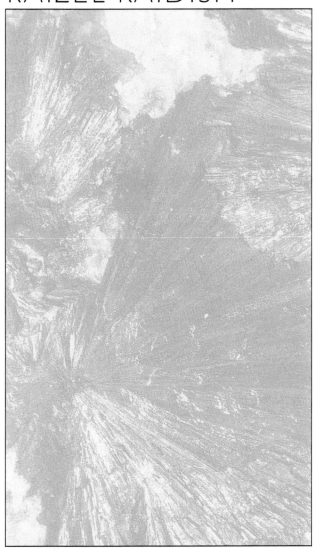

In 1945 the following incident took place in the death camp of Buchenwald.

There were two young Jewish girls, each the last survivor of her family, and they had become very devoted to one another during the few months of their imprisonment. One morning one of them woke up too weak to work. Her name was put on the death list. The other, Raizel Kaidish, argued with her friend that she, Raizel, should go instead. She would tell the Germans there had been a mistake, and when they saw how strong and fit for work she was, it would be all right. Someone informed on the girls and they were both gassed. The informer was rewarded with Raizel's kitchen job.

I'm named after Raizel Kaidish. My mother knew her from the camp. It's noteworthy that, though the war took all her family from her, my mother chose to name her first child, her only child, after an outsider—the heroine of block eight, Buchenwald.

My mother's moral framework was formed in Buchenwald. Forged in the fires, it was strong and inflexible. One of her central concerns was that I should come to know, without myself suffering, all that she had learned there.

My moral education began at an early age. It consisted at first of tales from the camp.

People in my real life were nice or mean, usually a little of both. But in the tales there were only saints and sinners, heroes and villains. I remember questioning my mother about this, and her answer to me:

"When times are normal, then normal people are a little

nice and a little mean together. But when there are hard times, when there's not enough to eat or drink, when there's war, then you don't find a little nice and a little mean mixed together. You find only greatness. Very great badness and very great goodness."

The people in my life didn't seem so real to me as the people in the tales. When I closed my eyes I couldn't picture the faces of my friends or family. All that I could make out of my father was a vaguely sad face around the glinting rimless glasses. Even my mother's features wouldn't come into focus, only the outline of her: tall and always erect, in the gray or dark-blue suit and the white blouse, her light-brown hair in a low bun at the nape of her neck.

But my images of the camp were vivid and detailed. The pink rosebuds on my wallpaper weren't so real to me as the grayness of the barracks, the brown of the mud. It seemed to me that I knew the feel through decaying shoes of the sharp stones in the main square, the sight, twice daily, of the terrifying roll call.

It seemed I, too, had quickly glanced up at the open sky, and wondered that others outside saw the same sky.

My father, like my mother a doctor, didn't approve of the tales:

"She's too young. You'll give her nightmares, traumas. A child this age shouldn't know."

"A child this age. You know you would never consider her old enough to know."

"And why should she know? Can't we forget already? Can't we live like others?"

"Would you really want it, Saul, to live like the others? To join the mass of sleepwalkers, with the glazed eyes and the smug smiles? Is that why we lived when all those others didn't? Is that what we want for Rose?"

And at this point I can hear my father's sigh, the deep drawn-out sigh so characteristic of him, which had always seemed to me, when I was young, to hold the slight tremor of a sob. My father's sadness was something I felt I could almost reach out and touch, like my mother's goodness.

The arguments between my parents continued throughout my childhood. And my father, so gentle, was a man who hated to fight. In the quiet of the night, awake in my bed, I would catch the cadences of their voices, my father's sad and low, so that I missed much of what he said, my mother's burning with the pure flame of her certainty.

And the lessons continued, the simple stark tales of cruelty and sacrifice, cowardice and courage, which always came back to the story of my namesake. My mother would tell me that she had honored both Raizel and me in choosing my name. She sometimes called me Raizel, or even Raizela, in rare moments of tenderness, stroking back my hair.

When I reached fourteen, my mother, deeming me to have arrived at long last at the age of reason (and also, perhaps not coincidentally, at the age at which Raizel had lost her life), began to instruct me in the moral theory she had worked out in Buchenwald.

The theory is elaborate and detailed, reminiscent of the German my parents spoke to one another: complications nesting within complications. The brief account I give here is necessarily inadequate, and perhaps not intrinsically interesting. But I feel that the picture of my mother is incomplete without a description of her moral outlook.

My mother believed that the ethical view is the impersonal view. One is morally obliged to look at a situation without regard for one's own identity in it, and to act in the way dictated by this impersonal view; to act in the way one believes will minimize the sum of suffering.

My mother's emphasis was always on minimizing pain and suffering, never maximizing happiness or well-being. She explained this to me once, when, much older, I asked her:

"I know what is evil. To know suffering is to know evil.

None of the attempts to identify the good have this same certainty."

So far there's nothing, except for its pessimistic cast, to distinguish my mother's view from the great bulk of utilitarian theories. The special twist comes in the foundations she claimed, and it's a twist that mirrors her personality: her uncompromising rationality.

Ethics, she believed, is nothing "separate"; it's a branch of logic. The moral obligation is nothing over and above the obligation to be logically consistent, and virtue reduces to rationality.

Why is this so? Because, she explained, to deny the obligation of acting on the impersonal viewpoint, one would have to maintain that one's self has some special metaphysical significance, that it makes a difference that one is who one is. And how can this consistently be maintained once one has recognized the existence of other selves, each of whom is who he is? Only the solipsist can consistently be unethical.

To use one of my mother's favorite analogies: the person who acts only in his own interest is like a person who says there is always something special about his own location, because he can always say, "I'm *here*," whereas everyone else is merely *there*.

Once one has granted that there are other subjects of experience, other selves who suffer, then one can maintain that one's own pain matters—and who would deny *that*?—only if one grants that the pain of everyone else matters in exactly the same way.

Raizel Kaidish's behavior was therefore, by my mother's accounting, paradigmatically ethical. Viewing the situation impersonally, this fourteen-year-old had seen that the stronger child would have a better, although slim, chance to survive. She acted on this view, undeterred by the fact that it was she who was the stronger, she who was unnecessarily risking her life.

In fact, I have no doubt at all that my mother's ethical view was the straightforward consequence of taking Raizel Kaidish as her paradigm, and not the other way round. The heroic action of that child was the real foundation of her theory—which, like my name, honored the girl's memory.

After the liberation my mother returned to Berlin to continue her formal training in medicine. She also began her lifelong study of philosophy. She was curious to see who among the philosophically great had shared her discovery.

She considered Kant to be the most worthwhile ethicist. Socrates she loved for his devotion to the ethical questions, for his conviction that nothing ought to concern us more than the questions of how to live our lives. Hanging over my bed, the only piece of embroidery I've ever known her to do, was the Socratic quotation: "The unexamined life is not worth living."

But for the most part my mother found the great philosophers of the past a supreme disappointment. The truth, so simple, had eluded them, because they had assumed the separateness of the ethical realm. Some had grasped pieces of it, but few had seen the seamless whole.

It was contemporary philosophers, however, particularly the positivists and their "fellow travelers," who aroused her genuine wrath.

For here were theorists who dismissed the possibility of all ethical theory, who denied the very subject matter of the field. Instead of conducting inquiries into the nature of our moral obligations, they offered analyses of the grammar of ethical propositions.

She would look up from some contemporary philosophical book or journal, her eyes blazing their blue fury:

"Positivists." The intonation she gave the word was similar to that she gave "Nazi." "They don't see, because their eyes aren't turned outward but inward, into the tabulae rasae of their own minds. To forsake the important questions for this dribble! To spend your life examining endless quibbles!"

And I? How did I feel about my intensive moral upbringing?

The object of so much attention, of all the pedagogical theorizing, the fights in the night: I felt ignored, unloved, of no significance.

And, especially as I grew older, I felt angry: an unvoiced and unacknowledged outrage.

It wasn't just a matter of the rigidity of my upbringing, the lack of laughter in a home where one could reach out and touch one's father's sadness and mother's goodness.

It wasn't just the fact that I was always made to feel so different from my friends, so that I often, though always with an overwhelming sense of guilt, fantasized myself in another family, with parents who were frivolously pursuing happiness, and didn't have numbers burned into their arms.

It was something else, more elusive and more potent, that infuriated me.

Of course, there's nothing unusual in a daughter's resentment of a mother. My friends, from early adolescence onward, were always enraged with one or the other of their parents. But theirs was the pure clean indignation unashamed of itself.

Hadn't she suffered enough? Shouldn't I try to do everything to make it up to her? By hating her, I joined the ranks of her enemies. I allied myself with the murderers.

And so the resentment was folded back on itself, again and again, always thickening, always darkening.

I never spoke it, not even to myself. Its acknowledgment came only years later, after my mother had died, during the years I spent deliberating over whether to have a child of my own. The mental delivery of that decision was so much more agonizing than the physical birth.

In debating the reasons for having a child, I asked myself

whether any reasons could ever be right, whether one was ever justified in bringing a person into being for some reason of one's own? But if not for one's own reason, then for whose? It seemed a moral inconsistency woven into the very fabric of human existence.

The solution really only came to me after I was a mother: It's possible—it's right—for the reasons one had for creating a child to recede into insignificance when faced with the fact of that child's existence. Whatever considerations went into the decision to have a child lose themselves in the knowledge of the child itself.

In my view, this is the essence of good parenting, and once I finally knew this I knew at last what I had felt all along to be wrong about my mother and myself. I had known what no child should ever know: that my mother had had me for some definite reason, and that she would always see me in terms of this reason. I sensed this in my mother, and I hated her for it.

I said that my anger never showed itself. Actually there was a brief rebellion, whose form was so typical of my family's peculiarity that now, years later, even I can see its comic aspect and smile.

My first semester of college, while my friends developed their own conventional modes of rebellion, I worked out mine. I became a positivist. I took Introduction to Philosophy with a self-intoxicated young professor, a new Ph.D. from Harvard, and, although this wouldn't be his own description, a neopositivist.

He told us during the first lecture that he was going to show us, over the course of the semester, why we were lucky, insofar as we were philosophy students, to have been born now; that it was now possible to see that previous generations had devoted themselves to pseudo-questions concerning the nature of Reality, Truth, and the Good; and that such questions were expressions of logical confusion. These fine big words don't name anything, and thus there is nothing there whose nature is to be explored.

I sat there, drinking in his words, thinking: "This is it. This is why I came to college."

All through that term, Monday, Wednesday, and Friday, from ten to eleven, while others dozed and doodled, I listened in a state of delirium, following the arguments with a concentration I've never attained since. My mind bubbled over with the excitement of this illicit doctrine, this forbidden philosophy.

And the most forbidden, and therefore enticing, view offered in the course was that devoted to ethics, or, rather, to the dismissal of ethics.

I memorized whole passages out of my favorite book, A. J. Ayer's *Language, Truth, and Logic*:

> We can now see why it is impossible to find a criterion for determining the validity of ethical judgements. It is not because they have an 'absolute' validity which is mysteriously independent of ordinary sense-experience, but because they have no objective validity whatsoever. If a sentence makes no statement at all, there is obviously no sense in asking whether what it says is true or false. And we have seen that sentences which simply express moral judgements do not say anything. They are pure expressions of feeling and as such do not come under the category of truth and falsehood.

I was inexpressibly moved by the sparse beauty of the arguments. How had I never seen it before, never seen that my mother's supposedly impermeable theory was nothing but an insubstantial confection fabricated of pseudo-statements?

My preparations for final exams were trivial compared with my cramming for the visit home during intersession. I arrived back about eleven at night, too late for philosophical debate. But my mind was so teeming with my professor's methods of query that when my mother wished me "good night" I almost challenged her: "What do you mean by that? What do you mean by 'good'?"

The next evening, after my mother and father arrived home from the hospital, we all sat in the living room, while Bertha, our housekeeper, finished dinner. I was waiting for the right moment for launching my attack, poised to pounce on any comment that was mildly speculative.

But my mother, with her practiced perversity, was being very concrete that night. She asked me about the food at school, about my roommate, even told a funny story about her own roommate, in Berlin, before the war. Then, finally:

"You were always so brief on the phone when I asked you about your classes. Tell me more about them. You seemed to have enjoyed them very much."

"They were wonderful. Especially philosophy. I'm going to major in it."

"Really? And are you thinking of this as a profession?"

"Absolutely. It's it. There's nothing else I'll even consider."

"Well, that's interesting. Very interesting."

"That's *all*: interesting? Are you pleased, horrified, what?"

"At the moment maybe a little baffled. To tell you the truth, I've always thought it a rather funny kind of profession. Every person should of course think about the big questions, but it seems an odd way to earn one's living."

"But what about teaching, Marta?" my father, the eternal peacemaker, asked. "Don't you think it's important to have people teaching philosophy?"

"Well, yes, that's true. Yet I suspect that most of them don't think of themselves primarily as teachers, but as thinkers, professional thinkers, however peculiar that sounds. Well, we can ask Rose here. What do you fancy yourself, a teacher or a philosopher?"

"A philosopher, of course. The need for professional training in philosophy is no different than anywhere else, no different than in medicine. People think they can just jump in and start philosophizing and that they'll make sense. They rarely do. It takes technical training. Years and years of it."

"Oh? I disagree very much, as you know, with this emphasis on technical training. Instead of humanizing the mathematical sciences, they try to mathematize the humanities. Translating into a lot of fancy symbols doesn't show the truth of what you're saying."

"But it does often show its meaninglessness."

I brought out this positivist buzzword with all the provocative emphasis I could muster.

"Do you think so?" responded my mother, not even lifting an eyebrow. "Yes, I can see how that might often be true."

Impossible woman! What was wrong with her? Her kindling point was usually so frighteningly low, but tonight she wouldn't burn. She wouldn't even flicker.

The explanation, of course, would have been obvious to anyone not occupying my vantage point. She was, quite simply, very happy to see me.

I had no more patience for her unwonted tolerance. I abandoned my hopes for a smooth transition.

"Mom, there's a question about ethics that's been bothering me."

There. I had opened the door. Now I had to walk through.

"Yes? Tell me. Perhaps I can be of some help."

"You've always said that the moral obligation is nothing but the obligation to be logically consistent. But why do we have to be logically consistent?"

My mother smiled.

"I must say, you surprise me. Such an antirationalist question. And after a whole semester of college! The answer is, of course, that the truth is important. And logical inconsistencies can't be true. If you ask me, as I can see you're about to, why the truth is important, I can't give you a noncircular answer. Anything I say is going to presuppose the importance of truth, as all rational discourse presupposes it. And this impossibility of a noncircular answer is itself the answer."

"I don't understand a word you're saying!" I exploded. "The Truth! The holy Truth! What's the Truth? Where's the Truth? Let me see you point to it! What can it possibly mean to say, 'The Truth is important'? What cognitive content can it possibly have? It's nonsense! Emotive nonsense! And the same with all the other so-called truths of your so-called theory! You claim to be so rational, so superior and so rational! But you're only emoting—eternally emoting—and I'm sick to death of it!"

My speech was not delivered in that calm voice of detached reason I had so obsessively rehearsed. Instead it tore out of me with a force that frightened me, sweeping me along.

The effect was immediate. My mother's face had the capacity for instantaneous transformation I've observed in my own young daughter. In fact, I often find myself wondering whether this is a trait characteristic of early childhood, or whether it's something my daughter has inherited from her grandmother, along with her name.

My mother had never raised her voice to me, and she didn't raise it now. As always, her eyes did all the screaming.

"Positivist!"

Her intonation wasn't the usual one. There was anger, but it was softened by sadness.

"After all that I have taught you, you lose everything in one semester of college? Do you have so little substance that at your first exposure to the jargon of these antithinkers you disintegrate?"

I had no answer for my mother. The brilliant arguments spilling over in my mind only the night before were all vanished. My head was so hollow it felt as if it were floating away from the rest of me. The deadening fog, of shame and guilt, was settling back over everything.

Dimly, I saw my father sitting there, staring out at us over the wall of his sadness. My mother's voice cut through the haze.

"You disappoint me. You disappoint us all. You aren't worthy to be named after Raizel Kaidish."

Soon after my wedding, when my mother was fifty-six, she learned that she had ovarian cancer and didn't have more than six months to live.

She reacted to the news of her impending death as if she had been preparing for it her whole life. She looked at it with her customary objectivity: Yes, she was relatively young, and there were still many things that she would have liked to experience, particularly being a grandmother. But that she, a Jew from Berlin, had been given these past thirty years was a fact to which the proper response was gratitude, not a greedy demand for yet more years.

She never complained. Her grief seemed entirely focused on the anguish her terrible illness was causing my father and me.

She died as I had always known her to live: with super-human discipline, courage, and rationality.

A week before she died, she told me that it had been she who had informed on Raizel Kaidish. She asked my for-giveness.

STRANGE
ATTRACTORS

Phoebe Saunders is on an Air France jet headed for Charles de Gaulle Airport, already miserably regretting her decision to accept an invitation to visit at the Institut des Hautes Etudes Scientifiques, located in the village of Bures-sur-Yvette, about thirty kilometers outside of Paris.

Among the many things Phoebe's now dreading is her having to get herself from the airport to Bures-sur-Yvette. She only hopes she can manage to find a cab to take her there, that she can make herself understood in the execrable French she hasn't had to speak since high school.

Phoebe's reluctance to travel, all expenses paid, is an eccentricity she shares with very few of her academic colleagues. Many of the mathematicians she knows are airborne at least once a semester, always poised ready to flit across the globe and deliver a paper at this conference or that.

But for Phoebe, each invitation, especially from abroad, initiates a tormentedly prolonged process of deliberation that culminates in her eventually sending her regrets. Each refusal is based on a thoroughly rational decision, really: the projected gains, measured in terms of professional exposure and any new mathematics she might manage to learn, are far outweighed by the psychological costs inflicted on Phoebe whenever she leaves known territory, where she speaks the language and is reasonably familiar with the public means of transportation.

But the invitation from Bures has come from Antoine Shahaza, with whom Phoebe is in love.

Antoine Shahaza is one of the world's great nonlinear analysts, and he's a god. Phoebe first saw him the semester before, in the spring, when he'd come for a brief jaunt to Princeton, though she's known his name—tagged onto a dazzlingly large number of solutions to notoriously difficult problems—for almost as long as she's been mathematically conscious.

But, until she saw him, she'd been unaware that behind the mathematical brilliance there stands a man embodying the sum of all perfections.

His sheer physical beauty had taken Phoebe's breath away.

Tall, towering above all the other men, the godlike face— clean-shaven except for a thin mustache, and the features strong and proud and noble—suspended above the crowd. He looks a little like Omar Sharif, with whom Phoebe had been in love when she was nine, after having seen *Doctor Zhivago*. (Her grandmother Sasha had taken her to the old West Side revival house, the Thalia, to see the film; and had told her, as they bought the tickets, that if Phoebe didn't come out of the theater completely in love with Omar Sharif, then she was completely insensible.)

Antoine Shahaza's accent, too, is something like Omar Sharif's: hard to place, but meltingly divine. An Omar Sharif who can do the most exquisite mathematics!

A god. There's no other word for him, really. Beyond it, Phoebe's at a loss to describe Antoine Shahaza, to express her wonder of him, her gratitude that existence contains him.

Phoebe's been in love before: many times. But before, she's always fallen for vulnerability, not invincibility. She's been smitten by some weakness in the armor, a glimpse of the stark mortality beneath, suddenly making a member of the alien race of males achingly familiar, doomed and inconsolable.

So Phoebe has very few words for this new love, which has as its object a being who stands in no need of her, or anyone else's, adoration; for that is the nature of a god.

O, I burn! I burn! I am on fire with thee, Apollo!

So Phoebe—whose mother, Chloe, is a classical scholar at Barnard College—remembers the words of Cassandra, the truth-seared seeress, after whom no mothers name their daughters.

Though Phoebe doesn't dream of asking anything from this love beyond the very love itself, still, there had been the question—after Antoine Shahaza had gone away from Princeton, all through the strangely blurred summer when she'd lost herself to the study of the beautiful math of his papers, merged with dense fantasies—there'd been the question of how she would be able to survive without another glimpse of him to sustain her; one more sight of the man behind the mathematics.

She'd sent her silent wish out into the universe, and the universe had attended to her; just as it had used to seem that the universe could heed her.

The universe had responded and Phoebe had received an invitation from IHES to come and visit at her convenience.

And so, with no deliberation at all, with an overflowing sense of gratitude sent back to the kindly universe, she'd agreed to come during the week in the autumn semester that Princeton still gives off for election day; she'd agreed to brave anything and everything for another chance to look at Antoine Shahaza, to hear Antoine Shahaza, to store up Antoine Shahaza for all the years to come.

Phoebe's flying first class. When the first-class ticket had arrived she'd thought there must have been some sort of mistake.

So she'd gone to Delia, the one really helpful secretary in the department, to whom Phoebe tends to go an awful lot. Though Phoebe is herself very reserved, she feels most comfortable with those who, like Delia, are free-and-easy, blunt, and down-to-earth, so long as they are very kind.

"It's first class," she'd explained to Delia. "Do you think

there's some mistake? Do you think I should get in touch with them and see if they meant to send this ticket to someone else?"

Delia had laughed and told Phoebe, as she often did, that she was too much.

"You just take that first-class ticket and you fly! And if there's some big shot that's gotta squeeze himself into economy . . . No, I'm just kidding, Dr. Saunders! *You*'re the big shot!"

The man sitting next to Phoebe, who's dressed in a gray silk suit, is fast asleep, so that Phoebe feels a sort of tenderness toward him, though they haven't exchanged a word, and she wishes that the young French couple who're sitting behind them wouldn't keep laughing so loudly. Phoebe doesn't know, and certainly wouldn't care, that the gray silk suit is by the Italian designer Giorgio Armani, though even she has noticed that her neighbor smells expensively good. But in sleep he looks unprotected and childlike, and Phoebe feels tender.

A stewardess is passing down the aisle, asking people if they would like to order alcoholic beverages. She sees that Phoebe's neighbor is sleeping and passes right on to the noisy couple behind, not even bothering to ask Phoebe.

Phoebe is used to this, and it doesn't trouble her in the least, especially since she wouldn't have wanted anything to drink anyway. She's used to being treated like a child. Until quite recently she technically was a child, or at least a student. She doesn't know how she would respond were people suddenly to start treating her like a grown-up.

Somewhere over the Atlantic the man in the Armani suit, a Parisian businessman, wakes up. Dinner's already been served, and he seems put out and rings for the stewardess and gets his food and wine, which he consumes with great concentration. When he's finished, his tray cleared away, he turns and notices Phoebe, who's been furiously drawing her equations all over her lined yellow paper.

The man smiles at Phoebe in a kindly, patronizing manner, to which Phoebe is more than accustomed and which she even rather likes, and asks her if she's doing her homework.

"In a way."

He smiles again and tells Phoebe she must be a very good student to take her work along with her on a plane trip. He asks her where she goes to school.

"I'm at Princeton."

The man expresses surprise that Phoebe is already so old as to be in college.

"I had thought you were no more than a young schoolgirl, all alone on a trip to Paris."

He looks as if he might reach out and pat Phoebe on the top of her shining head.

Phoebe, uncomfortable, very softly corrects the man's error.

"I'm actually not a student," she mumbles. "I teach there."

The man, unsurprisingly, hasn't understood what Phoebe's said and asks her to repeat it.

"I used to be a student at Princeton. But I actually teach there now."

"You *teach* there? Is that what you said? *What* do you teach?"

"Math."

"What? What did you say? Why do you swallow your words?"

"I'm sorry. I teach math. Mathematics."

"You're a regular professor at Princeton? Or are you just some sort of graduate student?"

"No, I'm regular, I guess. I mean I'm not a student."

"You have your degrees? All the degrees?"

Phoebe nods.

"But how *old* are you?"

"I'm twenty-six."

"Inconceivable!" His eyes, which have filled suddenly with scorn, sweep down over Phoebe.

Her thick brown hair is brushed away from her face and hangs down almost to her waist. She's in a pair of jeans and a blue-and-white sweater that Sasha had bought her for her fifteenth birthday. She's small and slight. She's always assumed that her father, whom she doesn't know, and about whom her mother clearly doesn't like her to ask questions, must have been a small, slight man, since both Chloe and Sasha are tall women, who carry themselves with a presence of which Phoebe is now, and will always be, entirely lacking.

"Inconceivable!" he says again. "Princeton used to be one of the great American universities!"

The man, who has taken great offense at Phoebe's being on the Princeton faculty, turns away from her without another word, calls for more wine from the stewardess, and takes out some work of his own from his attaché case. Like Phoebe's work, his, too, is full of numbers.

Phoebe, upset by her neighbor's surprisingly violent opposition to her academic affiliation, finds that she's not able to get back into her equations. Anger's always had a devastating effect on her, and, baffled as she is by the reason behind it, she finds herself going numb beside the man's cold enmity.

This is a mistake, she thinks. Why did I think I could just throw myself into a world of strangers and strangeness I can't begin to figure out?

She longs, suddenly and intensely, for the sense of safety she knows at home: the few friends she has in Princeton; the good students she teaches there; and Chloe and Sasha in Manhattan, only a train ride away.

Why did I come? she thinks. And for an answer, and for

solace, she lets her mind drift back onto the wonders of Antoine Shahaza.

Antoine Shahaza is a polymath. He knows everything. Not just mathematics. Everything. Inexhaustible mind. Infinite.

The talk he had given at Princeton had been extremely beautiful: crystalline proofs, with every step explained, a little bit after the fashion of "Nicolas Bourbaki"—the collective pseudonym used by a group of mostly French mathematicians, whose shifting identities have always remained secret, and who had begun, in the late thirties, to publish a methodologically startling survey of mathematics: nothing assumed, everything proved, with a severe insistence on the logical structure and the utmost generality.

But the pleasure Phoebe had derived from the lecture had been only the beginning.

After the lecture, Phoebe, already a little beguiled, had uncharacteristically agreed to join the group of her colleagues accompanying Antoine Shahaza to dinner at the Prospect Faculty Club, where, instead of the usual shop talk, the conversation, under the sublimating influence of Antoine Shahaza, had dwelled on far-flung topics: the operas of Mozart; the plays of Shakespeare, mathematical Platonism; the mind-body problem!

The breadth of his knowledge is prodigious; every facet of his complex mind glints with erudition and charm, turned out in long and elegant sentences. His memory must be photographic, for his conversation is studded with quotations. Chloe also tends to quote heavily, especially from the ancients, but that's her job. For a mathematician to be able to recite from Shakespeare and Derrida, the Koran and Niels Bohr, is godlike.

And all around Phoebe, at their table in the middle of the faculty dining club, the mathematicians were rising to the occasion of Antoine Shahaza. They were, to a man, revealing themselves to have thought of things outside their carefully defined specialties. Penetrated by the breath of his genius, everybody's conversation was sprouting wings and flying; while Phoebe, always too shy to say much with her colleagues, watched and marveled, as the spirit of this great man felt its way into all around him.

It had seemed to her as if the entire table of mathematicians was lifting itself off of the ground; wordlessly acquiescing in their collective transcendence, they were levitating upward toward the ceiling of the faculty club; while beneath them, over at the other tables, occupied by the wretchedly earthbound empiricists, the plodding art historians and chemists, literary theorists and linguists had continued to talk and chew their food; to get up and leave to go back to offices and lectures; taking no notice of the miracle that had embraced the table of mathematicians, defying physics, rising up on the unleashed powers of *a priori* genius.

At one point in the conversation the name of one of the absent Princeton mathematicians had come up. This mathematician, one of Princeton's most respected, had recently astounded them all by publishing a strange little monograph in a philosophical journal, in which he had indulged in some highly speculative, not to speak of downright dubious, claims concerning the philosophy of mind.

"And what do you think of our Himmel's efforts to resurrect Cartesian dualism?" one of the mathematicians now asks Antoine Shahaza.

"Ah yes," answers Shahaza, his eyes glinting mischievously, as they have on and off throughout the meal. "Your Noam Himmel. O! what a noble mind is here o'erthrown!"

And Phoebe, for a moment forgetting herself, for a moment altogether forgetting that she's terrified to speak before all these great men, breaks out into:

"Oy, sara geyst ahn aydelehr iz daw tzeshtert!"

And then she stops and finds herself staring back into the flabbergasted faces of her colleagues.

"That's Yiddish," she stammers. "That's that line of Ophelia's in Yiddish."

And still they all stare at her.

"You see, my grandmother was a Yiddish actress. One of her big roles, back when she was young in Warsaw, was Ophelia."

Himmel's Cartesian dualism is forgotten in the strange effect that little Phoebe has suddenly produced.

They're all asking her questions. But she only hears the questions of Antoine Shahaza, who professes much interest, having not known that the plays of Shakespeare had been translated into Yiddish.

Which plays? he asks her.

"I'm not sure. I think *Lear* and *Othello*. *Romeo and Juliet*. *Macbeth*. Probably more. Perhaps all the tragedies."

"All the tragedies," he repeats. "And you know Yiddish?" he asks her, smiling.

"No, not really. Just bits and pieces of my grandmother's old roles. Sometimes she'd perform them when she'd put me to bed, instead of reading me a story. It was pretty weird."

"Recite! Recite!" the mathematicians are all chanting now, so that even the duller-witted nonmathematicians of Princeton finally glance their way; and Phoebe, laughing, pinking with the strange attention she's attracted, tells them that she doesn't really know anything more, that she hadn't even known she knew what she'd just blurted out.

"Please," pleads Antoine Shahaza, in his melting Sharif accent. "Just the little you remember. You've no idea how charming it is to hear you."

And Phoebe, her stubby little wings just sprouted, finds herself looking down the long table at Antoine Shahaza, who is, improbably, requesting something of her; and somehow she finds herself declaiming, in the style of the Warsaw Yiddish theater of the early twenties, a few mangled fragments of Ophelia's soliloquy, of which none of them, including Phoebe, fortunately understands a word:

And I of all ladies
Am jangled out of tune, like a harsh bell,
Blasted with ecstasy: O! woe is me,
To have seen what I have seen.

Un ich, fun alleh froyen
Iz arup fun ton un rimpelt, vee ah ge'plahtster gluk,
Tze'shmeh'tert fun shiga'en.
Oy, vay iz mihr!
Ahz ich hub dus gezehn.

But it was only the next day that Phoebe came upon the innermost miracle of Antoine Shahaza: in the midst of all the other perfections dwells his perfect kindness.

He had been kind to her, to Phoebe Saunders, who, there in that Princeton constellation of mathematical stars, is a barely visible body, the barest nobody, the youngest assistant professor, who had only just received her doctorate the year before.

And what did the divinely gifted man—this mathematician who's like some sort of spectacularly rare comet shooting across the sky, with a tail of beautiful mathematical results trailing after him—what did he do? He actually took the trouble to attend a little insignificant talk that Phoebe Saunders was scheduled to give at one of the regular Thursday-afternoon meetings.

Phoebe had been so absorbed in her exposition of the geometry of soap bubbles, her specialty, that she hadn't even noticed the slight ruffle that had passed through her audience as Antoine Shahaza, arriving a little bit late, had quietly taken a seat in the back of the room. She'd only discovered his presence near the end of her talk, which was very fortunate, since the discovery had completely nonplussed her, causing her to lose, for a moment, her place in her proof, a humiliation she relived over and over again in burning recollection.

Not that it mattered what he thought of her. She loved him as one loves a god, with no expectation of being loved in return.

But he was sublimely kind. The day that he left Princeton to go back to Paris, Phoebe had found in her department mailbox a small wrapped box, containing a necklace that had as its pendant a little glass bottle filled with soap solution, the cap unscrewing to show a tiny attached bubble wand, which produced bubbles of no more than perhaps a centimeter in diameter.

And there was a note: "To the pretty little girl who does such pretty mathematics —A.S."

Phoebe's wearing the necklace now. The scornful eyes of her Air France neighbor had taken it in.

That man has now in fact decided for some reason to talk once again to Phoebe, which he is doing nonstop.

He's telling her how he started his own business, against the advice of all his acquaintances and family, only to prove them all, millions and millions of dollars' worth, wrong.

He's telling her that she could not begin to imagine the sums on which he sits; and that she has no idea at all how much creativity is demanded by business; how it's more an art form than a science. People like her have no idea.

And now he's telling Phoebe about the very beautiful woman to whom he's married, who stays at home and makes his house beautiful for him; and he's also telling Phoebe about the very beautiful woman who passionately loves him in New York. He's telling her about many women.

Phoebe's at a loss.

How has she attracted this man's strange disclosures?

Is this friendly or hostile, and how does one make it stop?

She wishes miserably that the man would go back to sleep, and leave her free, either to do her math or to think about Antoine Shahaza.

When Phoebe wakes up in the little flat she's been given on the grounds of IHES, it's already quite dark and it seems to be raining.

Getting to Bures-sur-Yvette had been pretty much the nightmare Phoebe had feared.

Oddly, unfathomably, the man in the Armani suit had offered to drive her to Bures-sur-Yvette; so perhaps his strange attention had been friendly after all.

But, as desperate with anxiety as Phoebe had felt about making her own way in a foreign country, she was even more desperate to get away from this man. So she thanked him politely and then bolted with her backpack.

It was raining.

Eventually she managed to find a cab driver who didn't just stare at her blankly when she pronounced for him the address to which she was to go; but not before, near tears, she'd considered chucking the whole mad scheme and trying to get herself back onto a flight home.

The drive from Charles de Gaulle had taken her on a highway that skirted the environs of Paris. Phoebe, staring at the city through the rain-streaked windows of the cab, with the bleary eyes of her sleep-starved night, saw only gray and gloom. Only Sacré-Coeur, miraculously white and ascendant on its hill, gave any suggestion to Phoebe of the sparkling city about which Chloe and Sasha, enthusiastic travelers both, had gone on and on.

The driver had a lot of trouble finding the Institut. Once in Bures, he stopped and asked someone, who answered at great length and with many gestures; but in spite of this,

Phoebe and the driver ended up circling the parking lot of a giant concrete department store or mall or something, called Carrefour, which looked about as unenchanting as anything in this world gets. Phoebe thought she hadn't seen its like in ugliness anywhere, not even on the universally maligned turnpike of New Jersey.

She felt the gloom outside moving into her, congealing into a something settled in her heart. Sometimes, once that happened, there was no expelling it, for days or even weeks, and Phoebe suffered in silence.

Finally, somehow, the driver, who at least was rather good-natured and amused about the whole thing, managed to find the address of the caretaker of the residence grounds of the Institut.

The residences, small attached stucco cottages, with one highrise for mathematicians without families, were arranged in an oval, at one of whose epicenters was a little dripping playground.

Phoebe approached the caretaker's cottage, and two lean black dogs, chained in the yard, bared their terrifying teeth at her and snarled.

The caretaker, as welcoming as his dogs, gave Phoebe a key to her flat in the highrise.

Phoebe got herself in, found the bed, and crawled between the sheets, which were cold and damp.

And when she wakes up now, it's dark and the rain's still falling, and she remembers exactly where she is from the gloom still settled within her, and she's famished.

In the kitchen cabinet she finds a case of Perrier, and in the refrigerator there's a bottle of fancy mustard and some candied violets.

Driven by need, she puts on her raincoat and ventures out into the miserable drizzle.

She knows the general direction of the one main street of Bures from her extensive ride in the cab.

Every shop along this little curving street is closed: the bakery, the butcher, the one small grocery store.

There must be a café, she thinks. Even a village this size has to have a café.

The thought of actually entering a café and having to deal with a French waiter in the French language doesn't appeal to Phoebe very much; but, since she's already growing faint with hunger, there seems no choice.

There's a man approaching from the opposite direction and Phoebe is determined to make herself speak to him: to ask him where in Bures she can get herself some food.

"Pardon," she says to him, trying to make it sound French, as he's going past her.

"Oh," he answers in accented English. "I don't speak French."

"No, me neither."

"Ah," he answers, "you're a mathematician."

"Yes, I am. Phoebe Saunders. From Princeton."

"I'm Oren Glube. Originally from Jerusalem. But now I've been here in Bures for twelve years."

"And you don't speak French?"

"Not yet."

Suddenly Phoebe feels at home.

"I just got here today. I just woke up. This is my first look at Bures."

He nods solemnly. He's a very solemn-looking young man. The two of them are standing not far from a streetlight and Phoebe looks up into a clean-shaven, regular-featured face, staring seriously down into her own, the bangs of his long straight black hair overhanging the dark frames of his glasses. He's wearing a rainhat from which water is dripping onto the little folding umbrella Sasha had given Phoebe for a bon-voyage gift.

"So you would like me now to take you to see the Institut, yes?"

"Well, actually I was thinking more in the way of a café or restaurant first?" Phoebe half answers, half asks.

"Really?" The eyebrows lift beneath the bangs. "Before the Institut?"

"It's just that I'm so famished," she explains apologetically. "I'm actually getting sort of weak from hunger."

Oren's face becomes even more somber.

"Ah. You're hungry. This isn't good. This is, in fact, very bad."

"Isn't there some sort of restaurant in Bures I can go to?" She checks her watch. "It's only a little after nine."

"Maybe. I think so. I think people have taken me to eat somewhere around here. But I couldn't find it."

"You always eat at home?"

"Never. That would be a trivial solution for us now, I think, if I had food at my home to give you. But I never eat there. I tried once a few years ago to turn on the oven and the entire flat filled with poisonous gas."

"How horrible!"

"Very horrible! I was afraid to go back into my apartment for days. I never go near the kitchen since then."

"So, then, how do you eat?"

"At the Institut. At their facility. It's very good food. But the problem is that it's too late to get anything there. It's after their hours. I'm sorry, but this is extremely bad."

They stand for several moments in silence, Oren staring off into the light of the streetlamp.

"I know what we'll do!" he says, breaking out suddenly into a wide smile. "We'll go to see Iphigenia Sorkin, my friend. She's very good at emergencies."

And so they turn around and head back down a little footpath that leads much more directly into the residence grounds than the way in which Phoebe had come.

The path takes them past a very large old house, surrounded by high walls, and a latched iron gate.

"That," Oren says in a low voice and with a little motion of his head, "is a lunatic asylum!"

And Phoebe, looking up into his solemn face as they pass beneath another lamp, can't tell whether he's joking or not.

They knock on the door of one of the little stucco cottages, and are immediately admitted: ushered out of the cold, dark drizzle into the wonderfully warm, cooking-smelling home of the Sorkins, Iphigenia and her husband, Danny, who are just getting up from dinner, but who very obligingly sit down again for Oren and his newfound friend, Phoebe.

Danny's a mathematician at M.I.T. who spends half of each year at Bures. Both the Sorkins are perhaps in their early forties, and have a grown son who's studying physics at Harvard. Phoebe's heard of Danny Sorkin, who's a very good topologist, but Iphigenia's a revelation.

Iphigenia's a poet. She's the first real poet Phoebe has ever set eyes on: a person who actually identifies herself as a poet. Of course, Phoebe knows that books of poetry are published, even in this day; but she's never really thought about there existing real flesh-and-blood poets, having husbands, eating dinner.

And Iphigenia is spectacularly flesh-and-blood. She doesn't at all conform to how Phoebe would have imagined a poet to be: ethereal and tragic and starved. Instead Iphigenia's brimming with the glow of robust animal spirits, and *Phoebe's* starved; and Iphigenia's feeding her with fresh bread and wonderful hot moussaka, and Danny Sorkin is pouring Phoebe glasses of a red wine that's surprisingly easy to drink.

Iphigenia is so beautiful and so self-assured that Phoebe's at first intimidated by her. She's tall, built on the scale of a goddess, with white luminous skin and green eyes and thick auburn hair that falls to her shoulders. She belongs to the fearless breed of women whom Phoebe admires above all others, the sort for whom life opens all its hidden places, yielding its treasures of experience.

Iphigenia's been enchanted with things French ever since she was very young. At seventeen, during a summer in Paris, she won the friendship of the owner of Shakespeare & Company, the celebrated birthplace of Joyce's *Ulysses,* and procured for herself the privilege of sleeping the nights in a bed that's hidden somewhere in the famous bookshop, which was started by the Presbyterian minister's daughter from Princeton.

Iphigenia's filled with little stories to illustrate the lopsided charm she sees everywhere here: from the guards who go with little bells each day at dusk to close the Jardin du Luxembourg, to the great respect with which, she claims, each Parisian regards his crotch; even that Carrefour that Phoebe had dejectedly glimpsed from the cab, and in which, if Iphigenia is to be believed, they sell everything from fresh truffles to machine guns, placed side by side in shoppers' wagons. Phoebe's overwhelmed.

But Iphigenia goes to work on Phoebe with such a practiced hand that, before the hour's out, Phoebe, given food and wine and the soothing sense of both the Sorkins' lively interest in her, again has that heady feeling that she's arrived home.

She's amazed with how good she's turning out to be at managing all by herself in a foreign country—like a real seasoned traveler!

Meanwhile, Iphigenia, discovering the sort of math Phoebe does, seems as dazzled by Phoebe as Phoebe is by her.

"The geometry of *soap* bubbles! The *geometry* of soap bubbles! Danny, why haven't you ever told me there's such a thing as the *geometry of soap bubbles?*"

"Perhaps I was afraid you'd give up poetry to take up math."

"Right. As if I could. You people are gods. You know that.

Mathematicians and musicians. Gods." She smiles at each of them—Danny and Oren and Phoebe—in turn.

"And what about poets?" Danny asks her.

"Poets are mathematicians and musicians—only without any mathematical and musical talent."

"Oh, come now." Danny laughs. "You only say that to disparage what you can do and exaggerate what you can't."

"No, Iphigenia's right. Mathematics and music *are* God's languages," Oren says to Danny, with his solemn air, and automatically translating Iphigenia's paganism into monotheistic terms. "When you speak them, Danny, you're speaking directly to God."

And Danny and Iphigenia gently smile at Oren, with about as open a display of love as any Phoebe, herself a much-loved child, has ever seen.

But now that Phoebe has been restored to life with Iphigenia's moussaka and Danny's earthy red wine, Oren's very concerned to take her away again. No longer being hungry, she is of course, he assumes, anxious to see the Institut.

"Oren, let the poor girl rest," Danny and Iphigenia both tell him. "She's only just gotten here. She can see the Institut tomorrow morning."

"Don't you want to go now?" Oren asks her.

And Phoebe, who would of course much rather remain put where she is, finds she can't really say that to Oren.

So sure, she says to him.

Iphigenia grins at Oren, her smile full of a mother's indulgence. "You always win, don't you."

He stares back at her as if he doesn't know what she's talking about.

"Come on," he says, giving Phoebe's hand a little tug to get her out of her seat.

Iphigenia, getting their coats for them, tells Oren that he can't put back on that rainhat he came in, that somehow he's managed to get it soaked through to the inside.

"Do you have another one he can borrow?" she asks Danny.

"Sure. That one he came in is mine anyway. Let him leave it here, and I'll go get him another one."

While Danny's doing that, Iphigenia's giving Phoebe good advice on how to adjust to the time change.

And so Phoebe and Oren are sent back out into the rain, again taking the winding path that leads up onto the main street, which they cross, continuing on over the railroad tracks—"They go to Paris," Oren tells Phoebe—turning up a dark street that leads to the stone gates of the Institut des Hautes Etudes Scientifiques.

Oren takes her to his office, which is small and spare, excessively tidy and with almost no books on the shelves. He sits down behind his desk, Phoebe sits across from him, he folds his hands on his desk, sitting up very straight, looks across at her, with his face full of expectation, and demands:

"Now, tell me about your mathematics!"

And Phoebe, again feeling unable to resist Oren's quiet obstinance, goes to work on the blackboard covering one of the walls.

The rate with which Oren takes in and anticipates what Phoebe says is astonishing. Phoebe's never seen the like before. In a little less than an hour Phoebe has covered enough ground so that she can explain to him the particular difficulties of the problem currently occupying her.

"Yes," he says. "Yes. Yes." He's looking down at the top of his clean desk, on which his hands still remain folded, like a good boy sitting as we were all taught to sit at our school desks.

Suddenly he stands up and moves to the board.

"What if you allow the objects under consideration to evolve like so?" And he quickly draws some symbols. "Then, if you represent this system by conformal coordinates, you recognize that the dynamics leads to a strange attractor, consisting of quasiminimal varieties."

He beams, like the schoolboy who's just given the correct answer, and Phoebe stares at him.

She hadn't considered looking at her problem in terms of a dynamical system; much less had she entertained the possibility that the concept of a strange attractor might have any value. This concept originated, she believed, with David Ruelle, yet another Bures great, who gave mathematical representation to the phenomena of chance and chaos. Ruelle, approving the "psychoanalytic" undertone of the term, had used the strange attractors to understand the dynamics of turbulence: the eerie chaos that lies just beyond the thin veil of order; and the even more mysterious order that lies deep within the chaos.

At first Oren's words don't stick, but then they attach themselves, and begin to stir something, so that Phoebe begins to see her problem shifting before her.

And how is it that Phoebe Saunders has never heard of this phenomenon called Oren Glube before? Of course, one does hear of him, sooner or later. Either one meets him here at Bures, as Phoebe's just done, or else one meets with his legend, which does travel abroad, even if Oren himself never does.

In the twelve years that Oren's been at Bures, he's left only a handful of times, and then only to go the thirty kilometers into Paris, a trip that invariably ends for him with some sort of catastrophe—to whose mathematical theory, born here in Bures, of the mathematician René Thom, Oren has contributed—and a desperate call to someone at Bures to help him out. And, though he lives and breathes mathematics, he's published next to nothing.

What he does do, and does sublimely, so that it more than earns him his keep at the Institut, is precisely what he's been doing just now with Phoebe.

Oren Glube talks with any mathematician that presents itself. He goes from one to another, like a honeybee sipping among the mathematical flowers. And, just like a honeybee, Oren's often responsible for important cross-fertilization.

For Oren mathematics is essentially a matter of conversation. He converses with his fellow mathematicians, and he converses with God, and in neither case does he feel the need to write up an account. What's discussed with the mathematicians is written up by them. And what he discusses with God they both keep to themselves.

Sometimes a look of transfixed bliss will come to him; and then those who know him know that he's just said something particularly nice to God.

So, even among the madmen of mathematics, Oren Glube is legendary, both for his genius and his eccentricities. There's a theory about the personalities of mathematicians proposed by the great Russian mathematician Andrei N. Kolmogorov, according to which a mathematician's emotional development is frozen at the precise age at which his or her mathematical ability first takes wing—and takes over. In Oren's case this happened particularly young, at perhaps four or five years of age. And what this means is that at times Oren Glube is impossible.

The people connected with the Institut compose something very much like a family. As in any other family, there are shared secrets, things that are not usually spoken about, and never before strangers. And Oren, as the precocious child of this family, has found out its secrets; some grown-up has been indiscreet enough to mention something or other in front of Oren, who can be counted on to blurt it out at the most inopportune time possible.

And now the sheer brilliance of Oren's suggestion has sunk itself into Phoebe's mind, and she goes to the blackboard, and begins tentatively to move some symbols around.

"I'm going home now," Oren announces to her. "It's quite late and I want to go to sleep."

"Can I stay here and work a little on this idea?"

"But of course."

"Is it safe for me to stay here all alone in the middle of the night?" Phoebe remembers to ask, Manhattan-bred child that she is.

Oren stares at her, completely baffled for a few seconds; and then his face clears.

"Oh," he says with a little smile. "You're a girl. That's why you ask that. I had forgotten it."

Phoebe had failed to act on Iphigenia's parting good advice; and so she arrives just after two in the afternoon at the Institut.

The chief secretary, Jeanine, to whom Phoebe must go to get her key, is one of those intimidatingly bustling sorts, with a hard face and cold eyes.

Phoebe asks her if she may speak English to her, and Jeanine shrugs a heavy shoulder and very uncordially invites her to try.

So Phoebe instead struggles to get out her request in a French that is even worse than inadequate—she has inherited none of Sasha's or Chloe's facility for languages—and Jeanine stares with blatant incomprehension, so that Phoebe finally gives up, and Jeanine hands her the key.

"Is it perhaps for this that you are trying to ask?"

But these transactions take place with the greatest air of hostility, so that Phoebe thinks that Jeanine is not at all a nice sort, not at all like Delia at home.

Phoebe's right. Jeanine's not a nice sort. There's another secretary in the office, Suzette, younger and a little softer-seeming, and Jeanine and Suzette exchange an arch look between them, directed at Phoebe's back, as she retreats out the door.

"Still, it's a pity when they're so young," Suzette says giggling.

It's a joke between them: that there's precious little difference between the "inmates" of the two institutions of Bures.

Phoebe finds a note taped to her door: to go to the office of Dr. Shahaza as soon as she arrives.

This is really happening, she thinks, as she walks down the hall, looking for his office. In a few moments I'll actually see him. I'm not dreaming this.

And then she hears voices, laughter, and there is a whole crowd of mathematicians coming up the stairs—they're just returning en masse from lunch—and Phoebe sees his beautiful head carried high above all the others.

She sees the second when he sees her, when his face registers recognition and he smiles: incomparable, divine.

"Look," he says to no one in particular. "It's Phoebe Saunders just come."

And he's walking toward her, and Phoebe feels that she might perform a solo re-enactment of the miracle of Prospect; that she might at any moment begin embarrassingly to float upward—or perhaps she already has.

Antoine Shahaza bends way down and kisses little Phoebe on both of her cheeks.

"So! You have made it to Bures!"

She nods.

"And," he continues, smiling very widely, "you've already met Oren and been fed by Iphigenia, so everything's as it should be!"

"No, it's not," says Oren, stepping up behind Antoine. "She keeps missing the meals!"

The little group, waiting a few steps behind, laughs. Antoine introduces each of them to Phoebe—they're visitors and permanent members, gleaned from every part of the world —and soon they all excuse themselves and disperse back to their offices; all except Antoine and Oren, who now says, still quite upset:

"And it was such a good meal today. Chicken."

"It's okay. I just woke up. I couldn't have eaten chicken."

"No, no, this won't do." And Antoine, smiling like Sharif, wags his finger at her. "I'll permit it only this day. But by tomorrow you must forsake the clock of Princeton and be keeping time by Bures! We mathematicians must be like the air-shuttle diplomatists. No time to waste on jet lag."

"But in the meanwhile what will she eat now?" Oren continues to worry.

"You have a good point, Oren. Shall I have one of the secretaries get you a little something, some fruit or yogurt perhaps?"

Phoebe shakes her head.

"No, nothing? Well, you know, you have only to speak to Jeanine if you change your mind. She or one of the others will take care of everything. Anyway, we must go to speak with her now, so that we can schedule in your lecture."

In the presence of Dr. Shahaza a completely transformed Jeanine and Suzette are revealed: sweetly docile and ingratiating, the hardness melting away from Jeanine's mouth and eyes, so that she looks almost young and dewy.

Jeanine and Suzette must also, then, be susceptible to manifest divinity; and Phoebe can only think the better of them for it.

"We have here," Antoine tells them, smiling, "a little case of jet lag."

"So," Jeanine says to Phoebe. "It's only understandable. He"—and she cocks her head in Antoine Shahaza's direction—"he can't understand any sort of physical weakness. No weakness of any kind. But we women are great experts in weakness, no? So, we schedule the lecture at eleven in the morning, instead of the usual nine—just to be on the side of safety," she adds, winking at Dr. Shahaza.

"Goodbye, Phoebe," Jeanine and Suzette both call out to her as she is leaving their office with him. "Enjoy your stay with us in Bures!"

Phoebe turns back to stare at them; and Antoine, too, turns back and says, with a flash of his brilliant smile:

"It's Dr. Saunders."

"So now," he says to Phoebe, in front of the door to her office, "you are completely set. Only one thing remains. Can you come this evening to my home for dinner? Around eight o'clock.

"Perhaps you have been practicing your captivating Yiddish Ophelia for me. If so, here is your chance."

Phoebe walks through the drizzle to Antoine Shahaza's house, which is large and of white stucco and surrounded by an imposing wall and dripping chestnut trees.

She's very nervous. She had spent the entire rest of the afternoon worrying about everything, even about what to bring to the house as a gift.

The little village grocery store sold wine, but she had absolutely no idea which bottle to buy. Here was yet another language in which she couldn't converse, this language of worldliness that Antoine Shahaza knew to perfection. She would be saying something very precise by the bottle she brought to someone like Antoine Shahaza, and she would have no idea what she was saying.

She finally decided simply to buy the most expensive bottle there, a bottle of Taittinger champagne.

And now she's carrying this bottle, its high price giving her no sense that its content is appropriate, and she's knocking at the large, heavy door of the Shahaza house.

A small thin dark woman answers, nods with barely a smile at Phoebe, and wordlessly takes Phoebe's raincoat and umbrella and the bottle of champagne.

She's Gabrielle Shahaza, Antoine Shahaza's wife.

She leads Phoebe into the large living room.

There are people already here: Phoebe sees, with a great rush of relief, the Sorkins among them.

There's a young American couple, the man a mathematician who's visiting Bures for the year of his sabbatical from the University of Utah, and it's his wife who had been speaking as Phoebe entered. After Phoebe's been introduced all around by Antoine and then seated beside Iphigenia on the white couch, the woman from Utah again takes up the plaintive thread of her interrupted story.

The couple are the parents of a young daughter who's attending first grade at the school in Bures, and this child is absolutely miserable—"great dramatic, hysterical scenes," her mother describes, "every single morning when she has to leave.

"And then the kids here come home for lunch, so there's that whole scene to repeat all over again at midday!"

Almost all the others present have been through this with their own children, and they all have stories to tell of their own offspring's miseries and eventual masteries as strangers in strange lands.

Only Gabrielle Shahaza, who sits beside her own daughter, who's thirteen—another daughter studies at the Sorbonne—says nothing. This is perhaps because Gabrielle never travels with Antoine, but has always remained at home with the children.

"It's of course very hard on your daughter until she begins to catch on to the language," Iphigenia is saying to the exasperated mother. "You just have to put up with the most aberrant sorts of behavior until then. Grin and bear it and all that valiant sort of parental thing."

"But *will* she catch on?" the mother asks, sounding frankly desperate.

"Of course," everyone assures her.

"Just as she eventually caught on to English," someone says. "It's a wonderful advantage for our children. They all become fluent, sometimes in three or four languages."

"It will take until Christmas," Iphigenia says, with the buoyant self-assurance that comes from her splendid animal spirits. She's wearing black tonight, and she's ravishing.

"I've seen it happen time and time again. They start school in September, and right around Christmas they're suddenly speaking French. I remember when our son, Sammy, came home from school, when he was in kindergarten here, and just calmly announced: 'I understand her now.' "

"Christmas," the mother echoes, sounding dubious. "That doesn't leave Karen all that much time."

Phoebe feels very worried for this child Karen, with whom she completely identifies.

Iphigenia makes the process sound like a phase transition of matter, stupid and mechanical. Just as water that's heated to one hundred degrees Celsius will certainly begin to boil, so Karen will at Christmastime break out into French.

But what if it doesn't happen for Karen? Phoebe worries. What if Karen never does arrive home calmly to announce: now I understand?

Around midnight, the guests all leave Antoine Shahaza's home together, and walk as a group back through a rain that's dwindled to something just a little more serious than a mist.

"What good food that was," Iphigenia says with a contented little sigh. "That woman is a wonderful cook."

"But you didn't hear a peep out of her," Karen's mother remarks. "It gave me the creeps, the way she and her daughter went tiptoeing around, waiting on us."

"That's the way to raise them," Karen's father jokes. "Nice quiet womenfolk, faultlessly serving their men."

"Well, at least she doesn't go around wearing a veil," Karen's mother goes on, sticking a playful elbow into her husband's side.

"Oh, she does," Iphigenia laughs. "Gabrielle Shahaza most definitely wears a veil."

Phoebe has an unprecedented case of jitters the morning of her lecture. Unsure of herself in most other situations, she's usually rather self-possessed when presenting her math.

She comes a few minutes early into the small auditorium where she's to speak, to begin to set up the wire frames she dips into her soap solution in order to form the soap films whose mathematical properties she describes.

Her bubble solution is homemade, consisting of roughly equal parts of water and commercial dishwashing detergent, with a small addition of glycerin to stabilize the films. She also has several wands with which to blow bubbles of varying diameters.

The mathematicians begin to filter in. Antoine walks in, talking with several men, including Danny Sorkin.

And then, surprising everyone except for Danny, Iphigenia herself makes an entrance.

Judging from everyone's reaction, this is something of an event.

Antoine asks Iphigenia if she's planning to write a poem about the geometry of soap bubbles.

"Perhaps." She laughs. "It certainly deserves one. Maybe Phoebe's math will be immortalized by me when I get back to Cambridge. You know that in France I hardly write any poetry at all. I get very prosaic here. All I seem to think about is the food."

They finally get started, quite a bit late. Antoine introduces Phoebe, very simply, and then she begins her lecture, starting first with the basic statement of the Plateau rules.

Oren comes in late—he's gotten confused because of the

unusual time of Phoebe's lecture—and he makes a good deal of noise getting himself settled down into the middle seat of the front row, his own special place. There have been several embarrassing scenes when visitors to Bures unknowingly sat themselves down in the place Oren considers his own.

And then he catches sight of Phoebe's soap films lined up invitingly on a table beside her.

"What are those?" he calls out, breaking into her sentence.

Phoebe explains very briefly to him how these particular configurations function in her exposition.

"May I see?" he asks, not waiting for an answer, but rising from his seat and going over to examine the soap films, which shimmer wonderfully as he picks them up to stare through them at the ceiling lights.

He pokes in his index finger and pops a few of the films, then dips the frames again into the bucket of the solution. He finds the wands arranged beside the bucket, dips them in, too, and, one by one, blows through each, breaking out into a peal of delighted laughter.

Everybody, including Phoebe, who finds herself now completely relaxed in this scene of almost hilarious informality, enjoys the spectacle of Oren Glube playing with the bubbles, clumsily chasing after them in the big black rainboots he wears all through the rainy season, so that he won't have to take notice of whether it's raining or not.

Finally, Iphigenia, deciding it's enough, tells Oren, with impressive firmness, that he must sit down and behave himself so that Phoebe can explain to them all her lovely mathematics—which she now does.

Phoebe is sitting in her office with Oren, who's had some more thoughts to share with her on her problem.

There's a knock on the door, and there stands Antoine Shahaza.

"Phoebe," he says. "I've come to take you into Paris for

the afternoon. You don't want to go back to Princeton without having even glimpsed the Eiffel Tower."

"May I come, too, Antoine?" asks Oren.

"No, no, Oren, little brother. You may go at any time into
Paris. There is for Phoebe only this one half of this one day,
and she and I must give it all our attention."

The rain has suddenly stopped. There's even a weak attempt at sunlight.

Antoine's car is parked in the driveway of the Institut, and
he opens its door for Phoebe. Though he would insist that
the secretaries give Phoebe Saunders the same respect they
give her male counterparts, yet he's full of these little anach-
ronistic gallantries, which Phoebe finds, because they're his,
to be full of a heartbreaking beauty.

They take the highway back into Paris. They take it at a
very high speed, Antoine's little Porsche maneuvering in and
out between the cars and trucks; and Phoebe is shown the
sights of Paris, in a manner of speaking.

Because the truth—sad or happy—is that, although Antoine Shahaza is flawless as a guide, Phoebe manages to take
in very little of the presence of anything besides himself.

I will store this up forever, she thinks. For my whole life
hereafter I will live off of this day.

He drives her through the Bois de Boulogne; perilously he
talks the entire time as he navigates around the Etoile and
down the Champs-Elysées, past the obelisk, the Tuileries, the
Louvre.

"I am worse than a bus tour," he jokes. "I don't even stop
and permit you to get out to take photos."

But they do park the car and go into the vastness of Notre-
Dame.

To Phoebe such interiors are foreign, almost frightening.
She knows very little of the Christian symbolism, having been
raised on her grandmother's Jewish atheism and her mother's
paganism.

She says something of the sort to Antoine, and he, who tells her that he's himself a Christian, laughs. The cathedral, he believes, was built on a Roman temple dedicated to Jupiter, if that will make her feel any more comfortable in it.

Phoebe feels as if she's drinking in Antoine's beautifully fluid sentences, with which he explains everything to her. The details carved into the stone quicken into life for her, and the strange hue of the light in the church seems to warm itself around her.

"If we had the time I would love to take you to Chartres," he tells her. "There's an Englishman there, he came, I believe, as a graduate student from Oxford, maybe twenty or thirty years ago, and he's never left. He's one of the people I most admire in the world. He wrote a truly splendid book comparing the architecture, the metaphysics, the everything, of the two cathedrals, of Notre-Dame and of Chartres, to the overall discredit of Notre-Dame, which he thinks the more shallow. One can arrange to have a private tour with this man that is a revelation. Next time you're here we shall perhaps do that, if you would like."

And when they finally emerge from Notre-Dame, the dusk is falling, and Antoine Shahaza says that this is perfect, because there is no better hour of the day to grasp the essence of Paris than at twilight, with the saffron sunset coming from the west of the city.

And it's even better, he says, on a bridge. So they go to stand on Pont Saint-Louis, with the lights from the Ile de la Cité before them, and the lights from the Ile Saint-Louis behind them, and Antoine tells Phoebe how it was for him, so many years ago, when he first arrived all by himself in this city, a young boy of sixteen from North Africa, gifted in mathematics, "but so terrified, so alone, under the crush of this alien culture so immense I despaired that ever I could master it.

"I would read all the newspapers on which I could get my

hands, perhaps six a day, trying to assimilate what it was to be a Parisian, a European, a Westerner.

"In my country I belong to the aristocratic class; I have even some Spanish ancestry, as many of those of my class do; but here I felt as lowly as only a young Arab boy, alone in the great capital of Western culture, can feel lowly.

"Have you ever read, Phoebe, *La Chimère*? But you have heard of it, of course. Oh, but you must read it, and also the brilliant biography of E. A. Worthinghouse that was published some years ago by that Princeton woman, I can't for the moment recall her name. I used never to forget a name. I'm getting old perhaps.

"*La Chimère* was of course written first in English, but for me, strangely, the English reads like a translation—a very *good* translation—but still a translation from the French. When you read it, you will see perhaps what I mean.

"I had found, haunting the *bouquinistes* down on the quais, a used copy of *La Chimère*, which I had bought for a few sous.

"Such shimmering prose. Such a strange ecstatic music in those pages. It was through those pages, their music, that I began to grasp what it was to be French, the sensibility of the people, the *être intime* of the life here; and to begin with this to become at home in this world.

"And is it not a most beautiful paradox: that the author of *La Chimère* was the sad and solitary Worthinghouse, a creature who was perhaps the most lonely in all the world? She, who first led me in, was herself the eternal outsider.

"This was a paradox on which I dwelled much at that time; and through it I found the intuition that saved me.

"Shall I tell you what it was, Phoebe? Very simply, it was the idea of the universality of our experience. Beneath the riot of differences, there's a universal language that makes us all accessible to one another.

"I know this is a most simple idea. There's nothing very

deep here, nothing to impress one's colleagues with its intellectual flash. No long proof, Phoebe. But for me it was a
magnificent intuition; as if I had discovered, at sixteen, the
proof for Fermat's last theorem or for Goldbach's conjecture.
In my loneliness I sipped solace from it as I would the sweet
milk from my mother. And in some sense I have never sur-
passed it.

"This is why I think, Phoebe, that I was so strangely moved
when I heard you reciting your grandmother's lines that day
in Princeton. Ophelia's sad speech spoken in Yiddish.

"Here is a language of exile, a language I, too, understand;
a language invented to be spoken in the margins, straining
to surpass itself, to encompass the text.

"It touched me to hear you, who are yourself so young to
experience, who seem to me as beautifully fragile and pellucid
as one of your soap bubbles, reciting the tragic lines in the
tragic language.

"So, Phoebe, I have spoken much here on Pont Saint-Louis.
It is the twilight that promotes these dangerous disclosures
—the twilight and your eyes. I have spoken much because I
have seen your shining eyes speaking so much back to me.

"Tell me: did your wonderful grandmother ever recite for
you, when she tucked you in as a child to your bed, the lines
of the dark Moor?

"My story being done,
She gave me for my pains a world of sighs:
She swore, in faith, 'twas strange, 'twas passing strange."

Phoebe is sitting in her office, in the late afternoon of her last
day in Bures, filled with confusion.

She had come to Bures so that she might fill herself up with
the sight of the god for all the years to come; and now he
has shifted for her, put off the god, to become a man whom
she loves beyond the god; and she leaves Bures filled only

with a sense of wild chaos, and desire that's like a demon entered in her.

Suddenly, there's a great stamping noise outside of her door, and Oren Glube comes bursting in, his normally pale face flushed as if with fever.

"Come! Now! *This* second, Phoebe!"

Her only thought is of fire, of which she's always been frightened: the Institut des Hautes Etudes Scientifiques is in flames.

She rushes to the door, and Oren grabs her hand and is pulling her down the hall with him, stomping loudly in his big black rainboots.

Antoine comes running up behind them.

"Oh, you have her, Oren! Good boy! Run, run!"

Antoine's taken Phoebe's other hand, and they run for the main door of the building; all of the mathematicians have come from their offices and are running for the door.

Only the secretaries sit calmly at their desks, typing and making their jokes about the "inmates of Bures."

"They're overexciting themselves again," says Suzette. "We'll have our hands full trying to calm them down this evening."

And outside the mathematicians all stand gathered together on the wet lawn, staring up into the western sky, where there's a rare double rainbow stretching itself:

The colors of the primary arc are intense and pure; and beneath is the secondary rainbow, with its paler inversion of the spectrum.

And all of the mathematicians are standing together in silence; on every face the same look of transfixed bliss.